LEAP IN THE DARK

The struggle of the Yugoslav Partisans was one of the fiercest and most blood-curdling campaigns of the second war. Its excitement and ferocity, which the author experienced at first hand, provides the background and the context for this unusual first novel.

It is not, in the ordinary English sense, a war novel. Much more it is a novel of war as so many continentals experienced it. For the British the war was continuous and gradual. There was no thunderclap, before which all was smiling and peaceful and after which black night and bitter hatred blotted out all the contours of ordinary life. But the effect of the Blitzkrieg and the occupation which followed was precisely this, that it struck ordinary people like a tidal wave, separating families and carrying individuals far beyond their friendly, familiar worlds into horrible extremes where decency and honour and loyalty could not possibly be reconciled. Mr McCandless has constructed his plot round one such family, and for all the humour and lightness of touch the tragedy of the situation is not evaded.

The involvement of British forces in the shape of an unexpected and unwanted Military Mission and of the Royal Marine Commandos provides the author with some notable opportunities both for comedy and for exciting action. The contrast between regimental soldiers, even when engaged in decidedly unconventional warfare, and those who played that deadly game by a far harsher set of rules is most effectively brought out. Mr McCandless never forgets that his Partisans and their rivals are potentially and sometimes actually members of the same family, however dreadful the things they are prepared to do to each other. What the reader will carry away from the book is, strangely, a sense of exhilaration at the courage and generosity of people in danger and difficulty. Like Evelyn Waugh and Peter Fleming, the author does not allow his appreciation of the military virtues to blind him to the ludicrous in the most valiant of soldiers and in the tightest of corners.

This well-written and vivid novel makes the debut of a writer who belongs in that distinguished tradition.

LEAP IN THE DARK

ANTHONY McCANDLESS

THE
COMPANION BOOK CLUB
LONDON AND SYDNEY

This edition, published in 1981 by
The Hamlyn Publishing Group Ltd,
is issued by arrangement with
William Collins Sons & Co Ltd, Glasgow

THE COMPANION BOOK CLUB

The Club is not a library; all books are the property of members. There is no entrance fee or any payment beyond the low Club price of each book. Details of membership will gladly be sent on request.

Write to:

> The Companion Book Club,
> Odhams Books, Rushden, Northants.

Or, in Australia, write to:

> The Companion Book Club,
> C/- Hamlyn House Books, P.O. Box 252
> Dee Why, N.S.W. 2099

---

*Made and printed in Great Britain
for the Companion Book Club
by The Pitman Press, Bath*
600872645
481/364

For Ruth

AUTHOR'S NOTE

This story is fiction. Aside from named public figures the characters in it are imaginary. Some of the organizations mentioned existed. Some still do. No. 49 Royal Marine Commando comes into neither category.

The historical background is based on published records and a measure of personal observation. Any errors are mine. The geography is right although I have made some minor local modifications. To the best of my knowledge there never was a Villa Ribar on the stretch of shoreline of the Gulf of Kotor described in the story.

Prologue

A complicated affray in a cottage in County Wicklow, involving gun-play, assailants in stocking masks, a Catholic priest and four middle-aged men, created a great stir. Four people were killed in the fight. It was believed, almost universally, to have been instigated by the Provisional Wing of the Irish Republican Army. The IRA's spokesman disclaimed responsibility.

He might have been right.

PART ONE

Chapter One

IVO BILIC, a wealthy Zagreb banker, bought the Villa Ribar in the late 1920s. Its previous owner had been a bisexual Hungarian alcoholic whose intrepidity as a Cavalry officer in the First World War had been legendary. The dissolution of the Hapsburg Empire had diminished his profits as a landowner, expanded his appetite for his expensive amusements, and left him living off capital. A Croatian aunt of his had lived in Zagreb and her jewellery had been lodged in the Bilic Bank. When the bills for running his costly stable of kept women and catamites took his bank account one lurch nearer the red, it was natural that he should try to dispose of an asset on which no horse could canter. His aunt suggested Ivo as a possible buyer. Ivo loved the Adriatic coast and offered the market price plus a little bit more. An austere man himself, he admired the panache of a gallant, spendthrift voluptuary.

The villa, Fisherman's House, was on a small island, artificially built of stones, of about three quarters of an acre. It was connected to the shore by a narrow stone causeway sixty yards long. The house, like almost every other house on the Yugoslav Adriatic coast, had a roof of red tiles and walls of white limestone. There were cypresses and a few casuarina trees. An area of the short, shallow-rooted Dalmatian vines was backed by a vegetable garden which provided mainly cabbages whose leaves were plucked from the outside in the local

11

thrifty custom, allowing for further growth and use. A stone-flagged section doubled as a terrace and a jetty. A two-roomed cottage housed a venerable watchman and intermittent odd-job man named Josip. Fresh water was pumped from a well sunk beyond the narrow cliff-lined road that ran along the shore.

The inside of the villa was cool, dark and sparsely furnished. Ivo loved it and so did his wife and the four growing children. They came every summer, Ivo for one month, his family for two, and they swam, fished, sailed, sun-bathed and worked. Ivo had always been insistent about the work. His children were privileged, he told them, and they must earn their privileges. In Zagreb there were servants. Here, at the villa, there would be none, aside from occasional well-meaning interventions, usually generating more problems than they solved, by old Josip. Gardening, shopping, cooking, house-cleaning, washing-up, bed making, boat painting, path clearing, fish gutting were the shared responsibility of Tomislav, Branko, Vlado and Karla, directed by their mother, shared in when he was there, by their father. They grumbled about the work, and liked it.

Ivo knew from the deeds and local tradition that the villa had been built in the middle 1850s. He was never able to discover when the island had first been constructed or how many houses had preceded the Villa Ribar. This was a land with an ancient history, physically beautiful, and strategically valuable, characteristics that it shared with the whole of Yugoslavia and that in a like manner had moulded its small blood-soaked destiny in waves of racial obliteration, assimilation and compromise. In the times before history there were Celts and Illyrians. Greeks established a settlement and were overthrown by Romans. The great Slav migrations disposed of this portion of a declining Roman Empire. Byzantium controlled it for a period. In the ninth century Saracens captured, looted, wrecked and

12

abandoned it. It reverted to Byzantium and then became the property first of Serbian, then of Hungaro-Croatian, then of Bosnian Kings. From 1420 until 1797 it belonged to Venice, a period that did most to shape its architecture and its culture. In the subsequent sixteen years it was briefly Austrian, Russian (the Gulf of Kotor was the headquarters anchorage of a Tsarist fleet for a year), French and Montenegrin. The Montenegrins were, in 1814, induced by a persuasive mixture of threatened force and diplomacy to give it to the Austrians again, which was where it stayed until the end of the First World War in 1918, when it was brought to the new Yugoslavia. And for many centuries during the latter part of this chronicle of shifting domination there had been the standing menace of attack by the Turks.

It was hardly surprising, reflected Ivo, that given this background the inhabitants of the Gulf's littoral looked to their defences, hedged their bets and knew a thing or two about looking after their persons and their property. Which would account for a discovery made early one morning by young Tomislav when he was clearing, with a spade, a weed-bestrewn patch beside the vines. There were really two discoveries. The first was that the weeds were thriving in a shallow base of impacted earth that had accumulated down the ages on a base of flat stone. Tomislav scraped it clear and looked with satisfaction on a terrazzo of large flag-stones, shaped by the precise care of craftsmen who grew up with, understood and loved stone. The second discovery arose from the observation that one of the larger stones, about a metre square, was not entirely flush with its surrounding fellows. One edge was perhaps a centimetre lower than the flag adjoining it. The opposite edge was a corresponding centimetre higher. Tomislav gave a casual prod of his spade at the down-sloping side and got the surprise of his young life. The stone pivoted on its axis, swung until it was vertical and

13

revealed itself to be the opening of a dry stone-lined pit about five metres long, four wide and two high.

Tomislav called over Vlado and Branko, who shouted for Karla, who ran for her parents. The whole family gazed contemplatively at their new asset. The boys jumped down and padded about inside. Ivo examined the ingeniously simple mechanics of the thing. A semi-circular groove had been carved down the centre of the underside of the flagstone. The groove fitted neatly an ageing horizontal steel bar set across the gap below. There was a small unobtrusive rectangular gap cut into one side of the stone, clearly for a small stone wedge. Ivo found its ruin among the rubble of Tomislav's earth shifting. It was crumbling and rotten with age and had been shattered by a vigorous swipe of Tomislav's spade.

For the rest of the day there was protracted family speculation on who had built the 'cache' as they came to call it, when, and why. Branko's fanciful theory that it was the work of a long-distant Byzantine predecessor anxious to hide his valuables from the Saracens was dismissed with scorn by Vlado, the historian. Much more recent. Probably put in by a Venetian as an insurance policy against Turkish marauders. Ivo's wife said that she knew little about history but her guess was that it had been prepared during that year when the Russian fleet was in the Gulf. Anyone who had the space and the materials to dig a hole and who didn't do it when Russians were around was asking for trouble. Tomislav spurned all this romanticism. It was obviously the work of a smuggler, designed to conceal his traffic from the revenue authorities of whatever nation happened to be ordering public affairs at the time. Little Karla had no views but greatly enjoyed the excitement. Ivo privately agreed with Tomislav but didn't say so. He was a father who liked to encourage his children to think, speculate and discuss and he saw no reason to curb their enthusiasm on this occasion.

At dinner that night he articulated a thought that had been germinating throughout the day.

'You know,' he said, 'I've been studying the cache. I don't think it's been opened for at least sixty years. The chances are that there are only six people alive who know it exists. Us. Between us we'll replace the metal bar and make a new wedge. Then we'll close it up again and cover it with earth. And plant some oleanders round it. And we'll tell nobody. This is a family secret. You never know when a thing like that might be of use. I can't think how, but I'm sure we'll not regret it.'

Ivo never did regret it. Quite a number of other people did though. Including some whose lives were further affected by Ivo's enthusiasm for oleanders. In addition to the ones he planted around the cache he put in a small grove where the causeway met the island and lined the track along the causeway itself with a further selection. By 1944 they had all matured.

Chapter Two

ON THE LAST day of the week in which he had calculated
that he would probably die, old Ivo Bilic followed his
normal routine. He was awakened at seven by Stjepan,
white-haired, stooped, palsied and loyal, bearing a
glass of fruit juice. A leisured but precise interval for
careful shaving, selection of clothing, dressing. A slow,
limping progress along the landing and down the broad
staircase, feet placed meticulously in succession, right
hand firmly grasping the huge and beautiful polished
banister that had been fashioned from the trunk of a
single oak from the family's forest in Slovenia. The
familiar business, with age now become irritatingly
complicated, of being helped by Stjepan with overcoat,
scarf, hat, gloves and gold-mounted walking stick.
Stjepan holding open first the front door and then the
gate set into the iron-railed high stone wall that
guarded the house from the street. The exchange of
affectionate courtesies.

    'Hvala ljepo Stjepan. Do Vidjenya.'

    'Do Vidjenya Gospodine.'

    The first painful uphill steps of the morning constitu-
tional, as his wife's English in-laws insisted on calling it.
Stabs of hurt from the ancient hip wound. A genera-
lized dull gnawing pain in the small of the back.
Stiffness in the knees. Heart beating over-
energetically. And then, as he worked into the rhythm
of a plodding, steady, determined stride, the forgetting

16

of his frailties, their replacement by an always fresh, appreciative awareness of his surroundings. This was his city, his country. The people around him were his people. They shared with him his culture, his cherished language, a common gallant, blood-soaked, indomitable, confused, sometimes prejudiced, on occasion (he had to admit) inglorious, history. He had travelled widely throughout the world. There was nowhere on earth that he would prefer now, at this moment, to be, walking up the tree-lined rising road of Jurjevska towards Cmrok, where public executions once took place. Nowhere else? Absolutely nowhere else. He must conclude, he told himself wryly, that there were some who might consider that for a man of his opinions, connections and public record, there were better places to be at the end of November 1941 than in German-occupied Zagreb, the capital city of the newly proclaimed Independent State of Croatia, presided over by Ante Pavelic. Pavelic daily gave ample confirmation of Ivo Bilic's earlier suspicions that the man was a psychopathic guttersnipe. Also there was that small part of Ivo's recent record, so far undisclosed, that could make those sceptical about the good sense of his happiness in being where he was even more, much more, dubious about his present position. Well, to hell with them. He knew what he liked and he liked where he was. If he were killed today it would only be an anticipation of the processes of nature by a few, increasingly physically uncomfortable, years. He had made his preparations.

At the crest of the hill where Jurjevska met Tuskanac, he turned back and walked slowly home. Extraordinary how inconsistent weather patterns could be. The leaves were down, the trees were stark and the earth was moist. But it was almost like a good spring day. The sun shone from a clear blue sky. There was an invigorating nip in the air. Behind him the beech-covered slopes of Sljeme looked down benevolently on

17

the city they dominated. To his left, across the valley, lay the long high wall and intermittent domes of Mirogoj cemetery that strangers thought looked like a Hollywood version of a Turkish barracks. His family owned a well-filled plot in there. Fairly soon, probably today, he thought sardonically and without self-pity, the number of its occupants would increase by one.

He reached the little church of Svjete Juraj, always one of his favourites. As a child he had played among its elderly lichen covered gravestones, their inscriptions barely decipherable, eroded by the years. For a moment he contemplated walking the extra few hundred metres down the hill into Gornje Grad, the ancient upper town of ancient Zagreb, the evocative fragment of his native city that had always come nostalgically to his mind when he had been on banking business in Paris or New York, London or Berlin. He would have liked a last look at the Stone Gate with its spread of guttering votive candles and its simple dignified messages of thanksgiving and beseechment to Our Lady. At the multicoloured roof of St Mark's, where he had been married, where Branko, Vlado and Karla had been baptized, made their First Communions, been confirmed. At the old ochre buildings of Radicev Trg and Jezuitski Trg and the gateways and courtyards. At the Sabor, where he had played a brief, honourable and ineffectual part in the sterile and vindictive politics of the new Yugoslavia in the 1920s. At . . .

It was time to stop being sentimental. Pavelic and his Ustasha colleagues were conducting affairs down there. There would be sentries and checkpoints and roadblocks and all the other disagreeable paraphernalia of a fanatical totalitarian regime that was simultaneously devoted to a barbarous ideology and unsure of itself; the sorriest of all combinations. This was no day for the meek establishment of his identity to an insolent, truculent and, more likely than not, violent Ustasha militiaman trained, armed and uniformed, by and modelled on, the Nazi SS. The old gentleman took a last look around, drew the vernal-seeming November air into his lungs and walked sedately over the road to his house. Stjepan, when he had finished his duties with hat, coat, scarf, gloves and stick and all were neatly stowed away on hooks, hanger and shelf in the big cupboard under the stairs, escorted him to the *mali* salon where coffee and rolls were waiting.

Stjepan also had the morning mail, which he presented formally on a silver salver. The mail consisted of a torn portion of a cigarette packet. On the plain side was printed in pencil one word. *Led.* Ice. Old Ivo Bilic looked at it, rose, walked over to the log fire, threw the message into the flames, watched it until it was destroyed, and returned thoughtfully to his coffee. His forecast had been accurate. He would not live to see the morrow.

Like most good ideas it had been simple, practical and not particularly original. Its outline had occurred to him on the eighth of April, two days after German, Italian and Hungarian troops had crossed the Yugoslav border and the second of the three days of Operation Punishment, in the course of which large parts of a defenceless Belgrade were bombed to rubble by German aircraft and seventeen thousand of its inhabitants had died in the carnage. An inept Yugoslav General Staff was trying ineptly to conduct ill-considered and badly co-ordinated land operations for the defence of Slovenia and Croatia. The details of the debacle were not of course available to people with even such highly placed connections as old Ivo, but it needed neither inside information nor much perception to read a clear message through the fog of rumour, chaos, panic and despair. The Germans would shortly be in Zagreb.

The bank over which Ivo Bilic presided, and of which he was for practical purposes the sole owner, had been founded on a modest scale by his grandfather in the

19

latter half of the nineteenth century when Zagreb was Agram and Croatia a part of the Hapsburg Empire. The bank's primary function had been the financing of industrial and agricultural development projects by the skilled negotiation of loans from the international money market. Almost without exception the borrowers were private enterprise magnates or consortia of magnates, who put up land, forests, property and art treasures as security. Their agents, the Bilic Bank, needed a rare degree of diplomatic talent, financial expertise and powers of persuasion to succeed in convincing sceptical European and North American money houses of the advantages of investing their tightly guarded capital in a notoriously volatile part of the world where pledged securities could become worthless overnight. The Bilic's had prospered because they had the right qualities, plus one more. Their probity was absolute. From this derived a second, almost casually founded, service provided by the bank. The rich of Croatia and Slovenia took to storing their valuables in the bank's vaults. Bilic's efficiency and reliability would keep them inviolate.

On 8 April 1941, Ivo Bilic opened up the triple steel doors that led to this Aladdin's Cave of expensive baubles and made a provisional mental selection.

It had taken him only a few minutes to work out what he wanted to do. He had no illusions about the imperfections of the young Yugoslavia with its squalid political jockeying between Serbs and Croats. He was resentful of arbitrary Serbian moves towards Serb hegemony and contemptuous of the sterility of emotional Croatian counter-measures. But regardless of the way things had gone he still held intellectually to the ideal of a State for the South Slavs. Archbishop Strossmayer and the others had after all worked it out here in Zagreb. Given the will, and the love, it could be made to work. It had to, if there were to be any future for the cultural and political prospects of a people religiously divided, racially diluted, but still with a rough coherence, a people placed by history and geography on the boundary between West and East, Christianity and Islam, Catholicism and Orthodoxy. In the past he had been as vociferous as the next man in his resistance to attempted Serb domination. Now, when it was necessary, he knew what he was. He was a Yugoslav. It followed that he did not share the views of several of his friends, men he otherwise respected, who held that the only hope for Croatia was an isolationist independence protected from the outside world – and the Serbs – by German force of arms. It also followed that he could strike a small blow for his beliefs if he could remove as much as possible of the treasure trove in his bank's vaults to somewhere beyond the clutches of the invaders. International bankers live in a small world and have their own subtle means of communication. Ivo Bilic knew well what had happened to similar private deposits in Poland, Norway, the Low Countries and France.

The principle established, there came the question of the practicalities. How on earth did you shift all this stuff? There were tons of it. And shift it where? Take the last question first. Belgrade? No. At this moment being bombed to pieces. The Germans would be there soon anyway. Somewhere in Zagreb? Pointless. The Germans would be here soon too. They were thorough and ruthless. If he buried it in his garden or bricked it into his cellars he would need transport, labourers. Labourers could be induced to talk by monetary rewards, torture. Take it to friends in the country, to Zagorje? Same problem. In any case this was all being over-ambitious. There was no transport. It had all been requisitioned for the fighting. Forget all ideas about hiding away massive quantities of old masters, statuary, gold bars and diamond tiaras. 'As much as possible' of the trove had been the initial idea. What was valuable and sufficiently portable to be carried without undue

21

discomfort by one person, travelling on foot across country? Simple answer. Diamonds. Travelling to where? Only one place with a secure hiding place of which he had detailed knowledge. And permanent access to. His villa on the Adriatic Coast between Kotor and Perast.

Three hours later old Ivo carefully locked the three gates of the vault behind him and went up the stairs to his office. In his left hand he carried two wash-leather draw-string bags each weighing about three pounds. He had no idea of the precise worth of their contents, but his previous experience of negotiating loans from American corporations against the security of miscellaneous Balkan valuables suggested a figure of about half a million dollars. In his right hand he held a list describing each item he had abstracted and the name of its owner. Below the list was a signed declaration that he took full responsibility for removing the goods to alternative custody and that he guaranteed their replacement in kind or cash when a more normal state of affairs prevailed. The Bilic Bank's reputation for probity was still intact. Ivo locked the bags and the declaration in the wall safe of his office. He now had a package and a destination. How was he to get the first to the second?

The times were so confused that Ivo was afterwards unable to remember the exact moments in the next few days when he ran into his two bits of luck. He kept a clear recollection of the circumstances of each. The first was an encounter in Ilica, the long straight street that bisected the city on an east-west axis. On the section of it that ran under the southern slopes of Gornije Grad, Ivo one morning met a strange little procession. An imperturbable middle-aged man in a suit from Savile Row, with brightly polished shoes, led a column of four panting clerkly-looking Croatians, each bent under a bulging sack.

'*Dobar Dan Ivo*,' said the British Consul General.

''Morning,' said Ivo in English. 'What's all this?'

'We're having a bit of a bonfire. Office papers. In my garden.'

'You're leaving us then.' said Ivo sadly. It was no surprise. But visual confirmation of the inevitable was painful.

''Fraid so. Got my instructions this morning.'

'Where to?'

'You will be less than amazed to hear,' said His Britannic Majesty's Representative in Croatia and Slovenia, 'that I have been strictly enjoined to keep my destination a secret. I will be less than amazed if it's not common gossip in Zagreb by tonight.' They smiled at each other. They were friends. Then they embraced in the Croatian fashion, kissed each other on both cheeks, and wished each other luck. Ivo watched the sack-laden party plodding wearily up the steps towards Strossmayerova.

That same evening, over a drink, whilst worriedly exchanging gossip and rumours with a neighbour in Jurjevska, a senior official in the Provincial Administration, Ivo was told casually and with no prompting by him some news that fitted admirably the little plot that he had been hatching. The British staffs of the Embassy in Belgrade and of the Consulate General in Zagreb were to be evacuated from Yugoslavia. They would leave their respective posts by road at noon on the following day. If their vehicles stood up to the appalling roads, and if there weren't civil chaos, and if the German armoured columns didn't cut them off and if they weren't bombed to hell by Stukas they would all be evacuated by a British flying boat or a British submarine that was coming to collect them. From Kotor.

Ivo limped with dignified haste to the big house with the Union Jack flying in the front garden and clouds of smoke blowing about at the back. Its ash-smeared custodian, shirt-sleeved and clutching a large glass of whisky, greeted Ivo affably, pressed an equally large

23

glass of whisky upon him and listened carefully to his story and to his proposal for rounding it off. At the end of the account the Consul General showed what Ivo regarded as uncharacteristic signs of emotion. Or perhaps it was a consequence of an afternoon's exposure to smoke.

'Ivo,' he said throatily, refilling their glasses, 'I congratulate you on a really splendid scheme. But it's not quite right yet.'

'Not right?'

'Well, it has two weaknesses. For planning purposes we must assume that I'll get through to Kotor. But I don't know what conditions will be like when I get there, or what arrangements will be made for embarkation. There may be no time for me to get to the villa. We may be rushed straight aboard.'

'Well?'

'Well indeed. You don't want your jewels ending up in some Maltese bank do you?'

'Why not? Better than in German hands.'

'But better still used for the purpose you want them used. Here. In this country.'

Ivo gazed at him in puzzlement.

'All right,' he said hesitantly, 'I don't think that that's much of a problem. But let's set it aside for a moment. The second weakness?'

The host flushed. Stared at his glass. Jiggled its contents about.

'Look at it this way. Technically you've stolen those gems or whatever they are. You give them to me. I'm then an accomplice to a theft. I get picked up by the Germans. I'm carrying stolen goods. Their propaganda people would make mincement of me. And my country. British diplomat plunders host country.' There was an embarrassed silence of perhaps half a minute. Ivo broke it.

'I've never been too good at English colloquialisms,' he said stiffly, 'but I think the correct usage is to say that you're talking balls. And you know it,' he added.

The Consul General looked at him diffidently.

'There is a solution,' he said at last.

'Oh yes?'

'There's room for one in my car'

'I can't go. My place is here. I hope that doesn't sound too histrionic. But it's true.'

'Someone you trust?'

'I can think of very few people I could trust in a matter like this. Fewer still with the local knowledge of the villa to hide the stuff. There's also the question of reprisals. It would be unfair to implicate outsiders.'

'Okay,' said the Consul General daringly. He was a classicist whose knowledge of English colloquialisms was not much more extensive than Ivo's. 'What about Karla?'

This silence was longer than the last. Ivo's breach of manners in topping up his glass from his host's bottle was uncontroversial. The lump in his throat was not evident. The filming over his eyes was. The fate of his daughter Karla, the only member of his immediate family still in Zagreb, was his greatest personal worry. He had thought that he had concealed it successfully. His host had evidently divined it. Ivo looked across the table with compounded admiration, friendship and gratitude. This was clearly a colloquial evening.

'Perfidious bloody Albion,' said Ivo happily. 'All this contrived cock about weaknesses. You just want to help by getting Karla out.'

'Balls,' said the Consul General, blushing again. They shared a final whisky.

Promptly at noon on the following day the little convoy set off for the South. Karla, a second-year medical student at Zagreb University, sat in the front passenger seat of the gleaming Austin saloon. She was dressed in the clothes that in happier days she had used for climbing in the Slovenian Alps or for Sunday walks up Sljeme. Climbing boots. *Lederhosen*. Calf-length cor-

25

duroy trousers that buckled below the knees. Heavy checked woollen Canadian lumberjacket, loose at the waist. Heavy Norwegian wool sweater. Fair hair in a coloured head-scarf. Flawless healthy skin, high Slav cheekbones, slightly slanted green eyes. Wide mouth. Ivo looked at her with love, respect and pride. As they embraced he could feel the small bulge of the two leather bags inside the top of her slacks, slung from her waist belt. Her rucksack was in the car's boot.

'*Do Vidjenya Tata.*'

'*Do Vidjenya Karla. Sretan put.*'

A last slightly tearful hug. The car drew away. Wavings. Uninhibited tears now. Kisses blown. The car vanished round the corner into Gornje Grad. Old Ivo mopped his eyes and stumped slowly back into his house. In the car Karla stopped sobbing, blew her nose, tidied up her face and looked sightlessly at the small silk flag blowing back from its metal stave on the top of the front right-hand mudguard. Union Jack with the Royal Cypher inset in the centre. She turned back to address the Consul General seated, as protocol required, in the rear right seat. He might be about to be bombed, shot or lynched, but he would take good care to ensure that his side of the transaction was conducted with decorum and according to civilized usage.

'Thank you,' said Karla, smiling. Two individual tears rolled slowly down her peach-coloured convex cheeks, incongruous complements to the smile.

'Oh that's all right,' said the Consul General off-handedly, 'I'm very fond of your father.'

Marvellous teeth this girl's got, he thought.

Slavko, the driver, threaded his way through the Baroque buildings of the doomed city and headed south towards Karlovac. He was a Dalmatian and had made clear his wish to face the uncertainty ahead among his own people. Karla, tired by nervous excitement, prepared to doze. Before she shut her eyes she carefully checked the contraband that nestled

26

around her waist. The two leather bags of diamonds and the ambiguously worded piece of paper in a flat pocket on her belt. It identified her to similarly minded people as a member of the Communist Party of Yugoslavia.

Well that departure had been more than six months ago reflected old Ivo, two hours after he had burnt the *Led* message. He had had no word of Karla or of his packages. But even if she had not reached Kotor he could congratulate himself on two modest successes. His beloved daughter, wherever she was, was clear of the horrors being practised daily in Zagreb. And the Germans and their Ustasha lackeys had been deprived of the use of at least some of the treasure of which he had been the guardian.

The time had now come, as he had always been certain that it would, to pay the price of his little operation. *Led* was the signal agreed with his secretary. He had chosen the word partly because he'd heard ice used as a slang word for diamonds in American gangster movies, but mainly because it was short, could be written briefly and compactly, and minimized the risk to Zdenka of handwriting experts identifying whoever wrote it. He had told her nothing of the background to his need for such a message. It simply signified that the team of Gestapo auditors and economists who had been examining the books, cash, securities and valuables in the Bilic bank had completed their work. They could have reached only one conclusion. Ivo had made no attempt at a cover-up. Even if an effective one could have been devised, which Ivo doubted, he would not have attempted it. In his view it would have been dishonourable. So all the evidence was there, available to the trained investigator. Even the signed declaration was neatly filed in his office safe. To another course that had theoretically been open to him, flight, he had given even less thought. By his lights that would have

27

been the ultimate dishonour. He had grown up and prospered in this beautiful land that he loved, whose people he loved and where materially he had enjoyed more than most. That he could do other than share the tragedy that had fallen on both land and people was not a matter for serious consideration.

He had however given serious consideration to the priorities of what to do on his last day on earth. He was at peace with God. On the previous Sunday he had gone to the Cathedral in Kapitol, made his confession and received Holy Communion. He owed a duty to Stjepan. Ivo called the old man (well, he's older than I am, thought Ivo defensively) into the *mali* salon and asked for sandwiches, olives and a bottle of *slievovica* to be left on a tray. That provided, Ivo handed over an envelope, told Stjepan not to open it until the following day and gently advised him to go and stay with his elderly sister for a few weeks. The money in the envelope would keep Stjepan going for a long, long time. The advice would be interpreted as an order. The grief and concern on the old man's face were incapable of consolation. From boyhood their relationship had been one of master and man. It had been supported by a deep, mutual respect and friendship. They embraced for the last time.

'*Puno hvala Stjepan. Do Vidjenya.*'

'*Do vidjenya Gospodine.*'

Time for some *slievovica* and reflection.

Before he poured his first slug of the day Ivo looked affectionately around the *mali* salon, the small drawing-room. It was high and octagonal, the outline proportions those of a jam jar. The ceiling was of intricately carved stained oak. The windows were tall, their inner section a layer of leaded ochre-coloured stained glass. The mantelpiece a vast creation of cream and golden porcelain like one side of Cinderella's coach. Meissen. In its lower centre the logs glowed comfortingly beneath a burnished copper awning. It was the oldest room in the house, part of a medieval tower that had once guarded the Christian marches of Croatia against Turkish Moslem enemies. Ivo's first memories were of this room.

One more thing to do. The heart tablets. Ivo had taken none for the past week. If he were to be submitted to violence he wanted a quick finish. This urge had worried him for a time because suicide was a mortal sin. An engineered discussion about a hypothesis, with a Jesuit he knew, brought reassurance. To take your own life was sinful. To neglect to prolong it with artificial measures was not. God bless the Society of Jesus. Ivo threw the pill-box into the fire, added some logs from the basket that Stjepan had topped up as a matter of course and lay back comfortably in an armchair.

The *slievovica* was good, made in his kitchen from the plum trees grown in the rather pretentiously named Park on the steep slope between the rose-bordered, oak-shaded lawn on the little upper plateau and Dubravkin Put, the path along the valley between Jurjevska and Tuskanac. Ivo knew each plum tree like the palm of his hand. Come to think of it, better. He'd never wasted much time on studying the palm of his hand. Incomprehensible expression.

Top up the crystal wine glass. Any preparations overlooked? Couldn't think of any. It all seemed to be working out remarkably well. Nobody to suffer except him. That would be disagreeable, but brief. Family all well out of it. My goodness, Nedo and Stefica and Beba, all those nice people in the kitchen, had really excelled themselves over this particular production of *slievovica*. No doubt about the rightness of sending them back to their villages just before the Germans arrived. Hope they're all all right. Nedo and all, not the Germans. Must get a tumbler. Shocking insult to drink this stuff from a wine glass.

Where was he? Yes. The family. Very good institutions, families. His, more than most. Something of a

29

triumph really. Nobody, of course, had ever said anything in his hearing but he had had no illusions about the sort of gossip that would have been rampant when he married Nadja. Young widow with a baby son. Thirty years his junior. The widow, not the son. Must formulate his thoughts more clearly. Yes. Particularly after his first sad marriage. Poor Tanja. Died in an insane asylum. Where were we?

The family. That's better. Patch of total clarity. Accentuate the clearness of the outline by refilling this extraordinarily useful tumbler. There was young Tomislav. Not his, but he loved him as one of his own. Nadja's by her first marriage to that wild English racing driver who'd killed himself at Le Mans. Quite right that Tomislav should have been educated in his father's country. Delightful to have had him out for the holidays. Thank God that Nadja had gone to visit him in Cambridge in February before all this started. Branko the regular soldier. Last heard of with his regiment in Serbia before the invasion. Shrewd, tough, capable. Branko could look after himself. Might be dead of course. If so he would have died well. Vlado? Nice, kind, dreamy, artistic, romantic Vlado. Painting showed real talent. Beautiful pianist. Brilliant thesis he'd done on Croatian history and culture. Been in Italy at some sort of conference at the beginning of the year. Still there at the time of the invasion. He'd charm his way out of any troubles. And sweet, pretty, sensible Karla, whose total indifference to politics, economics and anything other than healing and medicine had been a friendly family joke since her adolescence. Ivo chuckled. You could have any amount of worldly success but there was no substitute for fathering, cherishing and bringing up a close-knit family which you loved and respected and which gave you pride.

Very odd the speed at which the level in this bottle was going down. Perhaps it had a hole in it. Better check. No. Seemed intact. But sensible to fill up the tumbler again, just in case. Rather enjoying this conversation with himself. Eliminated controversy. Full agreement on all counts. God really had showered him with blessings. Good health. Expansive life. Wide range of interests. Wealth. Lovely wife. Lovely children. Lovely country. Never really thought of it in the round before. Only in bits. Must thank God. Courteous thing to do.

Hallo God. Ivo here. You've frequently heard from me before on a more formal basis, but since we're going to meet for the first time in a few hours, I thought that a few preliminary words of thanks . . . Old Ivo dozed. At four o'clock he awoke without start or fuss. It would be dark in less than an hour. Then they'd come for him.

He made his way slowly up the big staircase, washed his face and brushed his hair. A dressing-gown would be comfortable. He shed his coat, and his stiff collar and tie, slipped into his old brocaded dressing-gown and fastened around his neck the hideously coloured cravat that Tomislav had given him as a present two Christmases previously. Nice subtlety of choice this. The uniform of a Croatian regiment in the French service had once included red silk scarves, tucked into the collars of tunics. The Croatian word for Croat was *Hrvat*. The French, philological snobs so far as their own language was concerned, had been unable to cope with the pronunciation of somebody else's. They'd adopted the word to describe the scarf, but had adapted it to cravat. Ivo felt strangely proud as he smoothed out the front of the fold and tucked the ends into his shirt. There was much to be said for an obscurely patriotic gesture that would be meaningless to his adversaries.

Painfully down the stairs again. Ivo detested these little journeys. All the disordered nerves in his hip and back reacted more malevolently in descent than in ascent. Unless he sank his head to the point where his

31

chin was pressed against his collar-bone his bifocal glasses distorted the steps. Safely at the bottom he grinned suddenly. The problem would not recur. He had made that particular descent for the last time.

In the *mali* salon he threw three more logs on to the fire and looked critically at the *slievovica* bottle. About four centimetres left. Shame to waste it. He poured it into the faithful tumbler, took a gulp and opened the double doors to the *veliki* salon, the big drawing-room. He was seated there behind the Steinway Grand, strumming dreamily, surrounded by the oak panelling, the family portraits, the silver, glass and china, illuminated by the crystal chandelier, when they came. Noisily.

A vehicle, driven in low gear, roared up Jurjevska from Gornje Grad and skidded to a halt outside Ivo's front door. There were shouted commands. Nailed boots clattered on the pavement. A whistle shrilled. An answering whistle sounded from the park to the rear of the house. A single shot was fired and the street gate clanged open. Clumping hurried footsteps. Shattering glass. Another bang as the lock on the front door was shot open. Shouts in the hallway. Ivo, who had not bothered to draw the curtains, saw torches flashing on the lawn. Rather flattering, the elaboration they'd gone to, to secure an arthritic old man. Time to add his own contribution to the din. He downed the last two centimetres of *slievovica* from the tumbler that seemed to have made its own way to the top of the piano, shot the cuffs of his dressing-gown and crashed into the opening bars of the Polonaise Militaire in A major. Not Croatian, but sound Slav music. His choice had in any case been limited. It was the only piece that he knew.

The door from the hall was kicked open and Ivo was confronted with his executioners. They probably saw themselves as interrogators, but Ivo knew better. There was a pleasant-looking, rosy cheeked young civilian, hatless and in a tweed overcoat; and two apes, both in black uniforms, both nursing Schmeisser machine pistols. The tall one with the stupid expression and the thick wrists was SS. The shorter man, with the broken nose and the broad shoulders, who looked like a boxer, was Ustasha. Doubtless under instruction.

Ivo completed his musical exercises with a thundering chord. He rose to his feet, limped to the front of the piano and said, 'Good evening'. The young civilian remarked smilingly upon the beauty of the room, pocketed a silver-framed miniature of Karla, aged six, and kicked in the glass front of a cabinet of china. Ivo remained impassive. He was in a state of grace and anger and pride were two of the seven deadly sins. Besides, he was uneasily aware that he might have been a little over-familiar with God when he had addressed him earlier in the afternoon.

The three callers advanced steadily over the Persian carpet towards Ivo, the agreeable young man pausing only to throw a Sèvres vase at an oil painting of Ivo's grandfather. The ensuing conversation was as brief as Ivo could have wished for.

'Where are they?'

'Where are what?'

'You know perfectly well what.'

'Yes,' said Ivo. Lying was sinful too.

'I don't know where they are,' he added with truth.

'I really would like to know,' said the young man charmingly.

'I'm afraid I can't help you,' said Ivo staunchly.

The young man smiled and nodded to the Ustasha who looked like a boxer.

'Give him a little help to concentrate his thoughts,' said the young man.

The Ustasha carefully placed his Schmeisser on a glass-topped table and then gave convincing proof that he was indeed a boxer. He stepped towards Ivo, made a little jump to get his feet into position and lashed out with two quick punches, correctly delivered, all his

33

weight behind each, every one of his muscles in arms, shoulders, body and legs co-ordinated. The first punch, a left hook, broke three of Ivo's right ribs. The second, to Ivo's left side, crunched over his heart. Ivo's knees gave way, his back thumped into the piano and he slid slowly towards the floor. He was dead before his body reached it.

'You fool,' said the young man expressionlessly to the Ustasha boxer, 'I said a *little* help.'

So died a good, kindly, decent, anachronistic old gentleman who believed in God, love, honour, duty, patriotism and trust. The timing was right. He would not have liked what was to follow, either in his own country or in most others.

At the time when Ivo died the Bilic family was disposed as follows. Nadja, his wife, was living querulously in a seedy family hotel in the Cromwell Road in West London. She was running out of money. Ivo had provided generously for a three month stay in Britain. She was now in her tenth month. She spent most of her time intriguing listlessly with officials of the Royal Yugoslav Government in exile and she slept intermittently with a Conservative Member of Parliament.

Tomislav, her son by the late racing driver, had completed his post-graduate course in Slavonic Studies at Cambridge and was under training for a commission in the Intelligence Corps.

Branko, the regular soldier, had pledged his destiny to that of an officer whom he disliked personally and whose Pan-Serbian politics he abhorred. But Colonel Draza Mihaelovic was at least prepared to continue fighting Germans and that was enough for Branko to go along with. Branko, with a small band of bearded Chetniks, was marching through the woods and hills of Bosnia, on his way to Montenegro.

Vlado, the painter-musician-philosopher, had left his Ustasha training camp in Italy a day after Ante Pavelic in Zagreb had been proclaimed the Poglavnik of the Independent State of Croatia. Vlado had gone by sea to Zara, been sent to the borders of Southern Croatia and Bosnia, and had been put straight to work to help solve the problem of the one and a half million Serbs who in one way or another had come to live in Croatia. Vlado, the passionate Croatian patriot, found the task exalting, the means necessary but repellent. On the day of his father's death, of which he knew nothing, Vlado had supervised the death by hanging of seven Serbs, including two women, in an Orthodox Church. When he could get some leave he really must go to Zagreb to see the old man.

Lovely Karla, the medical student, with two years seniority as a clandestine member of the Communist Party, was with an underfed, under-trained, ill-equipped and ardent Partisan group in the Montenegrin hills to the East of Trebinje. Her journey with her father's friend the Consul General had been eventful, but successfully accomplished. It had ended in something close to farce. The Southern Adriatic coast had been an Italian objective in the invasion and the Italians had duly scooped up all the assembling diplomats and put them under an affable and courteous guardianship. There followed some urbane negotiations in the course of which His Majesty's Submarine *Regent* made its appearance in the Gulf of Kotor. An officer from the submarine came ashore to talk with the Italians while at the same time two Italian officers boarded *Regent* as surety against harm befalling the Naval officer. In the course of an agreeably conducted parley three unbriefed and unwelcome German Stukas flew into view and dive-bombed and machine-gunned the submarine. The submarine left smartly for Malta, taking its complaining Italian hostages with it. The diplomats were shifted to Italy, interned, and later repatriated according to civilized international custom. Karla slipped away in the confusion, planted her bundle in the cache at the Villa Ribar and went in search of a fisherman whom she knew only as Marko. Marko was efficient and discreet. His organization saw Karla to a pre-selected Communist Party rendezvous in the hills.

Chapter Three

IN JULY 1940, when Britain was the only country left in the fight against Nazi Germany; when the British Expeditionary Force had been evacuated from continental Europe through Dunkirk with the loss of many of its lives and almost all of its equipment; and when a German invasion of Britain seemed to be imminent, Mr Winston Churchill, the British Prime Minister, sent an instruction to Dr Hugh Dalton, the Minister of Economic Warfare. 'Set Europe Ablaze' was a quotation that summarized the message. The instrument for this licensed incendiarism was Special Operations Executive, which over the next five years instigated, arranged and succoured a variety of wartime activities in occupied Europe. SOE's work ranged from intelligence gathering and sabotage to the sustaining of guerrilla operations on a large scale. There were outstanding successes and dismal, costly failures. About the expediency, on occasion the morality, of some of these ventures there was controversy. From time to time there were deep divisions within the organization itself over policy, as was inevitable and up to a point healthy. Some of it was unhealthy. The nature of its task, the spreading of mayhem by means that had to be almost entirely devious, attracted to SOE people from an unusual variety of backgrounds: regular officers, diplomats, bankers, journalists, writers, politicians, engineers, schoolmasters, businessmen, university lecturers.

Among them were patriots, idealists, bums, Christians, Marxists, anarchists, agnostics, exhibitionists, heroes, homosexuals, conservatives, rogues, socialists and intellectual crooks. Their operations were conducted in a militarily necessary atmosphere of secrecy, which carried with it an inbuilt scope for ambiguity.

One of SOE's less celebrated contributions to victory occurred in the middle of 1944. It was called Operation Martingale and it was mounted from Bari in Southern Italy. It went wrong from every point of view; not least that of its progenitor, a lieutenant-colonel named Beverly.

John Beverly was suave, opulent and intelligent, a young former Cambridge don. Some years previously he had been recruited to Soviet Intelligence by the same source whose other protégés, MacLean and Burgess, were currently working in the Foreign Office. Another, Philby, was a senior officer in the Secret Intelligence Service, MI6. Beverly had met Philby and Burgess socially, but knew nothing of their true roles. At the time of his seduction his instructions had been explicit. He was to drop gently out of the left wing undergraduate politics in which he had been dabbling noisily and become the respectable academic figure that everyone expected him to become anyway. He did willingly what he was told. His amusing and recondite lectures on Balkan History had been widely attended. His two books had been well received by the critics, if indifferently rewarded by the book-buying public. His tutorials were greatly enjoyed. A substantial inherited private income enabled him to entertain extensively and his gifts as a raconteur, a shot and a horseman made him the welcome recipient of reciprocal hospitality at the country houses of the parents of some of his better-heeled students. It was on one of these visits that he first met a young man named Challoner, known to his family and friends as

Yeti. Beverly found that he had nothing in common with his host's son.

Very few people had much in common with Yeti Challoner although quite a few horses had. Yeti was squat, dark and hairy with huge feet and a tiny forehead. On the few occasions on which he spoke his words reflected the existence of a thought process of sorts, but one that operated at a slower pace and with less predictable results than was customary among his contemporaries. His voice had a quality of strangled surprise, tempered with resentment, particularly so when he found it actually necessary to string a complete sentence together. Yeti's life centred on the stables and the hunting field and he found it almost intolerably painful to have to listen with courtesy to the incomprehensible conversations indulged in by his father's sophisticated guests. He always made the effort though. Sometimes he contributed a statement, seldom of more than one sentence. He conceived these offerings to be his duty, but despite the worthiness of his intentions they were apt to induce paralysed silences. Two examples of this genre cropped up during Beverly's visit. Yeti, working hard with knitted brows at the fish course at dinner, and listening with total puzzlement to a conversation about modern poets, spotted something recognizable among the verbiage.

'Yeats,' he said slowly. 'I knew a chap called Yeats once. Caught him reading a book in the hunting season.'

With similar facility on the following evening he destroyed a discussion about music.

'Beethoven,' he interrupted unnervingly. 'Sounds like a foreigner.'

It was six years until Yeti and Beverly met again. Beverly found the encounter less than stimulating socially. But he at once recognized an instrument that seemed ideal for the furtherance of a purpose that he had in mind.

In the interim each had become embroiled uncomplainingly in the war. SOE's officers came to it in the only way that they could, by a process of discreet personal recommendation. John Beverly was a natural. Brainy, healthy, thirty years of age, well-connected, linguist, historian, travelled, intimate knowledge of Eastern Europe. He was interviewed and after a cursory security vetting was commissioned into the Intelligence Corps. He duly took up employment at 73 Baker Street, London.

It was the late summer of 1940. The young men of Fighter Command were establishing their legend. They accepted the need to be prepared to die for their country and set about with relish the task of ensuring that as many as possible of their opponents died for theirs. In the penultimate paragraph of the British Empire, New Zealanders, South Africans, Rhodesians, Canadians, Australians and the ambiguously placed neutral Irish, flew and fought alongside their British hosts of the Royal Air Force. So did Poles, Czechs, Frenchmen, Dutch and Belgians, bent on vengeance for the violation of their homelands. 'Never in the field of Human Conflict have so many owed so much to so few,' declaimed Mr Churchill in a phrase that caught at the hearts of his countrymen. (Sir Arthur Conan Doyle had used it years earlier in one of his works in a different context. In 1940 few knew and nobody cared.) The pilots, privately gratified by the tribute, chose to interpret it as a reflection on the size of their mess bills. They battled doggedly on, depleted, exhausted, spirited and indomitable. They won, just. It was possibly the last instance in Western history in which a small group of talented and trained individualists determined the course of the future. To John Beverly, working efficiently inside SOE, it was nothing about which to rejoice. It was an irritating episode in the last ditch defence of Imperialism. Molotov, Ribbentrop and their Soviet-German non-aggression pact proclaimed it so.

Beverly showed himself to be a capable, patient and imaginative staff officer. The requirements of his cover demanded a high standard of performance in his official duties. His early work included the collation of intelligence on the still neutral Balkan countries and the co-ordination of plans for the activation of agents and sabotage parties should they be over-run. He was in at the London end of the scheme for the mining of the Iron Gates on the Danube. On all these subjects he worked well and without deceit, in accordance with his hidden brief. In late 1941 he was promoted and posted to the SOE Headquarters in Cairo which was where, parallel to the impeccable discharge of the duties for which he was paid, he began to develop the project chosen for him by his Soviet masters. The Balkans were by now over-run by the Germans and Italians. Information was scarce and suspect. Beverly's task was long term. He was to divert such British resources as he could reasonably, and without suspicion, lay his hands on to the support of an armed nucleus in Albania who would play a minimal part in guerrilla fighting against the Germans, but who would be poised to seize power when, or if, the Germans were finally forced to withdraw. That group was to be Marxist, Stalinist division.

Beverly found it fairly easy to make himself the Albanian specialist in SOE. He was one of the few people in the organization who had studied the country's cultural and historical background. He had visited it in peace-time. Compared to Greece and Yugoslavia, which carried the main rail and road communications down the peninsula, it was of limited military importance. If Beverly chose in his spare time to absorb himself in the affairs of a barren block of towering rocks inhabited by brigands with unpleasant personal habits he was welcome to his little eccentricity. The way he did the rest of his work did him credit. Beverly cornered Albania and acquired an exiled Albanian patriot named Ali, who had escaped from Tirana to

Cairo in legitimate and exciting circumstances. Ali's lines of control were similar to those of Beverly. Both led back to Moscow.

The essence of Beverly's plan, which underwent a series of progressive refinements over the months, was to parachute Ali with a large sum in gold sovereigns and a reasonable supply of weaponry, explosives and equipment, into Albania. Ali had already arranged for a clandestine reception committee to meet him at a preselected dropping zone. The committee would be activated by an agreed phrase to be used in a news broadcast in Albanian by the British Broadcasting Corporation. Beverly was certain that in the course of time he would be able, by persistence and skilled advocacy, to get his superiors to authorize the use of an RAF aircraft for the operation. There should be no difficulty over the provision of weapons, and explosives. The gold would present greater problems, but they were not insuperable. The main stumbling block lay in the nomination of the British liaison officer who must accompany Ali, a *sine qua non* for any SOE activity of this kind. To suit Beverly's purpose the liaison officer must have an unusual blend of characteristics. Sufficient experience of war to make him look acceptable to the SOE hierarchy; obscurity of a degree that would not make him missed too badly when he was eliminated by Ali's associates, as was his ordained fate; and a rather special streak of stupidity.

Beverly had almost despaired of finding an officer who qualified for this job description when he met Yeti Challoner at a drinks party in the mess of the 99th British General Hospital in Alexandria.

Until a year earlier Yeti had found the war puzzling but enjoyable. As, for practical purposes, a hereditary officer in his county Yeomanry regiment he had embarked for the Middle East in 1940 with the Cavalry Division. In Palestine he and his comrades had been

42

deprived of their horses, an event that generated human and equine rage and sorrow in equal measure. Yeti had found himself the Commander of a Troop of three light tanks, a role in which he had never imagined himself and to which he adapted successfully in a curiously logical way. In his new calling he ignored all those elements of which he lacked knowledge, interest or experience. One of the advantages of military life, he discovered dimly, was that there always seemed to be somebody else available to take care of such matters. He was mechanically illiterate. His soldiers were mechanically adept. He knew, and cared, nothing of administration. His Troop Sergeant, an old sweat, filled in all the right forms, added a percentage for luck and corruption and ensured a constant flow of food, water, ammunition, rum, spare parts, petrol, oil and lubricants. Yeti had no knowledge of either geography or strategy. A chain of his seniors, starting with his Squadron Commander, leading to his Colonel and his Brigadier and fading out of sight through a series of Divisional, Corps and Army mandarins whose names he was unable to remember, ensured through their staffs that Yeti was in the right country at the right time, pointing the right way.

On the domestic plane, Yeti was ignorant of cooking or laundering. His batman, a former groom whom he'd known from childhood, kept him fed, clean and smart. Freed of the mundane demands that plague most people's lives, Yeti was able to concentrate on getting on with his part of the war.

In the Western Desert, to which his regiment went in early 1941, Yeti became something of a minor legend. A lifetime of fox hunting had developed in him a natural feel for country. He could sense how the land lay, what the going would be like. Atlases were meaningless to him but he used a large scale map in the way in which a great conductor uses a musical score. When the tanks of other Troops were bogged in the sand,

43

Yeti's were roaring ahead trailing plumes of dust. When others' tanks, silhouetted on a skyline, were being shelled remorselessly, Yeti's were snugly hull down, ensconced in folds in the ground undiscerned by most. An early grounding in contests of wits with fish, birds, deer and foxes had given him a fine instinct for minor tactics. The guns of his tanks he treated like brothers. It had taken him some time to achieve a working knowledge of wireless procedure but since he seldom said anything, and taciturnity on the air was a military virtue, he was regarded as sound in this respect. He was fearless. He looked after his men in a high-handed, paternalistic style that they liked. They would do anything for him. He had no disciplinary problems, which was just as well because he knew nothing of military law and did not know how to set about putting anyone on a charge. As a squadron commander he would have been calamitous. As a trooper he would have been wasted. As the troop leader of three light tanks he had found his niche.

For the better part of two years Yeti trundled dourly up and down the Egyptian and Libyan deserts, east to west, west to east, now advancing, now retreating, fighting, leaguering, over-hot, over-cold, bothered by flies, on rare occasions enchanted by the sight of gazelle or of wild flowers, respectful of the Afrika Korps, contemptuous of the Italians. He was awarded the Military Cross in the Crusader battles. He won a bar to it in the pursuit after Alamein. In the transient parochial life of an Armoured Regiment in the Desert where people came, were killed, wounded, went, Yeti was a fixture, a character, undisturbed by ambition, held in respect, awe. He seldom said a thing and didn't need to. He was the chap who'd done so well in the last battle but one, at Sidi Rezegh, Tobruk, the Cauldron. What was interpreted as one of his better witticisms was recalled, repeatedly and affectionately, throughout the Brigade.

The Colonel of an armoured car regiment had come across Yeti in an abandoned Italian school outside Sirte.

Yeti, in faded black beret, khaki bush jacket, polka dot silk scarf, corduroy trousers and desert boots, was making an earnest study of a globe on which was mapped the world. Yeti, burnt almost black by the sun, brows knitted together, was concentrating.

'Hallo, Yeti.'

There was a long pause. Yeti needed time to adjust himself to changed circumstances. He slowly identified the caller.

'*Morning, Colonel,' he said grudgingly, when he had absorbed the facts.

'What are you looking for?' asked the Colonel.

Yeti continued to stare at the globe, spinning it slowly around its axis.

'Where's Libya?' he asked finally. He'd been there for the past eighteen months. It was a genuine enquiry.

Outside El Algheila, after the pursuit from Alamein, Yeti's Troop led the Squadron, the Regiment, the Brigade, the Division. Yeti was the ace navigator, a fulfilled, gloomy-looking, happy man. He was standing up in his tank, coloured pennant flying, map in its talc-covered case in front of him, elbows on the rim of the turret. The off-side track ran over a Teller mine and the suddenly accumulated compressed air inside the tank blew Yeti out of the turret like a cork from a champagne bottle. Years of being thrown from horses had accustomed him to this manoeuvre, although the strength of the propellant force on this occasion was more than he was used to. He went through a perfectly proportioned arc, landed on his head and bounced. Stretcher-bearers picked him up. The Regimental Medical Officer diagnosed two broken legs, a fractured pelvis, a dented shoulder, multiple contusions and abrasions about the face and body, and a medically confusing absence of shock, a condition in which Yeti had no confidence. His driver was dead and his gunner had lost both legs. Later Yeti, without telling anyone, made financial provision for the widow of the first and paid for specialist surgical treatment for the second.

It took the doctors in Cairo more than a year to put Yeti together again. They were impressed by his physical toughness but frustrated by his unwillingness to describe his symptoms. Yeti had a strong proprietary feeling about his body and had no intention of discussing it with strangers, particularly with this crowd, most of whom seemed to be Irish and talkative, untrustworthy on both scores.

After some months the dispersed parts of Yeti had knitted together sufficiently to allow him to limp about tentatively on two rubber-padded walking sticks. It was a moment of triumph in Officers Ward B, Surgical; and not for conventional reasons of pleasure that a fellow patient was on his feet again. It was a relief to have the morose, wordless bastard out of the way. Week by week, month by month, he progressed. He was put on Light Duties, which in his context meant that every two weeks he became the hospital's orderly officer. He was unsure of the meaning of the term, indifferent to the job's significance and bewildered by its modest requirements. A Royal Army Medical Corps staff-sergeant, straight-backed and of clipped speech, guided him around wards, stores and gardens. Yeti stumped about gloomily after him, understanding nothing and accidentally stimulating efficiency by the expression of vacuous ferocity on his face. A year after he was wounded he was pronounced fit for duty but not for active service. He was promoted Captain and appointed to an administrative headquarters in Alexandria. Yeti said that he wanted neither the promotion nor the appointment. He wanted to rejoin his regiment in the Desert.

He was told, with incredulity, that his regiment was no longer in the Desert. Nor was anyone else. The Desert campaigns were over. The Germans had been beaten. His regiment had returned to Britain. The war had moved to continental Europe. Sicily had been captured. Italy had been invaded. The Fifth Army was currently engaged in a major fight at Salerno and the Eighth Army was moving slowly up the heel of Italy. This was news to Yeti and he was sorry to hear it. He couldn't work out where these places were but it was a nasty blow to discover that there would be no more Desert fighting. He had never enjoyed himself so much in his life as in the Desert. He went wordlessly to take up his job as Deputy Assistant Adjutant and Quartermaster General in the administrative headquarters in Alexandria.

Within three months he had done almost as much damage to the Allied War Effort as had Rommel in two years. At the hospital drinks party Yeti gladly accepted Beverly's cautiously worded offer of an interesting job of an unspecified but exciting nature and was not in the least put out when his superiors on the staff endorsed his transfer with an offensive enthusiasm. Yeti never had understood these chaps, whose reputation as it happened was at the time none too high with some of the fighting troops in Italy. A snowbound, mud-encased infantry division on the Sangro was blasphemously disposing of a consignment of pith sun helmets, sent to them with great care and at huge expense by an uncomprehending stroke of Yeti's awkwardly held pen. The matter of the crated tank spare parts, addressed by Yeti to Singapore two years after its capture by the Japanese, only emerged in its nightmare light some time after Yeti's departure from Alexandria.

Beverly worked tirelessly on his little scheme and Yeti was put into training. First, a parachute course. Yeti was fearless to the point of near suicide, and on a memorable jump had to be knocked unconscious by one instructor while the other hooked Yeti up to the static line, a precaution that Yeti had overlooked. Yeti's havoc-ridden progress through a demolitions course led to the hospitalization of three of the instructional staff, two with physical and one with psychological injuries. He flatly refused to attend a signals procedure course on the grounds that he already knew it. Attempts to teach him Albanian, admittedly a famously difficult tongue, were fruitless. At a refresher course on small arms – pistol, rifle, Bren, Tommy gun, Sten – Yeti came top. On a course in the encodement of messages Yeti came bottom, and indeed, with no marks at all, set a record. Reading the reports of the results of all this expensive education in subversion, Beverly was impressed. Yeti was undoubtedly the most unsuitable officer ever to be selected for an SOE operation. Beverly liked it that way.

The branch of SOE dealing with the Balkans moved to Bari, on the Adriatic coast of Italy. Things were warming up. Sabotage was going well in Greece. Useful operational intelligence was being signalled out of Romania and Hungary. In Yugoslavia it had been established that the earlier British favourite, General Mihaelovic, and his Chetniks, was no longer fighting actively against the Germans. His major enemies were now the Communist-led Partisans whom he saw as the real threat to the restoration of the Serb-dominated monarchy to which his loyalty was pledged. Mihaelovic had reached accommodations with the Germans and had co-operated with them in operations against the Partisans. The principle behind British policy was of fundamental simplicity. The post-war ordering of the internal affairs of Yugoslavia was for the Yugoslavs to determine themselves. The current British objective was to win the war as quickly as was possible and the present key question was who in Yugoslavia was killing most Germans? An exploratory British party, led by Major Bill Deakin, dropped to the Partisans in the midst of a merciless fight in which the Partisan main body was extricating itself from German encirclement on Mount Durmitor in Montenegro. Deakin reported that when it came to killing Germans the Partisans were ahead by a very long lead. Mihaelovic was abandoned. A British Military Mission parachuted to Marshal Tito's headquarters in Bosnia, with similar subordinate missions going subsequently to Partisan formations throughout the country. Weapons, ammunition, medicine, equipment, boots, clothing were airdropped, air landed, brought in by sea, following advice from these officers. Sustained by these stores the most successful Resistance Movement of the Second World War rolled inexorably on its way.

Beverly showed an efficient but, given his beliefs and brief, unenthusiastic concern for some minor operations in Albania in support of anti-German bands of no evident ideological commitment. He carefully prepared the ground for Martingale and awaited patiently the right moment to propose it, which would have to be a time when there was general preoccupation with a major crisis elsewhere. A German airborne attack on Tito's headquarters at Drvar in Bosnia provided the opportunity. Tito was to be evacuated to Italy, a major enterprise in itself and one that would be followed by complex discussion, strategic and political, demanding exhaustive briefing and the attention of most of the staff of SOE. The almost absent-minded acceptance of Beverly's plan for Martingale came after an absurdly easy passage. It was early in June, 1944.

As Yeti's wireless operator Beverly had selected a sergeant named Hicks. Beverly had picked him on the basis of the reports of Hicks' progress in training. Technically highly competent. Very lazy. Did precisely what he was told but no more. Lack of initiative. Unwillingness to accept responsibility. Just the

49

man for this job, thought Beverly happily. He and Yeti together would make a thoroughly beatable combination.

Yeti found Hicks something of a conundrum. Since Hicks would never do anything unless he was told to and Yeti could never think of anything to tell him to do, their pre-flight dealings assumed a strange, wordless passivity which both, for different reasons, found rather agreeable. Hicks early reached the private conclusion that Yeti was a dangerous nutter. Yeti and Hicks were, however, silently united over one matter, their view of Ali the Albanian patriot. Ali was slight, with oiled black hair, glittering brown eyes, a nose shaped like the centre board of a dinghy, a pencil moustache and gleaming white teeth. He was drenched in scent and he chattered ceaselessly in a high-pitched voice with an Oxford accent. He was pathologically secretive about his doings, a wasted precaution because Yeti would have been unable to understand them and Hicks wasn't interested. Yeti suspected grimly that Ali led an absolutely disgusting private life.

Encumbered by equipment, crowded by the containers that held their stores, almost suffocated by Ali's powerful perfume, and deafened by the noise of aircraft engines, this strange team of unreconciled components looked gloomily out of a Halifax bomber as it roared eastward towards Albania over the moonlit Adriatic. Ali knew exactly what he intended to do. Yeti was in his customary condition of dogged bafflement. Hicks didn't care.

Chapter Four

CAPTAIN KLAUS MÜLLER was tired, bored, irritated and standing in a small stony field near Viluse, an undistinguished village at a road junction in Montenegro. The early phases of his battery's journey from Athens had gone well, given the decrepitude of the vehicles that towed his light Flak guns, the state of the roads, and the unsoldierly incompetence of the men he had taken over three months previously. Müller was a soldiers' soldier. He had fought in Poland, France and Russia. Above all in Russia. He had lost a foot and two fingers of his left hand at Kiev and after prolonged treatment and convalescence had been sent to Greece to command this Flak battery. He had been appalled at what he found. These were not German soldiers as he understood the term. These were flabby, middle-aged, ill-disciplined no-hopers, soft after too long in the Mediterranean sunshine, debilitated by venereal disease and alcoholism. He had mercilessly beaten them into some sort of shape. He had welcomed the order to transfer his battery to Italy where there was serious soldiering to be done. He had nursed them this far on their journey. He had not been too surprised when the mechanical ailments of his aged transport had forced a halt on his march and the need for major maintenance. He had been outraged to discover that the nearest spare parts depot was at Mostar, over a hundred kilometres away in Hercegovina, and that because of

51

Partisan depredations he would have to wait for two weeks until a convoy escorted by armour could bring him what he required. And he had been incensed by the performance of the fat, shaven-headed old fool of a Colonel in Viluse, who had welcomed the battery to his command and officiously incorporated it in a ridiculous scheme for what he called his 'Allied Aircraft Ambush'. Müller had protested and had been told to hold his tongue. Thereafter he had obeyed orders, with a steaming resentment that he took out on his overhung, poxed-up soldiery.

Every night for the past eight nights he had stood behind his guns in the little field. Their crews slept around their weapons, one member of each crew awake and alert. Two miles behind them, further up the valley, others of the Colonel's minions waited around prepared bundles of brushwood, set out symmetrically in the form of an elongated cross. At the signal, if it ever came, they would throw petrol on to the brushwood and ignite it. The signal would be given when the sound of the engines of an Allied aircraft was heard. A few had been over in previous weeks dropping stores and, so Intelligence reported, at least one British liaison party, to Partisans in the area. Intelligence had also established that the Partisans guided the visitors to their dropping zones by the aid of fires laid out in a big cross.

So, thought Müller angrily, because that stupid lump of ageing pomposity, the Colonel, wanted to play his silly games in a futile attempt to lure the RAF and the USAAF to the wrong dropping zone he, Müller, was condemned to spend every night standing sleeplessly on a bleak, Godforsaken hillside in the most barbarous country it had ever been his misfortune . . .

At that point in his thoughts he heard the throb of aircraft engines, growing louder.

Like many of his generation Pilot Officer Ginger

Cartwright had been passionately addicted to the thought of flying almost from the time when he first learnt to walk. At the earliest possible moment, when he was seventeen and a half, he had volunteered for RAF aircrew. He had passed the aptitude tests and at eighteen had been called up. Tested again, he had been faced with a bitter disappointment. There was an over-abundance of better qualified applicants to become pilots. He would have to train as a navigator. Well, it was still flying. Cartwright made the most of it.

He was a pleasant, shy, gallant young man, covered in freckles and with, for his trade, an intermittent weakness. His mathematics were unreliable. Not hopelessly bad, but inconsistent. Usually he got his sums right. Sometimes he miscalculated. To insure against this unpredictable backsliding he had, during his training in Canada, resorted to extensive cheating. Help from compliant friends, some ability and some luck had seen him through the course. The last two attributes had also seen him successfully through seven operations. On this flight to Albania, carrying those odd looking bods in the back, his nineteen-year-old brain was slowly realizing that luck and maths had combined to let him down. He knew vaguely where he was to within a hundred miles or so, but conceded to himself that that was not good enough for a navigator in the Royal Air Force. When they came out of this pall of cloud he would have to make an embarrassing confession to his pilot, an old fire-eater of twenty-one with a devastating line in sarcasm.

The cloud thinned and they were suddenly in bright moonlight. Ginger Cartwright looked sharply downwards. Rugged, intricate peaks, rising from an upland plateau. Some patches of snow, still unmelted on the north facing slopes. Shadowed valleys. A cluster of shapeless buildings, a large farm or a small village.

'Whacko, Ginge. Bang on,' said a voice in his headphones. (The RAF spoke with the tongue of a strange, inbred sub-culture.) The pilot was heading for some clearly defined signal fires, laid out in the form of a cross. Ginger mentally thanked his luck and went back to alert the bods. The despatcher had already forestalled him. He was hooking up the three cylindrical canisters of stores, which were to be dropped first, on to the static line. The three bods were hooking themselves up, the miserable loopy-looking pongo officer immediately behind the canisters, the dozey clot of a sergeant behind him, and the foul-smelling foreign poofdah last of all. Ginger bawled 'Three minutes' into each of their ears over the row of the engines. He gave a thumbs up signal, tripped over the fastenings of the large leg pack attached to the poofdah's ankle, and returned to his seat beside the pilot.

'We'll make a pass straight down the valley over the fires,' said the pilot. 'And take a look-see. Then I'll circle for the jump.'

The second part of this programme proved to be unnecessary. Fifteen seconds after it was formulated Ginger and the pilot saw, below and in front of them, an eruption of familiar looking flashes. From these, lines of tracer, at first seemingly slowly, subsequently and disturbingly racing, poured towards the Halifax. Much of it burst wide of the starboard wing tip. The pilot wrenched the aircraft from side to side in an attempt at evasion. There was a colossal bang immediately below the machine's belly and the aircraft staggered about the sky temporarily uncontrolled. Two further bangs, uncomfortably close but less damaging than the first. For several seconds the aircraft wallowed about in a style beyond its crew's experience. A large strip of something detached itself from somewhere below, the aircraft bounced upwards as if relieved of a heavy weight and the pilot was through. The rear-gunner reported on the intercom that a bloody great lump of something he couldn't identify had blocked the approach to his turret and he was on his bloody tod. No he hadn't a bloody clue what had happened but before the skipper had had the good sense to bugger off out of the fucking flak he, the rear-gunner, had seen five parachutes descending in the moonlight towards a sharp looking mountain. He gave it as his private opinion that those bastards must be raving mad and was starting to add his reasons for this assessment when he was briskly ordered by the elderly, twenty-one-year-old fire-eating pilot to shut up. Affronted, he sulked all the way back to Foggia.

Captain Müller was enraged by what he thought had been the indifferent shooting of his clapped-out Flak battery. He had noted one very near miss and two not so near ones. It was, he told his cowed, sullen gunners, a disgraceful exhibition. No aircraft at that height, speed and course, would have survived in Russia. The fat Colonel, who had never been to Russia, berated Müller in similar tones. A brilliantly planned aerial ambush had been ruined by the uselessness, lack of training and ineptitude of Müller's command. Both the Colonel and Müller were wrong. The three close misses that Müller had observed had put paid to Operation Martingale, altered in emphasis if not in character the course of Albanian history, and led eventually to a Court of Enquiry on the activities of Colonel John Beverly. The findings of the Court effectively prevented him from ever again having access to knowledge of any of the classified activities, military or civil, of the British Government.

It was the very near miss that did most of the damage. Three smallish shell splinters penetrated the skin of the Halifax opposite to where Ali was standing. Of these one lodged in his liver and one in his brain. He died at once, his body collapsed towards the entrance to the crew's cabin. The third splinter severed the line by

55

which his leg bag had been attached to his ankle. These three splinters were but brief heralds of a more specta-cular development that followed their arrival fractionally later. Much longer, razor sharp, steel shards from the shell had sliced laterally into the underside of the fuselage, tearing loose a large half-circular section that hung for a second like the partly opened lid of a can of beans. Further miscellaneous structural damage and the sudden rushing through the hole of a com-pacted mass of high speed air attended to the rest. A length of underside was ripped jaggedly away, pointed downwards for a second or two, broke off, and blew into the night. The effect on Yeti, Sergeant Hicks and the containers, all hooked to the static line inside, was instantaneous. The floor disappeared from beneath them and they hurtled into the fresh air, feeling sur-prised. The despatcher, hanging by his hands from the static line, watched their departure with concern and then pulled his legs up and curled them round the static line too. Ginger Cartwright found him there ten min-utes later, shivering with cold and looking like a monkey on a tree branch. Helped to safety he reported that he had seen five parachutes open including those of the two bods. There had however been a couple of big bangs fairly close to them just after they had dropped out.

There had indeed. The first blew open one of the stores canisters and scattered its contents about the night sky. The second shredded Ali's leg-bag, which unlike its owner's body had fallen from the aircraft. Ali had been secretive about what was in it, referring mysteriously to an indifferent audience to the presence of 'State Papers'. The nature of these archives now became known to Yeti. He floated resentfully down under the canopy of his parachute amidst a cascade of falling gold coins from the stricken canister and a wafting litter of contraceptives, pornographic pictures and sharp fragments of broken scent bottles from Ali's leg-bag. These continued to blow about Yeti, or clatter dangerously down, according to their nature, when he had landed. He divested himself of his harness and looked morosely around him. He disliked what little he could see. Not like the good old days in the Desert.

On the following morning Yeti and Sergeant Hicks held what, in other circumstances, would have been called a conference. This particular moot was hamstrung by familiar symptoms. Hicks was prepared to put his skills as a communicator on permanent offer but had no intention of doing anything else unless he were ordered to do it. As he saw it, it was up to Yeti to work out the next move. Yeti had never been much of a man at working out any moves unconnected with horses and his nostalgically remembered tank, and he was faced with a problem that would have taxed the resources of people provided with a much more elaborate range of mental equipment.

As the morning mist was slowly burned away by the sun Yeti saw that he and Hicks were on a small, high, rocky limestone plateau, backed to the east by a craggy mountain and dropping steeply on the other three sides to a tangle of valleys and twisted old watercourses. At the northern end of the plateau was an unoccupied, roughly built stone hut. Shelter, on this summer pasture, for shepherds. Towards the middle of the plateau was one intact stores canister. A second had disappeared, who knew where. The contents of the third were spread about the ground, glinting capriciously amidst torn fragments of Ali's objets d'art and his socio-medical requirements. There was no sign of any life, human or animal. The first thing to try to establish, concluded Yeti, was where they were. He took his Albanian maps out of the map pocket on the front of his battle-dress trousers and tried to orientate himself. Nothing in this landscape coincided with any features shown on the maps. Discussion on Item One of the conference's agenda was short and inconclusive.

'Any idea where we are?' Yeti asked Sergeant Hicks.

'No,' said Hicks, without interest.

Item Two wriggled evasively about in Yeti's mind until he at last pinned it down.

'Better send a message,' said Yeti.

'Yes, Sir,' said Hicks. He assembled his set efficiently, tinkered with the aerial, twiddled some knobs and got himself on to the right frequency. That done he took the code book from his small pack, topped and tailed a message form, and handed it to Yeti to insert the message. Any message, so far as Hicks was concerned.

Yeti wasn't very good at messages. Instant oral communication on the RT set of a tank squadron's net was one thing. Writing his thoughts down was another. It took him several minutes of concentrated composition before he handed the completed form to Hicks. Hicks took it wordlessly, encyphered it and sent it.

'Arrived safely,' it read.

Bari told Hicks to stand by for a reply in one hour's time. This, when it came, consisted of a long series of questions about where Yeti was, what he was doing and what were his intentions. Since Yeti knew none of the answers he didn't bother to reply. Hicks did not contest this decision. It was none of his business. Besides, it cut down the work.

Yeti's third and last agenda item did involve Hicks in some work. Yeti decided to tidy up the plateau. They moved their equipment, the stores canister, the parachutes and the wireless set to the stone hut. Laboriously they combed the stony soil, collected the gold sovereigns, counted them and stacked them in neat rows beside the parachutes. Lastly they picked up all the fragments they could find of Ali's memorabilia, piled them together, and set fire to them, retreating rapidly up-wind when the flames reached Ali's intimate necessities.

During the silent meal that followed Yeti made a muddled, but on the whole adequate, attempt to muster the facts available to him and to draw conclusions from them. He and Hicks were on the side of a mountain in what he assumed must be Albania, although not the part of Albania in which he had expected to be. With Ali gone he had no means of communicating with the inhabitants, if there were any, a point on which he lacked evidence. There were ample supplies of compo rations in the stores canisters, which also held an assortment of weaponry, ammunition, clothing and boots. There was water from a small stream that tinkled on to the plateau from the high ground to the east. There was a weighty pile of gold sovereigns for which he probably held some sort of responsibility. There were two courses of action available to him. He could go swanning around the mountains trying to find out where he was, with the concomitant risks that he would probably make a fool of himself, or blunder into some Germans, or do both simultaneously. Alternatively, he could stay on his hillside, virtuously guard his hoard of gold and wait for something to turn up. Something undoubtedly would. At any rate it always had in the Desert. Yeti made his decision and his over-worked brain slipped automatically into its more customary gear, neutral. They would stay on the hill.

Yeti passed this news to a recumbent Sergeant Hicks who received it unemotionally. To Yeti's next question, posed some ten minutes later, Hicks said 'Yes, Sir.'

'Do you know how to play noughts and crosses?' Yeti had asked.

In Bari Lieutenant Colonel John Beverly was still

trying vainly to stitch together a rational hypothesis that could account for the fate of Operation Martingale. The first source of information arose from the debriefing of the Halifax pilot. Since he had had no reason to believe that Ginger Cartwright had navigated him to anywhere other than his planned destination, and since Ginger himself, despite his earlier doubts, was now convinced that he'd had it right all along, helped by his usual luck, the pilot had reported that the first leg of the trip had been uneventful. He had found the signal fires more or less on time and in place. He had been about to circle them, prior to dropping his passengers and cargo, when he had come under heavy and accurate fire from a light Flak battery. The underside of his aircraft had suffered severe damage, one of his passengers had been killed, and the rest and their accompanying containers had dropped successfully. On the return flight westward across the Adriatic the aircraft had briefly run into turbulence and the body of the passenger earlier killed by Flak splinters had unfortunately fallen through the hole in the deck and disappeared. And that was that. The report signed, pilot and crew went cheerfully off to a breakfast of coffee, bacon and eggs during which most of the conversation was devoted to banter about the simian adventures of the despatcher on the static line.

To Beverly this report was disturbing. The presence of the flak battery indicated that the Dropping Zone had been compromised at the Albanian end. Double treachery? Information squeezed out by torture? Willingly provided, for gain? It didn't really matter. Something had gone badly wrong in Albania and Ali was dead. Beverly's chief concern was to identify any elements in the fiasco that might point to his own ambivalent role. After prolonged thought he could still think of none. He was clean. His composure was shortly afterwards dented by Yeti's 'Arrived safely' message. A careful check with the signals centre confirmed that if the body of the message left something to be desired the procedure used in transmission had been correct in all respects. The cypher had been the one allocated theoretically to Yeti but practically to Sergeant Hicks. The security indicator, an unobtrusive phrasing in the layout of how the signal had been addressed, showed that it had not been sent under duress. The lack of subsequent response to Beverly's detailed questionnaire suggested three possibilities. Hicks' set had suddenly broken down. Improbable. Yeti and Hicks had been caught or killed by either the Germans or Beverly's Albanian associates. Possible. Yeti and Hicks had been surprised, had abandoned or were unable to operate the set, and were now on the run in the Albanian mountains. Also possible. All three contingencies were equally comforting to Beverly. Yeti and Hicks were unlikely to be heard of again. At the daily morning meeting Beverly made his report in competent and restrained terms. One of several SOE operations had run into trouble. It was an occupational risk and Beverly had his colleagues' sympathy.

Beverly was correspondingly put out when, three weeks later, a further fully authenticated signal arrived from Hicks, couched in terms that would have been recognizable to Yeti's old friends in the Desert.

'Where is Yugoslavia?' it read tersely.

This message had a slightly complicated genesis. Yeti's hillside might have seemed to him to be destitute of population but features on such massifs seldom are, particularly when they incorporate summer upland pastures. Since shortly after first light on the morning of their arrival Yeti and Hicks had been under observation by a ten-year-old boy named Bogdan Bojanic. He was a sad, resolute, self-sufficient and inarticulate lad and, as befitted the son of a Montenegrin shepherd, he had a developed aptitude for fieldcraft that would have earned the respect of a Pathan tribesman on the North

61

West Frontier of India. Immobile, unwinking, he silently set himself up amidst some loosely distributed rocks within a hundred yards of these strange people who had dropped from the sky. He watched. He himself was indistinguishable from the rocks that surrounded him. Experience and necessity had given him a keen sense of self-preservation.

Until his seventh birthday in 1941 he had led a hard, happy and secure life. His parents were peasants, as had been their ancestors back to their unrecorded origins. Bogdan had been nurtured with his elder brother and sister in a one-roomed, earth-floored stone cottage. The family grew sweet corn, vegetables and plum and apple trees. They had a pig or two, chickens, and some sheep and goats. They gathered firewood locally. Bogdan's mother loved him as the youngest and his brother and sister spoiled him. His father kept these processes from getting out of control, encouraged him and taught him the immemorial skills that he would need for survival. In the summer Bogdan accompanied his father to the upland grazing where Yeti had settled. There were produce-laden visits to the market in the nearest town, Risan. In the winter there was little to do except explore the rocky hills, watch his father get affably drunk on *rakija*, go to sleep at dusk and rise at dawn. This satisfying if limited routine had long since disappeared for young Bogdan.

The Italians were first. They raped his sister and bayonetted his mother when she objected. Bogdan went to help his mother and was knocked unconscious by a blow from a rifle butt. His father and elder brother had been out of the house at the time, selling a pig. On their return they comforted his sister, resuscitated Bogdan, arranged for an elaborate Orthodox burial for his mother and resorted to a traditional Montenegrin remedy hallowed by generations of resistance to Turks, Austrians and other outsiders and by equally lethal internecine blood feuds. They picked up their guns and took to the hills. Bogdan, aged seven, suffering from contusions, shock and grief, was left in the care of a half mad, pregnant fifteen-year-old sister.

Chetniks came next, wild, bearded, fur-hatted men, at that time fighting with enthusiasm and cruelty against the invader. They were welcome guests. Bogdan's father and brother were among them. There was much boastful, alcohol-inspired, belligerent talk and some haunting Slav singing. They left vinously to ambush a small Italian convoy, a deed they accomplished with the loss of one man, left seriously wounded at the site of the action. Bogdan saw his body the following day, hanging from a tree. His face showed marks of beating and burning. It was Bogdan's elder brother. Little Bogdan returned sightlessly to his sister and told her what he had seen. She had a miscarriage, nearly died and thereafter, broken-willed, broken-hearted, devoted herself listlessly to looking after Bogdan.

In the summer of 1943 the Partisans appeared. The Italians, although neither Bogdan nor his sister were to know of it, had surrendered, and the Partisans were engaged in a race to the coast with the Germans to secure Italian arms and equipment. Bogdan, now aged nine, and possessed of a precociously embittered understanding of the realities of life as he had experienced it, quite liked the Partisans. Hard, tough, intent people. There was, however, one thing about them that alarmed him. They made clear that one of their objectives was to kill Chetniks who they said had been helping the Germans. Had young Bogdan seen any Chetniks? Bogdan said no, lying. His father was around, somewhere, although Bogdan hadn't seen him for over six months.

The Partisans came back from the coast, laden with Italian arms, before disappearing again into the mountains. They spent a night around the Bojanic cottage, left some surplus cheese and fruit and also enough

63

evidence of their presence to arouse the fury of the mixed German and Ustasha force who were following them up. Bogdan's sister was beaten, raped again, watched the cottage being set on fire and was thrown into the flames. Bogdan, hidden in the rocks nearby, listened to the last of her screams and turned, half mad himself, to the mountains. In these, for over a year, he had led a lonely, almost independent existence.

The experience of his young life had taught him that contact with mankind led to suffering. He avoided mankind. It was not too difficult an aim to achieve in these wild mountains. He knew every valley, every peak, spur, cave, stream. The Germans, whose objective was solely to keep open secure lines of communications through the roads and towns, seldom came near the hinterland. The Ustasha were simply the junior component in German plans. They were mainly occupied on static guard duties on the roads. There were some Chetnik bands and a growing number of Partisan groups, but initially Bogdan kept well clear of both. A precocious cunning warned him that attachment to either would sooner or later involve him in further killing. He was skilled at evasion and survival and he went his solitary way, living on fish from the streams, snaring animals, gathering berries and roots and fruit from abandoned, mostly burned out, smallholdings. He survived the summer and the autumn. In the snows of the winter Partisans found him in a small cave, unconscious, starving and with a high fever. They were half-starving themselves, but they took him with them, nourished and warmed him from their meagre resources. The instrument of his recovery was a young girl doctor known as Olga, who wasn't really a doctor and whose name wasn't Olga. Bogdan came to worship her. For the first time since his mother's death he experienced the tenderness and love without which life for a child is an aching vacuum. But he refused to speak to her, any more than he would speak to anyone else.

These people, Olga above all, were as kind to him as they could be in the rough circumstances of their precarious lives. But if they found his father they would kill him. He knew by instinct that if he kept his mouth shut there would be less possibility of unconscious betrayal.

He passed the winter with them, in five separate camps, abandoned farms and caves high in the hills. Occasional parties went out on minor forays but the weather put an effective end to serious operations. On a spring morning Bogdan was found to have vanished. He had resumed his solitary life.

It was relatively uneventful. From time to time he heard the sound of distant shooting – spandaus going brr-roomph, shells and mortar bombs banging, demolitions exploding. None of it was near enough to trouble him. From a carefully prepared hide on a cliff-top he once caught a glimpse of his father, bedraggled and exhausted, marching wearily in a single file of Chetniks along a stony track below. Bogdan fought hard, and defeated, an urge to run to him. Best to know as little as possible of his father's movements. The Partisans had been gentle with Bogdan, but he had seen their way of getting information from people reluctant to disclose it. He wanted to know as little as possible. Only once at that time did tears come to his eyes. From another of his hides he overlooked a Partisan column swinging along a mountain path. It was the sight of Doctor Olga that moved him.

And then one night there had been the sound of rapid-firing guns, the roar of aircraft engines, flashings in the sky, and a brief sight, away to the east, of a few puzzling white mushrooms dropping slowly to the plateau which his father had once used for summer grazing. Bogdan was there by dawn.

As a form of remedial therapy for a tough, small boy who had been confronted brutally with too much horror,

65

bereavement, sorrow and suffering, a prolonged study of Yeti and Hicks was without equal. He certainly wouldn't approach them. He had seen too much of the murderously inconsequential behaviour of adult strangers to do that. But as he watched their incomprehensible activities, and contemplated the extraordinary nature of their arrival, Bogdan became slowly, subconsciously, aware that here was something that had been missing from his life since the death of his mother and his father's departure to the mountains. He remembered her fairy stories and his father's fondly told tales, the product of centuries of oral tradition, of bygone Montenegrin deeds of valour and romance. For nearly three years his deprivation from these sources of enchantment had been total. Now it was all here, in real life, in front of him. Bogdan watched in fascination. The necessary, self-preserving armour that would never altogether leave him while he lived took second place to a more serious consideration. He was a small boy again, bubbling with curiosity.

These magical creatures had dropped straight out of the sky, presumably from heaven. They seldom spoke, but when they did it was in an intriguing series of short grunts. On the first day one of them, the taller, thin fair one, had unpacked an oddly shaped box, put it on a rock, extended an almost invisible metallic shiny stick to it and had earnestly tapped out, with delicately poised fingers, a sort of rhythmic muted clatter on a small gadget with a knob on it. Then he had put it all away again. And what about those little round shiny things, glittering among the stones and then collected by these wondrous creatures? Bogdan's mother's fairy tales had had frequent references to gold. Could this be gold? He was sure of it. And the way the two men, or angels, or whatever they were, sat down opposite each other, a small rock in between, and alternately made a mark on a piece of paper with the pencil each clutched. And never spoke a word. For hours on end. No adult

Montenegrin of Bogdan's acquaintance would have kept quiet for a minute in the circumstances. At the end of an enchanting week of watching, Bogdan the boy, not Bogdan the skilled survivor, could keep these delights to himself no longer. He just had to tell somebody. That meant either his father or the woman doctor, Olga. He went methodically back into the mountains, moving with his habitual caution, in search of one or the other. He would share his secret with the first one he encountered. Fortunately for Yeti and Hicks it was Doctor Olga.

It had taken little Bogdan ten days to track down his old friends and protectors. They had just returned from a prolonged running fight with a Ustasha infantry screen that had been clearing the heights on either side of an upland valley. A column of German half-tracks, armoured cars and light guns had been moving slowly along the narrow road at its bottom. They had supported their Ustasha allies with mortars and occasional sustained bursts of long-range spandau fire. The whole affair had been messy and inconclusive. The Partisans had butchered a few Ustasha, taken their weapons, and stripped them of their clothing and boots. The German column had gone to wherever it wanted to go and achieved whatever its purposes were.

Doctor Olga, in the ruins of what had once been the shooting lodge of a wealthy Dubrovnik merchant, had just finished attending to four badly wounded, and two lightly hit, Partisans, all victims of eighty-one-millimetre mortar bombs. She had, with primitive instruments and without anaesthetic other than powerful doses of *rakija*, amputated two feet and one arm. Long usage, nearly three years of it, had made this sort of rough and ready surgery familiar. It had never dulled her sensitivity. It had been worse in Bosnia and during the break out from Durmitor during the Sixth Offensive. Then there had been no drugs whatsoever. Dressings had been used, washed, used again, washed again, until they had disintegrated. It had been better for a time after the Italians had given up and a large haul of their medical stores had been efficiently abstracted and distributed by the Partisans. It was worse again now. It would get better soon, probably next week. The competent looking liaison officer from the British Military Mission who had parachuted in a week previously, and whose manifold lists of Partisan requirements included her recommendations for her 'hospital', had sent his signal to Italy. The first drop was due. But knowledge of this imminent manna did not counteract the mixture of emotions that had always followed the surgery she had had to perform. Sadness; bitterness; doubt; admiration for the stoicism of her patients; amazement at their physical resilience, their powers of recovery, the men hopping around one-legged within forty-eight hours of having a foot taken off. She invariably felt drained and always wanted to cry. In three years she never had.

A laughing small boy, whose life she had first saved and then cherished, who had never smiled or talked in her presence, whose mind she had feared was irretrievably damaged, whose name she had never known, and who had run away on a spring night, came rushing towards her shouting through the overgrown ruin of the garden of a Montenegrin shooting lodge. She stared in astonishment. He threw his arms around her, put his head against her bosom and hugged her.

'Oh,' he said happily. 'Oh. *Gospodica* Olga.'

Gospodica Olga forgot the self-imposed discipline of three years of Partisan campaigning. She burst into tears. And she hugged little Bogdan hard, hard, hard and with love and relief.

Chapter Five

AT THE CONFERENCE held one hour later some time was wasted on irrelevancies. The Commissar and the Brigade Commander were logical, blunt and outspoken. Whoever the two men seen by Bogdan on the plateau were they must be secured and interrogated. If they resisted they should be killed. Henderson, the Croatian-speaking Captain from the British Mission, entirely agreed on the first count but urged restraint on the second. Bogdan, with his penetrating eye, had never seen British uniforms before but when he saw Henderson's he identified it at once. The men on the plateau were dressed just like Henderson. Henderson argued that on that testimony it must be assumed that the two castaways were British. If that were so, commented the Commissar, a dour suspicious pedantic Marxist who did nothing to disguise his view that Henderson was a presently useful, but otherwise despicable, capitalist lackey, what were they doing there? Henderson conceded that he didn't know. Well, said the Commissar cynically, that left two possibilities. Either Henderson was lying, in which case he was criminally involved in a British conspiracy to spy on, sabotage or betray the heroic, proletarian resistance of the Yugoslav people against the Fascist invader. Or he was telling the truth which would suggest that he and his British superiors were militarily inept. Henderson was already accustomed to the Commissar's dialectical skill at reducing the analysis of the simplest proposition to two impossible alternatives. Henderson had once had a Scottish trial as a hooker and he frequently dreamt of imaginary Rugby matches in which he played opposite the Commissar. This was no moment for such imaginings or for losing his temper. He made a brief, soldierly statement.

Normally, he said, he would have tried to clear the matter up by a wireless message to Italy. Because he, the Brigade Commander, and the Commissar had to leave within ten minutes for the Dropping Zone for the first ever supply of British, he repeated British, stores to the Brigade there was no time to signal. The strangers could be anything. Escaped prisoners of war. Baled-out aircrew. They might even have dropped out of that aircraft that he'd been told had been shot up from Viluse, just before his own arrival. The sure way to find out would be to take them and ask them. After all there were only two of them. If they were killed out of hand nobody would ever know where they came from. Valuable information might be lost. The Partisan Supreme Staff would be displeased. The Brigade Commander, who held himself to be as good a communist as the Commissar, but who was primarily a soldier who wanted to get his hands on those supplies, intervened hastily to end discussion on this side-issue. *Drug* Marko with ten men would go to the plateau and overpower the two interlopers by stealth or stratagem. The boy would act as guide. *Drugarica* Olga, who spoke English, would act as interpreter. It was a two-day march each way. The meeting adjourned. Twenty minutes later a hard marching party left for the plateau.

From the time of their landing Yeti had decided that with only the two of them it would be pointless to try to keep a permanent watch throughout the days and nights. He compromised by ordering a daily dusk stand-to, in which both he and Hicks took part for

70

twenty minutes, and a daily dawn stand-to which they took in turns. Shortly after dawn on a day when Hicks was supposedly supplying protection, Yeti was awakened in the hut by a hard kick on the thigh. When he opened his eyes he found himself looking down the barrel of a Schmeisser sub-machine pistol, held steadily by a sunburnt, unshaven man in a ragged German uniform jacket, stained civilian trousers and shoes made from rubber cut from old motor tyres. On his head was a khaki forage cap with a faded red five-pointed star stitched to the front. Behind this formidable apparition was a tired-looking, rather fetching girl, who somehow managed to look neat and feminine despite the multiplicity of patches and darns on her faded lumberjacket and worn corduroy calf-length trousers. She too had a red star in the forage cap she wore at an angle on her cropped blonde hair. Of the three of them she was the first to speak.

'Good morning,' she said in English. 'Are you British?'

Yeti gaped at her. Before he could articulate the thought that came to his mind his voice first disposed of another message that was already in the process of slow transmission between his brain and his tongue.

'Damn that idle sod Hicks,' he said solemnly.

The girl chuckled delightfully and said something in a foreign language to the alarming-looking chap with the Schmeisser. He lowered it and he too laughed.

'Okay,' said Karla Bilic, 'you're British all right.'

An awakened, unrepentant and indifferent Hicks, spurred by an indignant Yeti, cooked a breakfast gleaned from two twenty-four-hour ration packs. Marko and Karla watched the preparation of this technological triumph with admiration. Yeti, who had lived off the stuff more times than he could remember, watched with revulsion. The Tommy Cookers, solid paraffin blocks like small fire lighters, burned with a blue flame under Hicks' aluminium oblong mess tins. A tiny cube of combined tea leaves, sugar and dehydrated milk was put into boiling water and resolved itself into a fluid roughly resembling tea. Another cube, this time of oatmeal, was stirred in water in another tin and emerged as what its manufacturers described as porridge. The frying bacon was authentic but rubbery. When the creation was complete, Marko and Karla wolfed down their shares with the appreciation of people who had eaten sparingly, when at all, for three long years. Yeti restricted himself to a bar of plain chocolate and half a mug of the revolting tea. He was silent throughout the meal because he was thinking. Marko and Karla were silent because they were hungry.

Yeti's thoughts were even more confused than was usual because they were impeded by emotion. He had never been much of a one for the girls, who in his experience had been either simpering incompetents or beefy hearties on horses. But look at this sunburnt, short-haired girl here, with the delicious laugh, the gorgeous eyes, a shape that could only be guessed at, the air of responsible, workmanlike efficiency. Yeti was already besotted, to the extent that he willingly conceded to himself that this bloody mountain carried advantages that had not existed in the Desert. He did what he could to work out his ideas about what his next move should be, but found it impossible to disentangle the essential from the intrusive. Stocks. Bren guns. Food. Chuckling laugh. Slav cheek bones. Sovereigns. Ammunition. Blue eyes. Worn climbing boots. Medical stores. Shape under the lumberjacket. Short blonde hair. Sten guns. Grenades. Wireless message. Yeti was still trampling about mentally in the midst of all this confusion when Marko stated, through the girl, that they would now have a planning discussion. For good measure Marko produced from his pack a bottle of *rakija* and hospitably filled Yeti's mug with a measure

72

that would have felled a buffalo. This offering did little to help Yeti articulate his side of the conversation.

Marko was brisk and incisive. His orders, he explained, had been to come to the plateau and rescue, or capture, or if necessary kill the two strangers. He had now identified them as friends and had enjoyed his breakfast. But he had been given no instructions about the removal and disposal of their warlike stores, let alone the gold sovereigns. Little Bogdan's account had touched only lightly on these impedimenta and the Brigade Commander and the Commissar had understandably underestimated their importance.

Yeti, through a mist of *rakija* and enjoyable speculation about the contents of Karla's lumberjacket, remarked inconsequentially that he was very glad to have finally met the Albanian patriots he had been seeking. The girl laughed, thus further disordering Yeti, and told him that he was among Yugoslav Partisans and not Albanian patriots. Yeti asked how to spell Yugoslavia, provoked more distracting mirth, and wrote down the answer in his Field Service Pocket Book. He sucked his pencil for some moments, returned his mind reluctantly and relentlessly to duty, and threw a spanner into the works.

'I can't give you any of this,' he croaked throatily, waving his hand expansively towards the stone hut. 'Supposed to give it to Albanians, d'you see.' There was a murderously sharp deterioration in the mood of the meeting. It was Hicks, stirred from his lethargy by the sheer uncomplicated stupidity of this statement, who saved Yeti from being shot on the spot by Marko.

'Why not ask Bari, Sir?' he said sensibly.

The girl translated urgently. Marko's scowl moved up in the scale from homicidal intent to simple detestation. A shapeless argument ensued. Yeti's contribution varied capriciously as his thinking moved at random between an obstinate concept of duty and the imagined shape of Karla's legs. Marko tried to contain his wrath

in the light of Karla's insistent warnings of the consequence to future British supply drops if the Partisans
were to kill a British officer. In the sense that the
outcome was that British speciality, a compromise,
Yeti could be said to have won.

Yeti would signal Bari. Marko would send a messen-
ger to the Brigade Commander and the Commissar,
enumerating the extent of the stores and asking for
further orders. Meanwhile he, with the bulk of his
followers, would stay on the plateau. They shook hands
cagily on this accord, after which Marko, with Balkan
volatility, cheered up, grinned and poured another
damaging draught of *rakija* into Yeti's tin mug. Hicks
sighed enigmatically and the girl smiled.

It was at that point that Karla remembered Henderson, the Military Missioner, whose existence had been
overlooked in first the courtesy, and then the heat, of
the exchanges.

Henderson arrived on the plateau eight days later. He
was accompanied by a strong Partisan escort, three
mules, and Juraj, the Deputy Brigade Commander, a
sardonic former Royal Yugoslav Army Lieutenant
whom Henderson liked and trusted. As the party
clattered in through the pale grey grandeur of the
rocks, Henderson wondered gloomily why he had
volunteered to drop into Yugoslavia. He was, he
supposed, a scholarly tough. And, he also supposed,
(although nothing on earth would ever have induced
him to use the terms he thought in in discussion with
anyone else) he was an adventurer, a romantic and a
patriot. Helping to supply and sharing the hardships of
the finest guerrilla organization in Europe gave him
immense personal satisfaction. He was prepared to
endure the provocative loutishness of that bloody Commissar in order to help hardy and determined people
fight an invader whose political philosophy he loathed.
But to have to go nannying around tidying up the mess

left by some clown who, judging by the signals from Bari, was certifiably insane was a superfluous irritant that he could do without. Particularly since Henderson had been given an exhortation to possible authorized murder.

Henderson, after a familiarly acrimonious meeting with the Commissar, had sent his first signal to Bari as soon as the tidings brought by Marko's emissary had been digested. Henderson's message, like all his messages, was succinct and helpful. The first paragraph rehearsed briefly the facts as he knew them. The second made a firm recommendation; that the arms, ammunition and medical supplies should be immediately given to the Partisans. The third asked two questions. What to do with the officer and his wireless operator, both supposedly specialists in Albanian affairs? And what to do with the gold sovereigns?

The reply, drafted by the now perturbed Colonel John Beverly, was mostly unequivocal but incomplete. Weapons *et al* to go straight to the Partisans. Good. The next bit was about the Albanian specialist and was for Your Eyes, repeat Your Eyes, only. The man had clearly broken under pressure and was assumed to be mad. Although in possession of a fully working wireless set he had sent only two signals in the preceding three weeks. The first had been meaningless. The second, which clearly illustrated his mental condition, had read quote Where is Yugoslavia query unquote. Henderson must use his judgement on how to deal with this one-man inter-allied embarrassment. Alternatives were (i) get him to Italy soonest (ii) shoot him if he showed any sign of prejudicing relations with the Partisans. Destroy signal immediately. There was no mention of the gold.

There was no reference to the gold because its mention in Henderson's report had hit a vibrantly sensitive nerve in the short but comprehensive collective memory of SOE in Bari. They were thinking of the fate of Hydra Mission, an ill-starred SOE party consisting of a British officer, a Royal Jugoslav Army officer and an Irish wireless operator. They had landed by submarine near Petrovac in early 1942. They had been quarrelsome, devious and indiscreet to an extent that had provoked genuine fears among the Partisan Supreme Staff that the British, for their own political ends, were conspiring to destroy the allies they professed to want to help. Hydra Mission had compounded its shortcomings by bolting one April night from Tito's headquarters in Foca, in its British leader's case after he had dined with a senior member of Tito's staff. Less than two weeks later the group vanished, in circumstances that pointed with near certainty to their murder for gain by Bosnian Chetniks. They had had with them one million lira and about two thousand gold sovereigns. Never again did SOE parties in Yugoslavia carry large sums of negotiable currency. Never, that is, until Yeti had accidently dropped in as the custodian of a minor fortune. Henderson's report had caused a more or less controlled uproar in Bari.

Beverly had been ordered to make whatever arrangements he thought fit for the disposal of the weapons and stores and the recovery of his curious protégé. But the unwonted presence of a large sum of gold in a part of Montenegro that was being constantly fought over by Partisans, Chetniks, Ustasha and Germans introduced a complicating factor that would have to be contained, and preferably eliminated, with scrupulous care. The final decision must come from the top and could be reached only after extensive consultation.

Consideration of the problem was divided into two parts, the first of which dealt with immediate steps to be taken for the safeguarding and ultimate recovery of the sovereigns. An easily discernible helpful element was that they were held by the Partisans, whose puritanical military code would inhibit them from joining in the orgy of avaricious throat-cutting that would certainly have taken place if the treasure had landed among any of the other contestants. A corollary of this was thought to lie in Marxist dogma. Despisers of capitalism would, it was hoped, despise capitalist gold. In any case they would hardly advance their pleas for more and more supplies if they pinched valuable property belonging to their potential benefactors. That had them fixed on both ideological and practical counts. So far so good. It was a reasonable likelihood that the Partisans would not be averse from handing it over, possibly to the accompaniment of some wounding dialectical irony. How to get it out?

By air seemed an obvious and possible answer. The British Military Mission had expanded notably since the arrival of its leader at Tito's Bosnian headquarters in September 1943 and in addition to organizing a steadily increasing number of air drops it was in some areas operating improvised airstrips, capable of taking Dakotas. These would offload their supplies, turn around hastily, and depart laden with Partisan wounded for attention in hospitals in Italy. If the gold could be got to one of the strips it could be put into a returning Dakota. But alas, two snags. Could a hard-pressed guerrilla army really be expected to divert some of its limited resources to transporting and escorting somebody else's property, property that by its very nature epitomized capitalist depravity, to its destination? Almost certainly not. And if it just could, how did a British Mission officer explain to his Partisan hosts at the airstrip that he was giving loading priority to a sordid sum of money over badly wounded Partisans who would probably die if they were not evacuated? Couldn't be done.

By sea? At first glance could be feasible. The map reference in Henderson's signal showed Yeti's position to be not too far from the Gulf of Kotor. As with the hypothetical airstrip, the transport problem to the taking off place remained. Assuming its solution what craft were available to pick it up. Submarine? None left in the Mediterranean. Their task accomplished they'd all gone off to fight the Japanese or someone. Jugboat, the schooners used by the embryo Partisan navy? They wouldn't play. Royal Navy landing craft or one of the motor gun boats based on the Dalmatian Island of Vis? They could probably do the job but the Navy would be reluctant to divert one of them from its proper operational role, particularly without air cover, which the RAF would not want to provide on the grounds that it would be a diversion from Balkan Air Force's proper operational role . . .

It was eventually concluded that the best, perhaps the only, way to set about things was to ask the Partisans to secrete the sovereigns under Henderson's supervision in a secure place such as a remote cave. Henderson could blow in the opening with explosive. It was essential that as few people as possible should know of its location. Its choice would be at Henderson's discretion. Subsequent recovery would depend upon the progress of the war and might have to await the peace.

Instructions were drafted and signalled to the headquarters of the British Mission attached to the Partisan Supreme Staff, by then on the island of Vis. The instructions were received querulously, implemented resentfully, and achieved their purpose at the expense of a degrading three-quarters-of-an-hour-long sermon on the sinful bankruptcy of capitalist morality. Messages, given top priority by the British and bottom priority by the Partisans, worked their way downwards through an assortment of subordinate headquarters. Henderson's orders reached him three hours after Vis had confirmed to Bari that the scheme could go ahead. Henderson's putative collaborators in the plan, the Brigade Commander and the Commissar, got theirs

78

five days later through the agency of a boy courier, aged twelve.

The wheels thus set in motion, SOE in Bari turned their attention to the second part of the problem posed by Yeti's misadventures. Their initial conclusions were only tentative but they felt it prudent to transfer Colonel John Beverly to less sensitive duties, to put an unobtrusive watch on him and to open a special file on his observed activities.

Although Henderson had an exact inventory of the stores sitting on the plateau, a personal plan for their distribution, and a range of alternative ideas about how to deal with the gold, he was faced with one totally unknown factor. Yeti Challoner. Henderson knew only two things about him. His name, and the fact that Bari had said that he was mad, providing in the process some necessarily brief supporting evidence. But what sort of mad? Lying silently twitching, sucking his thumb and calling for Mummy? Issuing grandiose unenforcible orders, imagining himself as Napoleon or Captain Bligh? Roaring aggressively about, threatening to shoot whoever disagreed with him? Foaming at the mouth and barking like a dog? Henderson was inexperienced with madness and his imagination ran wild. It would look pretty good, he reflected bitterly, if an operation conceived amidst a frenzy of vituperative ill-will from the Commissar were to start with an exchange of violent abuse between two British officers, followed by gunplay, before a crowd of bemused Partisans. Henderson could see himself standing over Yeti's prostrate body like a screen sheriff in a Western, blowing the smoke away from the muzzle of his pistol and giving a terse account of his motives to an interested audience of Communist-led guerrillas.

'Sorry folks,' he would have to say, 'It just had to be done. The guy was crazy. Bari said so.'

To Henderson's extreme relief this worst-possible-case scenario showed no signs of developing. As he walked cautiously on to the plateau a correctly shaved, creditably turned out, swarthy British captain in a black beret and khaki battle dress approached with an air of glum benignity. Henderson noted that he wore above the pleated left-hand pocket of his blouse the mauve and white ribbon of the Military Cross, a silver rosette on the ribbon to denote that the award had been won twice, and the predominantly sand-coloured ribbon of the Africa Star. Superimposed on this second ribbon was the figure eight, which showed that Yeti had served in the Eighth Army under General Sir Bernard Montgomery, a distinction of which Yeti had been unaware at the time and was still ignorant of what it meant.

''Morning,' said Yeti, holding out his hand, 'I'm Yeti Challoner.' Henderson shook the hand, returned the greeting and identified himself.

'Henderson,' he said, with Scottish reserve.

There was a long silence. Yeti couldn't think of anything to say and so, as was his custom, said nothing. Henderson was looking for signs of lunacy and could detect none. Eventually Yeti suggested tea.

'Tea?' he said.

'Thanks,' said Henderson.

Hicks made a distressing brew from two of his magic preprocessed cubes and under its influence conversation prospered. At the end of this almost entirely monosyllabic discussion Henderson had reached some firm conclusions. Yeti was sane. He was clearly brave. He was also the biggest bloody fool that Henderson had ever met and should never have been employed by SOE. The sooner he could be got out of Yugoslavia the better. His departure should be accompanied by a firm caveat that he should never return and a suggestion that the circumstances of his recruitment should be investigated. There was also one tantalizingly familiar, but irritatingly evasive, element in Yeti's make-up that Henderson could not pin down. The symptoms kept surfacing, a wistful dreaminess that tempered the

80

grunted baffled replies to questions about Yeti's arrival, his supplies, his intentions.

When they were joined briefly by Doctor Olga, Henderson at last recognized it. Not only was this military comedian lost, in the wrong country, in possession of hideously embarrassing quantities of gold, and periodically sending half-witted wireless messages that further stirred up the cloud of confusion that shrouded his activities. He was in love. Not even just in love. But in love with a member of a guerrilla force which for political reasons vetoed personal relationships with capitalist foreigners and for practical reasons of survival forbade sexual connections amongst its own adherents. The penalty for transgression on this score, and for its sister military crime, pregnancy, was death to both parties. Oh Christ, thought Henderson.

In the late afternoon, when the sun was lowering itself towards the irregular jaggedness of the limestone mountains to the west, and the shadows were beginning to lengthen, a conference was called by Juraj, the Deputy Brigade Commander. It was a formal affair with a set agenda. Juraj, for the Partisans, was supported by Marko. Henderson, for the British Mission, was hindered by Yeti. Karla interpreted and because of her experience and common sense was encouraged by Juraj to intervene whenever she thought she might usefully do so.

The distribution of the weapons and stores was the first item. Henderson had already offered them to the Brigade Commander who had welcomed with delight this unexpected enhancement of a fire power already enhanced by the first drop arranged by Henderson. Juraj's job was simply to organize their transportation to the main body of the brigade. He intended that every man on the plateau should carry back an additional weapon. Ammunition, clothing, food and medical stores would go on the mules. Any comments?

Excellent scheme said Henderson. But timing would depend upon Item Two, disposal of the sovereigns. The Commissar and the Brigade Commander had agreed that the mules should first be used for shifting the gold. The wrinkles at the edge of Juraj's eyes began to expand and contract and he stroked his widespread moustache with a broad, sunburnt hand that hid his mouth. Henderson, at first puzzled, saw that Juraj was trying to conceal laughter. It was not scornful or malicious laughter. It was simple mirth, born of the recollection of the extravagant hullaballoo that had raged when this very point had been in contention three days previously between Henderson and the Commissar. The Commissar had disliked his orders but he was a loyal Communist and would obey them. As he saw it this obedience in no way detracted from his right and duty to point simultaneously to the deficiencies of the system Henderson represented. Henderson hadn't thought much of his orders either. They had made him short-tempered, and although he had far too much sense to essay a criticism of the Commissar's system he had managed to inject into the discussion some subtly ambiguous insults, expressed in idiomatic Croatian, about the Commissar's interpretation of how his system should operate. Juraj, in silent attendance, had hugely enjoyed these exchanges. Discipline and loyalty required a sublimation of his amusement. Protocol and good inter-allied manners demanded that Henderson should not be seen to have observed it. He turned to Yeti as if to ask the last thing he wanted, Yeti's opinion, and at once realized that even if he had wanted it he wouldn't have got it. Yeti's mind and eyes were both elsewhere. His head was cocked to one side, there was an idiotic half-smile on his face, and he was gazing with undiluted admiration at the conference secretariat, the interpreter Doctor Olga.

Oh Christ, thought Henderson for the second time that day.

Juraj and Henderson recovered their poise at about the same moment, each aware of the reason behind the other's momentary preoccupation, each unaware that the other had perceived it. The talk flowed crisply in Croatian with Karla making a totally useless simultaneous translation for the benefit of Yeti.

Juraj agreed that the mules should of course be used for moving the sovereigns. But where to? Henderson said that he had no specific place in mind. It could be buried. Put in a cave, as Bari had suggested, and the cave opening subsequently blocked by a demolition charge. Had Juraj any ideas? There were three desiderata. The gold must be securely hidden. It should preferably be put in a place that would not involve too many difficulties over its eventual removal to British hands. And as few people as possible should know where it was. Greed was an international affliction that crossed all ideological boundaries, said Henderson in a phrase that he would not have tried on the Commissar, and as one soldier to another he could say frankly that even the admirably iron discipline of the Partisans could be undermined if some of their weaker brothers were distracted from their duty by the prospect of sudden wealth. Juraj grinned and agreed.

They ran through various possibilities. Each had something to commend it, something against it, the disadvantages mostly being concerned with future transport complications when the time came for the British to collect their property. Henderson, a methodical man, marked each suggestion on his map, graded X or Y or Z according to its attractiveness. Doctor Olga, presumably by now reconciled to the unnerving whimsicality of Yeti's devoted gaze, temporarily abandoned interpreting and took an active part in affairs.

'From your point of view,' she asked Henderson, 'I take it that somewhere as close as possible to the coast would be best?'

'Yes. Or to a place where an aircraft could land.'

83

Juraj poked a large finger at the dark brown hachuring on the map and then at the blue representing the sea.

'The sea's closer than any possible site for an airstrip.'

'Okay. But the Germans and Ustasha hold the coast.'

Juraj laughed.

'The towns on the coast, yes. And some of the villages and some of the old Austro-Hungarian forts. They cover the rest by patrols. Or if they're pushing a big convoy through they use heavy road escorts and an infantry screen to clear the ground on either side of the road.'

'But if we go for the coast we might run into a patrol. We'd be stuck with all this bloody gold if we did.'

'Highly unlikely. Regular habits our enemies have. Their patrols leave every week on the same day at the same time on the same roads. It keeps things tidy for them. Also it makes sense. All they really want to do is keep communications open. They know we're short of explosives – or were until you came along – so we can't block roads by blowing in cliffs. They keep static Ustasha guards on bridges and things that we could damage by more primitive methods. And every so often they send out a punitive column to try to beat us up.'

Henderson pondered on this insight into Partisan warfare.

'You're saying that with luck you could get a party, with heavy loads, through to the coast?'

'No. The other way round. I'm saying that only exceptionally bad luck could stop me.'

Henderson was impressed.

'All right,' he said at last. 'Let's accept that in principle the coast it is. The nearest bit of coast is the Gulf of Kotor. Any likely spots along there?'

Doctor Olga thought fast while the two men bent over the map again. She concluded that if she handled things sensibly her daughterly responsibility to her capitalist father's jewels need not necessarily be compromised by her Marxist duty to help in the safe keeping of treasure belonging to her country's capitalist allies. (It was as well that Karla was a woman.)

'I think I know a place,' she said suddenly, and thrust her pretty finger without hesitation at a point on the map on the eastern shore of the innermost bay of the Gulf.

Yeti drooled.

Juraj and Henderson found no difficulty over accepting Doctor Olga's recommendation. Juraj had passed the villa many times and knew the cross-country approaches to it. He could, he said, guarantee to get the party along tracks to a point immediately behind the high cliffs that backed the road and overlooked the causeway. Henderson was pleased both because of the convenience for eventual loading to a naval craft and because of Doctor Olga's reassurance that the uncovering of the cache would be an impossible task for anyone without precise knowledge of its location and its workings. She was coyly evasive about the details. She would, she suggested, explain them when they got there. And, if Juraj agreed, she thought that when they arrived the escort should stay on the cliff-top and the final stage of carrying and stowing away should be the task of only four people – Juraj, Henderson, Yeti and herself. In that way dangerous knowledge would be limited.

The escort would know that the sovereigns were somewhere on the island, but faced with pressure or temptation would be unable to go further than that. The hiding place, she repeated, was fool-proof.

Juraj smilingly disagreed. Four was too many. They could count him out. For himself he preferred ignorance.

The little column set off along a narrow stony track at dusk. Juraj navigated, followed by a four-man escort. Behind the escort marched Henderson, Doctor Olga, Yeti and a sullen Sergeant Hicks, disgusted by the compulsory physical exercise. Behind them a rearguard of six more Partisans, leading mules. There had been much discussion about how big the party should be, whether the plant should be made by night or day, and what dispositions should be made while the job was being done. Juraj settled on a total of fifteen as a party strong enough to look after itself if surprised and sufficiently mobile to be able to move fast. The question of day or night was effectively settled by a comment of Karla's. To open the cache she would need to see clearly what she was doing for a period of several minutes. The light of the new moon would be inadequate. Torches shining continuously would, decided Juraj, attract attention, curiosity, and probably comment followed by investigation. They'd do it at first light.

The matter of dispositions was, to everyone else's surprise, determined by Yeti. Juraj's original scheme had had the merit of simplicity. It was based on the fact that the German known patrol between Kotor and Risan came out at dawn on Fridays. This was Tuesday. Juraj's intention was to take the whole party down a path that wound down the cliff face, cross the road, and move along the causeway to the leafy shelter of the oleander grove. There all but those engaged at the cache would drop off and cover the causeway.

Work at the cache, it was estimated, would take about forty minutes. When it was completed its three executants, plus the mules, would join up with the others and they would all walk away, down the causeway, over the road and up the cliff again.

'Nonsense,' said Yeti. This was minor tactics. For the first time in weeks conversation was centred upon a topic that he could understand. 'What you do,' went on

86

Yeti with an uninhibited incisiveness that irritated Henderson, amused Juraj and amazed Doctor Olga, 'is this. You put a two-man stop with a spandau at the bend in the road on the northern side of the cliff. You put another at the southern bend. And you leave a lookout on the cliff. That way we'll get warning of anyone who comes along and the stops should be able to hold them off long enough for us to beat it up the cliff. Then we cover the slope while they rejoin us.'

It was the longest statement anyone present had ever heard from Yeti. Henderson suddenly realized that if this man was a disaster as a soldier-diplomatist he was nobody's fool on at least one subject.

'Nobody will come,' said Juraj.

'Don't bet on it,' said Yeti.

'Your idea would leave us with only five men to cover the causeway. If you're right, and somebody does come, that's not enough.'

'Take Hicks,' said Yeti, 'and stick him up the cliff as the lookout. That'll give you one more.'

It was so agreed.

The approach march lasted for only six hours, but it was weary work. In a dim silvery light from the new moon and a proliferation of stars they wound slowly down stony zig-zag tracks, sweatily up hills, around spurs, up, down, up, up, down. Juraj's navigation was faultless. The mules behaved themselves. The Partisans, Montenegrin hillmen all, took these sort of journeyings as a matter of course. Henderson and Yeti found the going and the pace exhausting but kept doggedly, uncomplainingly closed up. Hicks straggled, with curses.

Shortly after one o'clock in the morning they reached their destination, a small upland valley a kilometre or so on the inshore side of the villa. Juraj posted sentries and they laid up.

At first light Juraj, Henderson, Yeti and Doctor Olga lay behind a cluster of boulders on top of the cliff and scrutinized the villa through binoculars. Three years of war and of casual occupancy had done it no good. There were two large holes in the roof. Some of the shutters had been torn away for firewood. The vines and the vegetable patch were a mass of entangled weeds. There was a litter of rubbish and broken glass on the terrace. Only the avenue of oleanders along the causeway, the grove at its end and the clump around the cache looked as pristine and natural as the blue sea beyond. Yeti gazed at them with distaste. At this stage he saw them as a tactical hazard. Doctor Olga admired their flowers, some pink, some white, standing out charmingly against the density of their thick green leaves. Juraj and Henderson were indifferent to them.

'Seems clear,' said Henderson.

'Yes. We'll start,' said Juraj.

The first part of the operation went impeccably. The two pairs of stops trotted to their positions and set themselves up behind the cover of rocks by the roadside. Juraj led off down the winding cliff track, with three Partisans close behind him. The cache contingent followed with the mules. Three Partisans provided a rearguard. Hicks stayed sitting on the cliff-top and looked like a man who had won first prize in a lottery. Progress over the causeway was uneventful. At the oleander grove Juraj beckoned to the main party to stay where they were and set out with his three warriors on a tour of inspection. He was back, grinning, in five minutes.

'Clear,' he announced. Then he hammed a charade of ostentatiously turning his back on the villa and covering his eyes and ears with his huge hands.

'See no evil,' he intoned. 'Hear no evil. Speak no evil. All yours, Doctor Olga.'

Karla chuckled, Henderson smiled and Yeti looked puzzled. They led the mules forward, stopped at a non-descript barren patch surrounded by oleanders, unfastened the two spades included in the mules' loads at Karla's instigation, and scraped effectively at the surface. In six minutes it was clear. Karla kicked out the wedge, thumped one side of the flagstone with her boot, and enjoyed Henderson's expression as he watched the stone swivelling on its axis. She didn't bother to look at Yeti. His look of gaping idiocy was both predictable and familiar.

Karla jumped into the hole and unobtrusively checked that the two little wash-leather bags with their draw-strings were still in position in the corner where she had placed them over three years before. They were.

The off-loading of the mules proceeded efficiently and smoothly. The sovereigns had been repacked in clusters of five hundred, each cluster in a sacking bag. Yeti gentled the mules, emptied the panniers systematically, and one by one handed the bags to Henderson. Henderson took them to the cache and lowered them to Karla. Karla stacked them below. Three-quarters-of-an-hour later the sovereigns were installed, the cache was closed, the wedge was in place and a deposit of earth and rubble was scattered over its surface. Henderson gazed at it critically. It loked obvious that the earth had been disturbed. Karla guessed at his thoughts. 'No problem,' she said reassuringly. 'A few hours' sunshine and no one will be able to tell the difference.'

They returned with the mules to Juraj at the grove. The stops had been silent. So had Hicks. Juraj was jubilant and pointed out to Yeti that his suggested precautions, though wise, had been unnecessary. The German garrisons in Kotor and Risan had continued to garrison Kotor and Risan. The Ustasha static guards had continued to statically guard whatever they were statically guarding. Yeti, possessed suddenly of a feeling of deep, instinctive unease, grunted and to the mild amusement of the others drew and cocked his Colt .45 pistol. Something, experienced tuition told him, was about to go wrong.

It went wrong when Juraj was leading the small party towards the road, at a bend in the track through the oleander grove. Juraj's Schmeisser was slung over his shoulder. Close behind him, overconfident, were Henderson, his pistol still in the holster on his waist-belt and Karla, unarmed. Three yards behind came Yeti, pistol in hand, forefinger along the trigger guard. What nobody had allowed for was the possibility that a group of starving Chetniks, desperate for any chance of food, would be brought to the villa by a man who recalled from pre-war days old Josip's vegetables, fish and chickens and who thought, mistakenly, that he might just be still cultivating, catching and tending them respectively. The Chetnik officer had brought his hungry followers down a narrow re-entrant that flanked Hicks' cliff-top position, had crossed the road quietly behind the backs of the outward-looking stops (of whose existence he was unaware) and along the bush-lined causeway. He and his ten bedraggled bearded men were suspicious and alert and all their weapons were held at the ready. The subsequent significant action took place within a period of about forty seconds, immediately following Juraj's startled confrontation with these menacing strangers as he rounded the curve of the track.

The Chetnik officer, at four yards' range, fired a short burst from his machine-carbine that shattered Juraj's shoulder. Juraj collapsed on to the path. Yeti, with bitter thoughts about bloody Hicks asleep again, took two great leaps forward, pushed Karla violently into the bushes and shot the Chetnik officer neatly between the eyes. A second Chetnik, brandishing a long curved knife, launched himself towards the recumbent Juraj. Henderson took the knife man with a springing tackle below the knees that would have enchanted the Scottish Rugby Football international selectors. The knifer's ankles, locked together by Henderson's arms, were knocked roughly from under him and he fell forward. Yeti kicked his teeth in as his face approached the ground and then jumped heavily on the back of his neck with both feet. Henderson rolled to the right, narrowly evading a burst of spandau fire and dragged out his pistol. Yeti stood steadily in the middle of the track, pistolled two more Chetniks and went down from a concentrated burst of Schmeisser bullets in his chest. The Partisan escort burst through from behind, firing from the hip. Somebody threw two grenades. Henderson shot a wild-eyed, slavering, bearded adversary who came running at him. This was little Bogdan Bojanic's father. Karla, sobbing, ran to the prostrate forms of Juraj, the Chetnik officer and Yeti, bunched together on the track. The noise of the fracas cracked and echoed among the rocks and it awakened Hicks, who from his cliff-top vantage point settled the issue. He had a perfect field of fire down the causeway and he shot four Chetniks in the back with four carefully aimed rifle shots.

Yeti died two minutes later. Three thoughts intermingled tiredly in his evaporating consciousness. Idle bugger Hicks. Who on earth were these non-Krauts he'd been fighting? And Karla's insistent sobs. So she had loved him. Yeti died happy.

Karla, to the amazement of the still conscious Juraj, was weeping over the body of the Chetnik officer. She had recognized her brother Branko behind the unfamiliar beard, just before Yeti had shot him dead.

Chapter Six

IN SEPTEMBER 1944, No. 49 Royal Marine Commando returned in two Landing Craft, Infantry, to Bari in Southern Italy after ten months of operations based on Vis, the Dalmatian island the furthermost offshore from the Yugoslav mainland. In February, when the Commando had first landed, Vis had been isolated and threatened. All the other islands in the group were in German hands and there was good reason to believe that an early attempt might be made to overrun Vis as well. It was crowded with resolute Partisans, but they were indifferently armed and trained. The Commando, and its companion Army Commando from the same Brigade, would have given a good account of itself in any invasion attempt, but its equipment was designed for amphibious raiding operations of up to forty-eight hours duration. Its heaviest weapons were four Vickers medium machine-guns and four three-inch mortars. The rest were Bren light machine-guns, Thompson machine-carbines, rifles, pistols, grenades, two-inch mortars and a scattering of PIATs, Projectors Infantry, Anti-Tank, capricious drain-pipe-like gadgets not well-loved by their handlers. Aside from the heavy weapons, all these, in the military phrase, could be carried on the man. They were invaluable when the Commando was employed on the purposes for which it had trained. Whether they would have sufficed, in company with the tenuous armament of the Partisans, even with the help of an aggressively directed flotilla of Royal Navy motor gun boats, for the defence of a barren rocky beautiful island, crowded with refugees, in the teeth of a determined German assault mounted from near-by bases and supported by aerial bombardment was, perhaps fortunately, never put to the test.

This potentially dangerous phase was not prolonged. A steady stream of more powerfully-armed reinforcements crossed the Adriatic Sea from Italy. Light anti-aircraft guns. A Field Regiment of Royal Artillery, equipped with twenty-four 25-pounder gun-howitzers. Spitfires of the Royal Air Force came to base themselves on an airstrip bulldozed out of the vineyards in the centre of the island. There were weapons, equipment, uniforms, boots for the growing army of Partisans assembling on the island. Hospitals were set up. Badly wounded Partisans and civilian Yugoslav refugees were evacuated to Italy. The Partisan Supreme Staff accompanied Marshal Tito to Vis, after the all-but-successful German airborne attack on his headquarters at Drvar in Bosnia, and he established his headquarters in a cave on Mount Hum.

Throughout all these comings and goings 49 Commando was engaged on comings and goings of its own, to the other islands. There were reconnaissances in Jugboats and from LCAs, Landing Craft Assault. Boarding parties captured German coastal craft. There were ambushes, small raids, big raids, and actions that weren't raids at all but minor set-piece battles involving assaults with artillery support on positions protected by barbed wire and mines, with the German defenders dug in in concrete and rock block houses. The company in these actions varied. Sometimes it was from other Commandos, Army or Royal Marine, in the Brigade who came to Vis for longer or shorter periods and then disappeared to take a hand in other Balkan coastal forays to Corfu or Albania or wherever. Sometimes it was with Partisans, whose courage, spirit and singing were much admired, but whose inability to perform agreed manoeuvres at agreed times was not. Sometimes it was the whole Commando, unaccompanied. Sometimes, three, two or one of its Troops, or a Section of one of its Troops. Hvar, Korcula, Brac, Mljet and the Peljesac peninsula received visitations, most of them bloody, all of them exhausting.

Back on Vis, bodies were buried, weapons were cleaned, wounds were patched up, owners of bad wounds were sent to Italy, vino was drunk, songs were sung, training was carried out, defensive duties were performed, suntans were perfected and curses were cursed. Some of these last were the usual meaningless curses but most of them were directed at a single phenomenon not previously encountered in any other country in which the licentious soldiery had served. Although the island was teaming with girls they were unavailable girls. They wore khaki forage caps fronted by a red star, British khaki battle dress, ammunition boots and grenades attached to their webbing waist-belts. They marched tirelessly, carried heavy weights and danced vigorous *kolas*, the traditional Slav folk manifestations in which the participants, usually alternately men and girls, formed a circle, arms around their neighbour's shoulders, and stamped and sang beautifully in a wheeling, rhythmic abandon. The marines often joined these and were welcomed laughingly and hospitably. They learnt the tunes and some of the words of the hauntingly harmonious Partisan songs. But for all the laughter and the friendliness, tempered by Marxist sloganizing, there was an impassable barrier as effective as that imposed by the vows of chastity honoured by an enclosed order of nuns. The most lubricious of the visitors early conceded that even if they could overcome the aesthetically repugnant obstacles posed by the battledress and the boots, and the daunting possibility of heterosexual consummation being interrupted by the close range detonation of

94

fragmentation grenades, man's primal urges could only wither in the face of the knowledge that the risked penalty for the loved one was not the universal chance of pregnancy or a nasty disease. It was drumhead court-martial followed by death by firing-squad. Continence prevailed.

If the return to Italy was greeted with pleasure by most members of the unit, what might be termed the negative fornication factor was not the only reason. The island was spectacularly lovely, the swimming was superb and the vino plentiful and potable. But even to young fit men accustomed by years of training and experience to living rough, life on Vis was rough, because the roughness was unmitigated by change. In Italy troops went up the line, fought battles, suffered casualties and were withdrawn to rest. The facilities provided in the rest areas would not have satisfied the more exacting requirements of later hedonistic generations but there were at least billets, baths, canteens, cinemas, occasional concert parties, occasional periods in the 8th Army Leave Centre and the surviving attractions of normal urban life as modified by the asymmetrically distributed destruction of the Italian campaign. There were also, of course, women, ungarnished with grenades and ammunition boots.

But from Vis the troops went by Landing Craft to the scenes of their fighting, marched and fought over hilly islands, and returned to resume their domestic lives amidst the meagre amenities available. They lived in shelters fashioned from tents, tarpaulins, old ammunition boxes and rocks. Water was at first scarce and brackish and subsequently became plentiful and brackish after the Royal Engineers built a pipeline. Because the needs of the islanders, the Partisans, and the civilian refugees had to be given priority an order prevailed that forbade the consumption of local food. British troops were fed from Italy on a monotonous diet that was nutritionally inadequate. There was a regular proportion of sufferers from desert sores, painful suppurating ulcers. Sanitation was by carefully disinfected holes in the ground. Lighting was by storm lantern. The only radios available were the operational 38 and 48 sets. There were few books and magazines. There was an erratic supply of newspapers from Italy, although a lively locally-produced broadsheet named *Vis-à-vis* did its best to fill this latter gap. It was all tolerable but it was frugal and it lasted unbroken for nine months. Many troops in many other theatres of war lived more uncomfortably for longer periods, a fact to which 49 Commando were entirely indifferent. They were glad to have been in the islands, and the ageing survivors still talk of them with nostalgia. But they were also glad to leave Vis for the bright lights and fleshpots of Italy.

After an interval of two weeks, of which one had been devoted to debilitating relaxations in and around Bari, they were told that they were to return to Yugoslavia.

'Oh Christ,' they said.

They embarked stolidly in the two LCIs that were to take them to Dubrovnik. Some of them looked like spent salmon.

Two days before this embarkation the Commanding Officer of No. 49 Royal Marine Commando had summoned his officers to a briefing. There were twenty-seven officers. Three from each of the five Fighting Troops. Three from the Heavy Weapons Troop. From Commando headquarters came the second-in-command, the adjutant, Intelligence Officer, the Signals Officer, the Administrative Officer (the Commando equivalent of a Quartermaster), the Doctor and the Padre. For the first time in months all were dressed in their best battle dress and carried short swagger sticks. Their faded green berets had their leather bands one inch above their owner's eyebrows. Their burnished brass globe and laurel cap badges, worn by their predecessors since King George IV in 1827 had decreed them to be 'the most appropriate emblem of the Corps whose duties carried them to all parts of the Globe in every quarter of which they had earned laurels by their valour and good conduct', were at a point on the left side of their berets mid-way above their left eyes and their left ears. Since they were officers, the small crown that surmounted the emblem was separated from the two tips of the laurel wreath and was fastened on the inside of the berets by a separate splayed pin. All wore khaki shirts and khaki ties. Battle dress blouses and trousers were neatly pressed. At the top of their sleeves, near their shoulders, were the honourable designations of their corporate identity which, to their irritation, they had been forbidden to wear in the islands because of an unrealistic preoccupation with 'security'. There was a small square 49, stitched in scarlet on a navy blue background. In the same colour scheme came below 'Royal Marines'. Below that 'Commando'. Below that again a triangular shield bearing an upthrust fighting knife, the symbol of Commando Group. It had previously been the Special Service Brigade, but the letters SS had been discredited by the opposition and thus foresworn. Black boots were highly polished. Brass fittings on white blancoed webbing belts and anklets glistened.

They were fit, deeply sunburnt and relaxed. Most of the subalterns and two of the Troop Commanders looked ridiculously young, as they were. Four officers, including one of the older subalterns, wore on their left breasts the ribbon of the Military Cross. One subaltern wore the ribbon of the Coronation Medal which had been awarded to him for singing treble in the choir at Westminster Abbey while His Majesty King George VI was being crowned. All sat on and behind the desks, designed for the small children of a small race, in the schoolroom that had been requisitioned for the conference. They chatted unselfconsciously. They had recently often met in odder surroundings.

The second-in-command saw that the Colonel was about to enter through the door behind the assembly and called them to attention. They stood up and stayed motionless, swagger sticks under their left armpits, eyes gazing steadily ahead, feet together at an angle of forty-five degrees, hands lightly clenched, thumbs pointing vertically down the seams of their trousers.

The Colonel reached the front and acknowledged the second-in-command's salute and report.

''Morning, gentlemen. Sit down please. Smoke if you want to.'

There was the scrape of chairs, the scratch of matches and an air of wary interest. The Colonel had with him a strange officer, a captain with Intelligence Corps badges.

'Well,' said the Colonel. 'We're getting ready to go to Dubrovnik on Thursday. After that we go to Montenegro to protect Gunner 25 pounders. You know all that. I'd thought, and I suppose you had too, that Montenegro would be much the same as Vis, if colder. And I understand that that's about right. Only I heard that there might be some differences of emphasis, so I consulted the I Corps. They kindly lent us Captain Daunt. Here he is. He'll tell you what to expect.'

The Colonel sat down abruptly and lit a cigarette, elegantly. He was compact, dark and moustachioed, twenty-six years old, debonair, brave, competent, ambitious, successful and, in the view of those who knew him well, a complete shit.

The I Corps captain had sad brown eyes and a brisk manner. He was no word-waster and his audience listened with impressed attention.

'As your Colonel said,' he began, 'it'll be like Vis, but much colder. Most of you will be in the mountains and the snow will be heavy. But by the nature of your

98

task you'll have to stick with the guns and there shouldn't be too much wandering about on your own.'

A surge of slight resentment fluttered through the schoolroom. Intelligence officers housed in comfortable premises at headquarters should brief actual combatants with tact. Daunt ignored it.

'But what I really want to talk about is the political background. It's changing. When you first went to Vis there was all that *Smrt Fascismu Sloboda Naroda* stuff painted on the walls, and plenty of hammers and sickles and red stars and clenched fist salutes. You had to put up with a measure of Marxist guff but as you'll recall you were very welcome. You were helping a nationally based resistance movement, which happened to be Communist-led and very well led too, to fight the people who had occupied their country. You may have noticed that towards the end of your stay things became a bit less cordial. Old chums you'd fought alongside for months became reluctant, or unwilling, to join you for a drink. Numbers of pompous, self-important chaps in well-cut uniforms, none of whom had been much in evidence when the shit was flying, began to interfere in agreed decisions and to veto things. Some were bloody ill-mannered. Right?' They nodded. He knew what he was talking about.

'Well,' went on Daunt, 'I doubt if any of you give a damn about Balkan politics. But you should know of some recent Yugoslav internal developments that will affect the job you have to do. The first is that although the Partisans will continue to fight the Germans hard, their expulsion is no longer the Partisans' primary objective. The Germans will go anyway because of pressures elsewhere. The main Partisan aim now is to exploit the current situation with a view to establishing a Communist regime in post-war Yugoslavia.' The padre looked worried. So did a practising Catholic and two conservatives. A public-school socialist and a former Welsh miner showed pleasure. Nobody else showed anything.

'The second point is related to the first one,' continued Daunt. 'The Russians are now going through Serbia and have taken Belgrade. The Partisans' internal enemies, the Chetniks and the Ustasha, are in disarray. The Communist leadership is confident of success. I won't bore you with Leninist theology, and dear old Uncle Joe Stalin is one of our closest allies so I can't speak out of turn about him. But unless something pretty odd happens you can take it that on an official level at least the good old happy camaraderie of the islands is over. You'll be used and exploited. You won't be thanked. You may be insulted. And let me say carefully here that I'm quoting British policy, not making it, you'll just have to take what comes to you. Within reason. The calculation is simply that the more Jerries the Gunners stop from getting out of the Balkans back to Germany the shorter the war will be.' He paused. There was some discontented murmuring.

'Lastly,' said Daunt, smiling gently, 'something to cheer you up. In my judgement the Montenegrins are some of the best people on earth. They're proud and touchy. But they're tough, hospitable, humorous, generous and full of guts.'

'Well that's something,' said a voice.

'But the Montenegrin Partisan leadership,' concluded Daunt, grinning, 'is the most bloody-minded of the whole bloody lot.'

'Thank you,' said the Colonel standing up. 'Any questions?'

Curiosity was muted for the very good reason that it was time for pre-lunch drinks in the mess and there had been little of those for a year. Further discussion would postpone them. The Colonel knew his officers. He looked ostentatiously at his watch. 'I didn't think there would be,' he said blandly amidst chuckles. 'Paddy, stay behind will you. The rest of you can fall out.'

They rose to their feet, saluted and tramped out of the schoolroom. Captain D. J. O'C. Madden RM, the officer commanding Y Troop, saw the last of them go. As he was closing the door he heard a voice that articulated the collective sentiments of the officers of 49 Commando.

'Fine fucking winter this is going to be,' it said cheerfully. Madden walked to the desk at which the Colonel and Daunt were sitting.

'Sir?' said Madden.

'Sit down, Paddy. I've kept you behind because there's a peculiar sort of job you'll have to do in addition to your normal one. You'll be working with Daunt here.'

The Colonel turned to Daunt.

'You'll be with us a lot. What's your Christian name?'

'Tommy, Sir,' said Daunt.

'With Thomas here,' said the Colonel, who liked his calculated informality to be met half-way.

'No, Sir. Not Thomas. Tomislav,' amended the half-brother of scholarly Vlado, soldierly Branko and pretty little Karla.

Tomislav had been with the Yugoslav section of SOE since the summer of 1942. For most of the first year he had spent his time in London collating and evaluating intelligence. There was precious little to evaluate. Fragmented and irregular wireless reports from the small British Mission that lived uneasily with, and later was ostracized by, General Draza Mihaelovic's Chetnik headquarters. Accounts, mostly parochial and biased, from a thin skein of refugees who had managed to get out of the country and who as often as not found their way to Istanbul. Assessments by a few British officers who had helped to land agents or exploratory small missions by submarine on the Adriatic Coast, and who brought back what snippets they had gleaned in the process. Intercepts of German and Italian military wireless traffic. Analysis of news broadcasts from

Radio Belgrade and copies of old Yugoslav newspapers that had somehow found their devious way to Cairo or to London. Loaded and unreliable gossip from his mother's friends in the Royal Yugoslav Government in exile in London.

The overall picture was incomplete and unsatisfactory, but as the months went by it began to give Tomislav an increasing feeling of unease. The British were fully committed to the support of young King Peter's Government. Its internal resistance forces were commanded by Mihaelovic, whose constitutional position had been strengthened formally by his being appointed Minister for War. But evidence began to accumulate that suggested that in operational terms he was doing less and less. His defenders at SOE argued that this decline in activity was perfectly explicable. The Germans took savage reprisals against civilians when guerrillas killed their soldiers or sabotaged their communications. Why should Mihaelovic risk his men's lives and expose civilians to atrocities with futile pin-prick encounters of no long-term strategic significance? Was it not more sensible to maintain an armed nucleus at large in the mountains and forests and to recruit clandestinely a large potential force to join the nucleus at the correct moment? And there would be a strategically correct moment. The whole lot would go into action to supplement an Allied landing in Yugoslavia much as the French Maquis subsequently did after the Normandy landings. This made military sense and was economical of human lives.

There were some at SOE who saw weaknesses in this *apologia*. Nobody knew when, or if, the Allies would land in Yugoslavia. Could any guerrilla leader hold together indefinitely a force that because it was inactive would inevitably decline in morale and might well disintegrate altogether in the course of time? Was there not more to be said for the doings of a body calling themselves the Partisans about which reports were filtering through? They were led by someone or something Communist called Tito. They killed Germans, blew things up and accepted the consequences. If the Germans butchered thousands of civilians in reprisal it was tragic, but this was war and the matter must be looked at in the light of military arithmetic. Even the Germans couldn't massacre the entire population. After a few unhappy examples those exposed to reprisals would take the obvious step of joining the Partisans, if only for self-protection. And such moves would swell the numbers of the Partisans, undermine further the Yugoslav economy and tie down more German troops in an attempt to counteract the nuisance. Looked at in overall terms of benefit to the Allied war effort, Tito was a better bet than Mihaelovic, went this argument.

Tomislav certainly began to think so. His convictions were strengthened when it became evident that Mihaelovic, far from lying up in the hills preparing to support a future invasion, was in some areas entering into local truces with the Germans and Italians and in others collaborating with them in operations against the Partisans. Tomislav could see the point of a Serbian monarchist leader trying to dispose of a Communist movement that by definition would work to get rid of the monarchy. The Slav side of his nature and background gave him an instinctive understanding of the convoluted thinking and plotting that must be going on on both sides. But he was a British officer charged with assessing intelligence and presenting it as accurately as he could in order that policy recommendations could be made for the furtherance of British interests. He became a firm, and because he was no communist, a reluctant supporter of the Partisan faction in SOE. He foresaw all sorts of post-war troubles but he believed that the immediate priority was to beat the Germans first. And his knowledge of the characteristics of his mother's fellow countrymen left him sceptical of their prospects of remaining for long as a tame colonial dependency of an Empire governed centrally from Moscow.

In the middle of 1943, Tomislav was transferred to Cairo. Early the following year he spent a few weeks on Vis. Later he was parachuted with a mission into Croatia and for a busy and harassed few months was liaison officer with a Partisan brigade operating around Plitvice. He was wounded in the leg when the brigade headquarters was dive-bombed by Stukas. He was evacuated to Italy with Partisan wounded, by an RAF Dakota. It was when he was fit and had reported for duty at SOE headquarters in Bari that he first met Henderson, recovering from wounds sustained in a fight with Austrian mountain troops in Montenegro.

Tomislav and Henderson liked each other, drank together and exchanged views and reminiscences. They found that their impressions of life in wartime Yugoslavia had many common threads. Admiration for Partisan courage and cheerfulness. An immense, simple liking for most of the people they had been in contact with, peasants who were called peasants, unselfconsciously called themselves peasants and would continue to be called peasants after a Communist government assumed power. Respect for the integrity of most of the Partisan leadership coupled to exasperation at the unimaginative doctrinaire rigidity of some of it. Affectionate irritation at a people who seemed to plan nothing until the last moment and then miraculously achieved spectacular triumphs, usually different from what they had originally intended, but just as good, or better. Love of the singing and the dances. Appreciation of the vino and the *rakija*. Sympathy for the appalling problems posed for individuals by the conflicting pulls of competing ideologies in a three-cornered civil war in which a man might for honourable reasons opt for Croatia or Serbia or Yugoslavia or the

King or Communism or straightforward National-Liberation-first-and-sort-it-out-later, or some combination of the options, and pay with his life and the impoverishment of his family if he made the wrong choice. Distaste for the casual callousness with which prisoners were despatched.

On this last point there was a closely argued difference of opinion, lubricated by whisky. Killing prisoners, to Henderson's mind, was unforgivable and a matter for unqualified disgust. Tomislav, half-Croat, found the practice repellent but understandable. After what the Germans had done in Yugoslavia it was hardly surprising that they should be repaid in their own coin. In any case what could the Partisans do with prisoners? They had nowhere to keep them. True enough, said Henderson, but why not undress them and turn them loose? He himself had been mixed up in a sort of Wild West shoot-out with Chetniks on a small island near Kotor. The shooting was fair enough – he'd shot two of the bastards himself – and so was the subsequent stripping of the bodies of useful clothing, boots and equipment. What had revolted him was the way in which five surviving badly wounded Chetniks had had their brains bashed out with rifle butts. There had been a marvellously tough young female doctor present, a sweet girl whom he'd never previously known show any emotion other than mirth. She'd sobbed uncontrollably throughout the shambles and had hardly said a word for about three weeks afterwards. His sympathies were entirely with her . . . Tomislav, realizing that the intensity of Henderson's feelings on the subject would make further discussion unprofitable, diverted the conversation by remarking that he knew the Kotor area well. Where precisely was this island and what had happened there? Henderson told him. Twenty minutes later a poker-faced Tomislav went thoughtfully to bed. He had quite a lot to think about.

The Beverly enquiry was by then well under way. The days of discreet surveillance were over. They had been revealing but inconclusive. Sufficient evidence had been accumulated for two senior security officers from SOE in London to fly out to Bari and to confront Colonel John Beverly with some courteously put, insistent questions. Beverly was nobody's fool and had for weeks prepared himself for this sort of inquisition. Like all convincing liars he kept as close to the truth as he could. Where the truth was too inconvenient he suppressed, embellished or denied facts. It was an altogether impressive piece of mendacity.

Q   Why did he spend so much time in the company of Major Orlov of the Soviet Military Mission in Bari?
A   In peacetime Orlov was a fellow academic, a professor of Balkan History at Leningrad University. They knew each other's work. It was natural that they should get together. In any case, association with Allies was respectable wasn't it?
Q   Okay. But why then take such elaborate precautions to hide the fact that the meetings had taken place?
A   The precautions couldn't have been all that elaborate if the questioners knew about the meetings.
Q   Point taken. Whose idea was it to drop in a large sum in gold sovereigns to the Albanian Resistance?
A   Beverly's decision, but hardly a new idea. British political officers in India, the Gulf and the Middle East had been furthering policy with gold subsidies to potential helpers for generations.
Q   Who had authorized the provision of the sovereigns?
A   Beverly had. He was controlling the operation and he had delegated financial authority to draw up to £5000 sterling.

A pause for the inevitable question that most worried

106

Beverly. He had prepared the answer with care and had decided to prejudice his future rather than ruin it.

Q   Yes. £5000. Challoner had told Henderson that an unquantifiable number of sovereigns had been lost when the container had been hit by flak. Yet Henderson had checked Challoner's count and had confirmed that twenty-two thousand seven hundred and forty-one sovereigns had survived and were now safely hidden. Where had the balance come from?
A   From Beverly.
Q   Beverly?
A   Yes. Beverly was personally rich. He was dedicated to his task of helping the Albanian patriots. He had asked for and been refused, permission to exceed his official authorized financial limit of £5000. For some months previously, in anticipation of this decision, he had been using his personal fortune in dealings on the Italian Black Market in old masters and jewellery. Yes, he was aware that this was a serious disciplinary offence. No, he was not prepared to disclose the identity of the RAF pilot who had smuggled out the cash withdrawn from his bank account in Cambridge. But the interrogators were welcome to check that the withdrawal had in fact been made (which it had. Beverly's precautions had always been thorough). No, he had no documentary evidence of his Black Market transactions and most of his dealings had been with unidentifiable front men. Damn it this was the *Black* Market. The only man he could identify positively was the owner of a small private Neapolitan art gallery who had paid £1000 in Black Market sovereigns for a gold statuette of Diana the Huntress. Yes, he could give his name and address. Unfortunately the man had been run over and killed (at Orlov's instigation) in a motor accident six weeks ago.

The interrogation was adjourned and resumed again and

again over a period of eight days and for hours each day. Beverly's testimony remained unshaken. He knew that he was discredited and could be cashiered. His object, which he achieved, was to avoid a charge of treason. Before his days as a Soviet agent were ended, however, he did a final mischief. He managed to have drawn reluctantly from him some false information. He himself, he said modestly, while moderately know-ledgeable about the art treasures in which he had dealt, was inexperienced in the authentication of gold coins. He had accepted at their face value the sovereigns offered to him from various sources, now unidentifiable. He had kept back some from the largest single consignment and out of curiosity had taken them to a goldsmith to be valued. They were duds. If they were a representative sample it was a fair assumption that about £15,000 worth of the sovereigns dropped in with Yeti Challoner had been counterfeit.

It was this piece of disinformation, supplemented by an accurate contribution by Tomislav Daunt, that led to the selection of Madden for the 'peculiar sort of job'. The appalled hierarchy of SOE in Bari saw at once the consequences to the reputation and credibility of their Balkan operations if the Partisans decided to seques-trate the gold, which given the way relations were fraying was not impossible. Arguments about genuine sovereigns would have been embarrassing enough. To have to try to explain away an apparent British attempt to bribe other people to fight for them for payment in worthless coinage was a prospect that turned normally nerveless men into fidgeting neurotics. Henderson, cross-examined for reasons which were not explained to him, gave some comfort by stating that so far as he knew only he and a woman Partisan doctor named Olga knew exactly where the stuff was hidden.

Tomislav, unaware of the interrogation of Beverly and of the questions put to Henderson, diminished the comfort by a unilateral initiative. On the previous night he had listened to Henderson's story about events at the Villa Ribar with a growing absorption. Because he was by nature of a cautious disposition he had deferred a decision about whether to tell Henderson that he was pretty sure that the sweet Partisan doctor was his own half-sister Karla and that he, Tomislav, was one of the six people alive, plus Henderson, who knew how to work the cache. He slept on it and thought it over again while he was shaving. He decided to come clean. He could think of no particular harm that could come of disclosure to a reliable fellow like Henderson and besides he wanted to hear all he could about Karla. He said his piece over coffee after luncheon and was surprised by the reaction it provoked. 'Oh Christ,' said Henderson sorrowfully, 'I've just been questioned by the brass about all this for some reason or other. I told them that only this girl Olga and I knew how to open the place up. I'll have to tell them about you.'

'Okay. Go ahead. But you'd better include the others.'

'Others?'

'Yes. There's also my stepfather, my mother and two half-brothers.' Henderson stared at him.

'Oh Christ,' he said again. 'You'd better come with me.'

The brass said grimly that they were glad that Tomislav had said what he had when he had. They were unable to tell him why but it was important that he answered their questions very carefully. First, where was his stepfather?

Last heard of in Zagreb in '41. Tomislav, when he'd been operating around Plitvice a few weeks previously had heard a rumour, unconfirmed, that the old man was dead.

His mother?

In London.

Good. That was something. His half-brothers?

He hadn't heard of them since '41. One had been a regular officer in the Royal Yugoslav Army stationed in

Serbia when the invasion came. The other, an academic, had been somewhere in Italy, Tomislav had never known where. He assumed that Vlado had probably been locked up by either the Italians or the Germans.

They thanked him. They might send for him again.

Tomislav saluted and withdrew. He was followed by the GI (Intelligence) who hastened to his office, sent for three files, glanced through them, swore, and returned to the meeting. 'I'm afraid it's getting worse, Sir,' he said despondently when he was asked what he had to say. 'I knew that Daunt's mother was that old bitch Nadja Bilic who's always gossiping and intriguing with the Royalist Government in exile. Her name's recorded in Daunt's personal file.'

He tapped the file, lying on the table in front of him.

'Well even if she's a raving keen Chetnik supporter she can't queer our pitch over this. She's safely in London.'

'For the time being. But it's this I'm more worried about.'

He opened another file, one entry of which was a captioned photograph taken from a two-month-old Ustasha newspaper, printed in Zagreb. It showed a man in Ustasha uniform addressing a parade of Ustasha soldiers. The caption described the speaker as Lieutenant-Colonel Bilic, a senior political officer on the staff of Ante Pavelic, the Poglavnik.

The GI Intelligence passed it round the table. 'We only got this rag yesterday. I think that's the missing half-brother in the picture. The one who was in Italy in '41.'

'Why? Yugoslavia's swarming with Bilics. It's a common name.'

'Well, Sir. First the timing fits. Pavelic was in Italy too in '41. That's just circumstantial. But the vetting people recently came up with some interesting stuff on Daunt's background. They're in no doubt about *him*. He's straight. In fact it was some of the more outrage-

110

ous indiscretions of his mother in London that led indirectly to this new stuff. MI5 began to take an interest in her because she was sleeping around all over the place and some of her bedmates had access to classified information. She's an unreconstructed gossip and there were fears that some of her chums might have become too talkative between the sheets.'

'Never mind her sex life. What's all this got to do with Daunt?'

'One of her lovers was a Member of Parliament. One night he found her very upset. She said that a Jug friend who'd just returned from Istanbul had met another Jug there who'd bluffed his way out from Zagreb. God knows how. There'd been talk of old times and present conditions. In the course of the discussion the Bilics cropped up. The Zagreb Jug said how amazing it was that one of the Bilic boys had teamed up with Pavelic. Not only teamed up, but he seems to be one of the biggest bastards in Croatia. He . . .'

'Keep it short will you?'

'Yes Sir. When the friend got back to London he reported it to Nadja Bilic. She told the MP and got very tearful about the ghastly plight of a mother with one son in the British Army and another who was collaborating with the Germans. The MP thought that he'd better report it all. MI5 passed it on to our vetters.'

'Has Daunt been told?'

'No, Sir. The whole thing was looked at very carefully. It was decided that it was in Daunt's own interest not to tell him officially. It might not even be true. After all by the time it reached our people it was fifth-hand information that had passed through a bar in Turkey and the bed of an over-emotional self-dramatist. There seemed no sound grounds to undermine the morale of a good operator. If his mother chose to tell him, that was her affair. He's more experience than most of judging the likely accuracy of her information.'

111

'What makes you so certain that the MP's Bilic is the same as the one in your press photograph?'

'I'm not absolutely certain. But the rumour, the photograph and Daunt's account of his brother's whereabouts in '41 all seem to me to point firmly in that direction. There are too many indications for them all to be coincidences. Of course one way to find out would be to show the photograph to Daunt and ask him if he can identify the chap in it.'

There was a long reflective pause. Then: 'No, don't do that. I've another idea. I'll just sum up. It's essential to get that bloody stuff out of that cellar or whatever it is as soon as possible. Three people know it's there, Henderson, Daunt and this Partisan girl Olga. Of the three, we can rely completely on Henderson and Daunt. The girl sounds all right, but if the Partisan party line changes on all this, hers will too. At best she's a benign neutral. At worst she's a potential menace. In addition to these three, four others know how to open the magic cave. One's a neurotic nymphomaniac for the moment contained in London. One, the old man, is rumoured to be dead. If he's still alive he's unlikely to have the health or the inclination to go swanning around in Montenegro, even if he'd be allowed to, which he wouldn't. One son, the regular officer, is a question mark about whom we know nothing after '41. The other son, who may or may not be a Ustasha, but who for planning purposes we must assume is, is the main danger. If he's Ustasha he's senior enough to be able to go wherever he likes, he sounds highly intelligent, and he probably realizes that his crowd have lost the war. If he has a little nest-egg for the future, and he'd be a fool not to, he's likely to go for that cellar and plant his loot or compromising papers or whatever it is. Then we'd be up the creek. We'll have to move fast.'

'Get the Partisans to knock him off you mean, Sir?'

'No. Too crude and too chancy. Ask 49 Commando to mount an operation to get the stuff out. Some of them

112

will be around Risan with Foxforce in a week's time. Henderson and Daunt can go with them.'

'Henderson's not fully recovered from wounds yet. He's on Light Duties.'

'Then Daunt can go alone. If this girl Olga really is his half-sister that's a plus. Daunt can soften her up a bit. And don't say a word to Daunt about the possible Ustasha Bilic. He'll need an uncluttered mind for this job.'

Chapter Seven

THE EMBROILMENT OF 49 Commando in the recovery of a collection of unspecified goods from a hiding place in a villa on the Adriatic Coast, at a time when the Germans were using an adjacent road in a full-scale attempt to break out of the Balkans, provoked much wrangling and ill-will. The Brigadier commanding No. 5 Commando Brigade told SOE that in principle he would commit units in his Brigade to almost any conceivable job provided that three criteria were met. It must have a worthwhile objective. There must be a reasonable chance of success. And if there were to be a likelihood of heavy casualties he must be personally convinced that the importance of the objective justified the risk. If SOE were going to persist in refusing to tell him, personally and confidentially, what his troops were supposed to collect from this damned Jug villa he was unable to reach a judgement on criteria one and three.

SOE said that they could only tell him that it was a matter of National Importance. The Brigadier remarked that if they couldn't do better than that they could think again. If he were ordered to carry out the operation he would of course do so. He certainly wouldn't authorize it in response to a request from SOE. They should know, also, that his wasn't the only finger in the pie. He had a final veto over any operations proposed for 49 Commando but in Montenegro they would be under the command of Foxforce. Their job was to protect the gun positions of a Regiment of 25 pounders of the Royal Artillery. Assuming that he himself agreed, and on the information so far offered he had no intention of doing so, SOE would also have to get the agreement of the Foxforce commander. At this point the Brigadier added to his temporary unpopularity by chuckling sardonically. The Foxforce commander was a famously touchy defender of his rights in military demarcation disputes.

SOE tried him, though, in a rather clumsy and immoral attempt to circumvent the Commando Brigadier. The result matched their worst expectations. They were told that to ask him, the Force Commander, to divert troops from their planned role in order to collect whatever it was that they weren't prepared to describe to him was not just military idiocy, it was plain bloody insulting. He wouldn't waste time in speculating on what they had lost but it was pretty obvious that SOE had, not for the first time, made a really spectacular cock-up. They needn't expect him to mend their bloody fences, pull their chestnuts out of the bloody fire and open the door that they had closed after the bloody horse had bolted. In a thick cloud of confused metaphors the SOE representatives departed with fleas in their ears, their hearts in their boots and their tails between their legs.

When attempted co-operation failed, SOE, as was their wont, resorted to coercion. Coded signals flashed between Bari, London, 8th Army Main Headquarters and back again. The day after their debating triumphs with the SOE negotiators the Commando Brigadier and the Foxforce Commander became the recipients of unambiguous orders from 8th Army. At the personal request of the Minister for Economic Warfare they were directed to mount with whatever resources they considered to be desirable an operation designed to achieve the object set by SOE in Bari. There was a palliative, insisted on by a sensible staff officer at 8th Army. For their own information, the material to be recovered was a large sum of money in gold sovereigns. If, and only if, they thought that it would help materially to achieve their set task they were authorized to disclose the nature of the goods to the smallest number necessary of 49 Commando officers directly involved, of the seniority of Captain and above.

*

'What'll we call this job?' asked the Foxforce Commander, sipping his Scotch.

'Goldbrick? Golddust?' suggested the Commando Brigadier, sipping his.

'Too obvious. If the troops get on to this there'll be a bit of a drain on SOE's gold reserves.'

'Moral Turpitude?'

'Immoral Turpitude? Have the other half.'

'Thanks. Brass Tacks?'

'Brasserie.'

'Brassiere.'

'Tinplate.'

'Tinpot.'

'Copperbottom.'

After several other halves, and with the slightly guilty expressions of two grown-ups who have enjoyed a children's game rather more than they were prepared to admit, they settled on 'Operation Croesus'. Their calculations were that the name bore some relation to the nature of the task in hand but was impenetrable enough not to excite the cupidity of those members of 49 Commando with a knowledge of classical mythology. If there were any which, cynically, they doubted.

After the Colonel had explained the requirements of Operation Croesus to Madden, with the aid of a large-scale map and some supplementary topographical detail furnished by Tomislav, he told Madden to do two things. The first was to make a preliminary study of the tactical problem posed and to go to discuss it with the Colonel at 1600 hours that afternoon. On the basis of conclusions reached at that discussion he was to produce a provisional plan, or if it seemed necessary in the current absence of essential information, a series of alternative plans covering different contingencies. This, or they, was to be presented to the Colonel at 0900 the following morning. Had Madden any questions?

'Yes, Sir. Precisely what resources will be at my disposal?'

'I've told you. Your whole Troop for a week. I'll get X Troop to look after your Gun-protection duties.'

'I meant from outside the Troop. I've obviously not had time to think it out, but I can imagine circumstances in which help from the Heavy Weapons Troop or the Gunners or the Sappers might be useful. Can I ask for 'em?'

The Colonel thought for a moment.

'I should think so, within reason. I'll put it to the Force Commander if your plan calls for it.'

'What about some collapsible boats if we have to go in by sea?'

'Same answer. If we need them I'll ask the Force Commander to tell the Sappers to bring some along.'

'Once we've recovered the loot how long do we have to look after it?'

'I'll take bloody good care to ensure that it's as short as possible. As I understand it the idea is to get it to Dubrovnik and away, fast.'

'Last one, Sir. Can I consult this fellow Henderson that Tommy's been talking about?'

'Okay by me. I'll ask SOE to send him over if they can spare him. Since it's their own bloody gold they've lost I can't see them saying no.'

The Colonel left them to their labours. Madden, who was one of those who knew the Colonel well and regarded him as a complete shit, was well content. He would rather be commanded by an efficient shit than a good-hearted incompetent.

The Colonel was well content too. He knew Madden's opinion of him because some years previously, before the exigencies of differing rank had supervened, Madden had made a point of telling him, repeatedly. They had joined the Corps together in 1936 as Probationary Second Lieutenants in the same batch. The Colonel was the son of a General and meant to let nothing stand in the way of his becoming one himself. Madden's father had been a Judge in the Indian Civil Service and his uncle a member of the Irish Republican Army, a curious conjunction that outraged the embryo Colonel's sensibilities and that Madden took a corresponding pleasure in flaunting. Whereas the Colonel's plans for his personal future involved a rigid adherence to the rules, Madden stuck only to those rules that seemed to him to make sense. The rest he disdained. Early in their respective careers the Colonel was marked as a star-turn likely to reach the top of his profession, a potential Adjutant General, Royal Marines. Madden was assessed as a man who discharged all his duties with great efficiency, who on occasion could be brilliantly unorthodox, and whose amiable and sometimes aggressively irresponsible eccentricities made a firm prognosis about his probable future an unrewarding waste of time.

When the Second War started in September 1939, they were both Lieutenants, the two outstanding members of their batch. Five years later the chances of war and a violent indiscretion by Madden had brought them to their present respective positions. The Colonel had served first in the Royal Marine Brigade and stayed with it when it was expanded to the Royal Marine

118

Division. Through no fault of its own it never achieved much. It trained hard and it stood by to defend Britain when invasion seemed imminent in 1940. The original Brigade, including the Colonel, went in August 1940 to Senegal on an abortive Anglo-Fighting French expedition whose exploits were commemorated comprehensively in song by its dispersed survivors in subsequent campaigns the world over, to the tune of 'Alleluia I'm a Bum'. It is possibly the most succinct piece of military history on record. It rhymes too.

> 'To Dakar we went
> With General de Gaulle
> We stayed their six months
> And we did sweet fuck-aulle.'

Because the army in 1940 had had perforce to abandon most of its weapons at Dunkirk, and the Royal Marine Brigade which hadn't been there still had theirs (and insisted that it still would have had them even if it had been) there was a strange reversal of historical roles. The Brigade was kept intact to defend Britain. Its traditional task of providing 'a striking force . . . immediately available for use under the direction of the Naval Commander-in-Chief for amphibious operations, such as raids on the enemy coastline and bases . . .' fell to the newly formed Army Commandos, formed from selected volunteers for 'special service of a hazardous nature'. It was inevitable that as time passed and things settled down, the Corps – or some of it – would revert to doing what it was supposed to do. The Colonel had been a founding member of the first Royal Marine Commando. He took part in its first operation, the Dieppe raid in 1942, a still controversial unsuccessful fiasco in which more than half of the unit were killed or captured. He was with 40 Commando in Sicily and at Termoli. He took over 49 Commando when their previous Colonel was killed at Anzio. He had the island campaigns behind him, wore the ribbons of the Distinguished Service Order and the Military Cross, and calculated that he was set on a true course for high command.

Madden's earlier war had been different. He had been Captain of Marines on a series of cruisers, an aircraft carrier and a battleship. In these his primary duties had been to supervise the manning of the Marine turret in each. He had been bombed extensively off Crete and in Malta convoys. He had been in at the sinking of *Bismarck* and had been torpedoed in the Atlantic. He had acquitted himself admirably and had been reported on accordingly. This trend had ended abruptly after a late night wardroom discussion about the handicap imposed upon the Royal and Merchant Navies in the Battle of the Atlantic by the Irish Government's refusal to permit the use of Irish ports by Allied escort vessels, a decision capable of logical political justification that nevertheless caused the deaths of thousands of Allied seamen. Madden had done himself well at dinner and was still so doing himself. Purely as a matter of the enlightened self-interest natural to a man who had served in the war at sea for three years, he was privately in favour of the Irish ports being made available. He was not prepared to acknowledge this sentiment to a red-faced Commander RN whose voice, personality and habits he disliked and he put up a masterly and spirited defence of the Irish case. The Commander, whose wine bill was running neck and neck with Madden's, lowered the tone of the discussion by a reference to priest-ridden bog rats. Madden lowered it further still by breaking the Commander's nose. The ensuing court-martial publicly deprived Madden of three years' seniority and privately advised him to apply smartly for a job in one of the seven new Commandos being formed from the still largely unemployed Royal Marine Division. Thus, Madden came to 49 Commando. With them he had done Anzio, Ornito and the Dalmatian Islands. Now he was planning for Operation Croesus. His Troop had found him competent, determined, willing to take almost any risk himself but only calculated risks where their lives were at stake: cheerful, understanding, relentless over discipline and turn out, fanatical over training. Sometimes very funny and sometimes downright alarming. It was a good Troop.

As the Colonel awaited Madden's preliminary findings he reflected on two things. If the dice in earlier postings had fallen differently it could well have been Madden who was now the Commanding Officer and he himself one of Madden's Troop Commanders. And if it had turned out like that he knew that he could never have adapted as philosophically as Madden had to the subordinate role. He would have been as punctilious in his 'Sirs' and general military courtesies as was Madden. He would have been outwardly as loyal. They were both professionals. But by God he would have resented it. In an odd way he rather envied Madden's serene acceptance of what life had to offer. Envy him or not he was damned glad to have him around.

Madden brought Henderson as well as Tomislav to report on his preliminary study. He had a marked map and a brief list of headings in his Field Service Pocket Book. They sat round an old kitchen table that served as the Colonel's desk.

'Okay, Paddy. Shoot.'

'One firm recommendation, Sir. And three possible plans ranging from dead simple to pretty complicated. Which one to adopt will depend on the intensity of local German activity.'

'All right. What's the recommendation?'

'That whatever we do we first send a small recce party to establish that the gold's still there.'

'Why? What's wrong with doing the whole thing in one go? That's what they did when they put it in.'

121

The Colonel always asked why when something was recommended to him. He found it a useful device to clear both his own mind and the recommender's. The question did not necessarily imply disagreement.

'Times have changed. When they put it in the opposition was garrisoning towns and guarding bridges. German patrol times were known. Even then the party ran into bad luck with Chetniks. Now the whole bloody German army seems to want to get out by the coast road. If this stuff's so important then clearly we must fight for it if we have to. I can't see much point in risking casualties and then finding that someone's already pinched the loot and that we've been wasting our time.'

The Colonel smiled cryptically.

'I wish you'd stop calling it loot, Paddy. It's Government property.'

'Figure of speech, Sir.'

'Anyway, loot or not, you're quite right. I agree to a recce. Now for Simple to Complicated.'

'Simple. Depends on a fairly trouble-free land route, like the one Henderson's party took, and not much going on on the road. We leave a firm base on the cliff-top, put out stops on the road, and about six of us cross to the villa and collect the loo—, the gold. Then back to the cliff-top and away for home.'

'Henderson's plan in reverse in fact?'

'Yes. With two modifications. There'll be more of us and we'll be able to load quicker than his crowd unloaded. And the stops will use their judgement on whether to stop German traffic or keep their heads down and let it through. If there's not too much of it that would be the sensible thing to do. Wait for a lull and then we nip over the road again.'

The Colonel pondered.

'Right,' he said, 'that's a good enough basis for me on Simple. Let's have Less Simple.'

'Background would be a land route so cluttered with German posts, piquets, patrols and all, that a large party

122

would risk being spotted on the way and bogged down in a firefight. A working assumption would be that a small group, say three or four, could get through to the cliff. Their job would be to establish that the villa and the island were clear and to signal by torch or radio that it was. The lifting party would come in by storm boat. One subsection would block the causeway and one would go into defensive positions around the island. A few odds and sods get the gold. Once the job's done, we pull in the cliff party and all go home by boat. That's the outline. There are some refinements.'

'Such as?'

'We'd need the gunners to bang about loud enough to cover the noise of the outboards. Unless it's a very clear night with something close to a full moon, we'd want a Vickers from the Heavy Weapon Troop to give us navigational help by firing tracer over the Gulf at the villa.'

'Two Vickers would be better. Firing from about a hundred yards apart. You could steer between them. I take it that there's some sort of suitable embarkation point?'

'Yes, Sir.' Madden pointed to a small cove marked on the map. A winding track led to it.

'Henderson reckons this is adequate.'

'Okay. We've had Simple and Less Simple. Now let's have Bloody.'

'Bloody assumes the worst possible case. Land route totally impassable. Lots of traffic on the road. And the villa and the island occupied by Jerry troops.'

The Colonel interrupted.

'I can think of a worse case than that,' he said.

'What?'

'The villa and the island occupied by German troops in prepared defensive positions.'

They considered the point. Henderson was the first one to comment. 'I suppose that's just possible, Sir, but from my own knowledge of the ground I think it's highly unlikely. If the Jerries are moving large quantities of stuff up towards Risan they might conceivably use the island as a maintenance park or a staging post or a place to tidy up traffic congestion. Or some such. But they won't worry much about a seaborne landing. They've sunk most of the boats in the Gulf and the local Partisans have always operated strictly on land. If there's anyone on the island, I think they'll be pretty relaxed and confident of a peaceful stay. Any defensive position is likely to be on the cliff-top, facing inland.'

After a further contemplative pause the Colonel said that for planning purposes he'd accept that. He asked Madden to continue. 'The thing about Bloody,' said Madden, 'is that we wouldn't know what to expect. No reports from the cliff-top about whether there was anyone, or how many armed with what, on the island. We'd need to go in prepared to find it empty and do a Less Simple. We'd also need to have enough resources on standby to deal with a really rough night.'

The Colonel, a firm believer in keeping paper work to the minimum, had the earlier two scenarios registered firmly in his mind. Now he produced a fountain pen and prepared to take some notes. 'I'd like to use the whole Troop,' went on Madden. 'Embarked in storm boats in two waves each of one Section. If it turns out to be Less Simple the first Section can do the job alone and the second can admire the scenery. If there's opposition I'd like the best I can get in the way of a comprehensive insurance policy. This would include a concentrated mortar stonk and machine-gun shoot on to the cliff-top. Enough twenty-five pounder gunfire to make the road impassable at two points about a hundred yards on either side of its junction with the causeway. Under cover of this I'd take in the second Section. We've no idea of what we'd be up against so from there we'd have to play it by ear. There'd be a lifting party of six with orders to concentrate on the job. The rest of us would sort out the opposition on the island and secure the causeway. Then we re-embark, still covered by gunfire, mortars and the Vickers.'

The Colonel looked up from his jottings.

'You could do with some smoke for the withdrawal,' he said.

'Yes, Sir. That would help.'

'What are your ideas about communications? They could be tricky.'

'I'd have a 48 set with me to call down whatever fire was necessary.'

'Take two. Signallers get shot and sets go on the blink. And take a Gunner officer and one from the Heavy Weapon Troop as well. That way you can concentrate on clearing the island if you have to. They can earn their specialist pay.'

Madden nodded.

'And take an extra medical orderly. X Troop's will do. And I'll bring along the Butcher to set up his Aid Post handy for where you land when it's over.'

They went over a few more details. Tomislav and Henderson offered some minor suggestions, with diffidence. The detailed planning of this sort of job was outside their training or their experience. The Colonel kept discussion rigorously to the point and finally adjourned the meeting.

'Well, that's about as far as we can go at present,' he said.

'We'll see what it looks like on the ground next week.'

'Do you think the Gunners will play, Sir?' asked Madden as he left.

'I can only tell you, Paddy,' said the Colonel wolfishly, 'that I'll put all this to the Force Commander tonight.'

He looked towards the door to ensure that Henderson and Tomislav were out of earshot.

'If he doesn't agree, there's going to be a bloody awful row.'

125

The Force Commander did agree, with enthusiasm. Too much indeed for the Colonel's liking. The Force Commander, forgetful of his earlier abrasiveness with SOE, entered into the spirit of Operation Croesus with a daunting zest. He thought the plan sound. 49 Commando could tap every available resource of Foxforce in support of it. What about more help from outside? The RAF for example. The Navy. A detachment from the Parachute Brigade. The Colonel passed an exhausting evening demolishing tactfully a series of imaginative ideas that at their most elaborate involved simultaneously an airstrike on the Villa Ribar, a parachute landing on the cliff-top, and supporting shellfire from a mixed flotilla of motor gun boats and submarines. About the only thing the bastard hadn't mentioned, thought the Colonel bitterly, was a torpedo attack on the causeway followed by a landing by ski-trained frogmen armed with claymores accompanied by a pipe band playing to divert the enemy's attention. After two hours of patient argument he had secured approval for the outline plan in much its original shape. As he said goodnight and saluted he felt a slight twinge of guilt, as if he had confiscated a bone from a dog. The success of his advocacy had deprived the Force Commander of the chance of some absolutely first-class rows with all three of the Armed Forces of the Crown.

The Colonel had, however, been able to offer one sop in this direction. He had no intention of allowing Madden to lead the recce party. It was a subaltern's job. Eighth Army's orders had specified that knowledge of the existence of the gold should in no circumstances be revealed to anyone below the rank of Captain. The Colonel had asked the Force Commander to try to get this embargo lifted in the case of one subaltern in Y Troop. The Force Commander had agreed. After the Colonel's departure this relatively minor administrative matter became the subject of a rousingly insulting *démarche* to SOE.

126

Chapter Eight

SIX DAYS AFTER the Force Commander had fought and won a profanely acrimonious argument with SOE over briefing the subaltern, the subaltern concerned sat with Madden and Tomislav on the forward slope of a high limestone ridge overlooking the western shore of the northernmost inlet of the Gulf of Kotor. Madden and Lieutenant Ken Kershaw wore faded green berets, leather jerkins over their battle dresses, camouflage nets as neckscarves, webbing anklets and studded, dubbined black boots. The brass fittings on their webbing equipment had been painted over to eliminate the chance of glitter betraying a position. They wore no cap badges in conformity with an obscurely reasoned security requirement designed to prevent enemy Intelligence from identifying their unit should any of its members be captured or killed and left behind. Madden, at that time and place, found himself brooding wrongly and incongruously over an irrelevant irritant instead of focusing his mind on an important reconnaissance. The cap badge business was one of those ill-thought-out, well-intentioned measures that enraged Madden and most others. If they were captured their green berets would mark them as Commandos. When interrogated the only information they were allowed to disclose was their name, rank and number. Since all their numbers were prefixed according to their home divisions by Plymouth, Portsmouth or Chatham they could only be

Royal Marines. In the Mediterranean there were only two Royal Marine Commandos, both with identical establishments. For practical German Intelligence purposes did it matter which one they were? Madden was willing to concede that troops deprived of their cap badges were unlikely to burst into tears, and that some of them couldn't care less whether they wore cap badges or not. But they were a small indication of corporate identity, an ingredient of that quality, elusive of definition, morale.

Tommy was allowed to wear his cap badge, thought Madden. There it was, on his black beret, the Intelligence Corps insignia of a bewreathed Rose of England, known alternatively as a pansy resting on his laurels. Well Tommy was no pansy. He'd shown himself in the past week to be a tough nut, even if he did insist on wearing that extraordinary looking sheepskin garment, produce of Croatia, over his battle dress.

Madden wrenched his mind back to what he was here to do. The others were picking out features on their maps, examining bits of ground through their binoculars, generally getting the feel of the area. To Tomislav the blue water of the Gulf, the grey and white limestone of the hills, three thousand abrupt feet high surrounding it, the red roofs of distant houses and the turquoise coloured sky made up as hauntingly beautiful a sight as it had always been to him from the time when he first came here as a small boy. Madden, listening to the guns booming and rumbling away to the left at targets in Risan and the old upland forts defending it, thought to himself that this was good-looking country right enough. Kershaw, trying to rough in on his map a route through the hills to the villa, considered the lovely view before him in strictly practical terms. So far as he was concerned it was a right bastard.

'Now,' said Madden, 'we've had a general look around. Either of you want a further shufti before we get down to specifics?'

They said not.

128

'Okay,' continued Madden, 'we're just discussing things at the moment. All suggestions considered. I'll give detailed orders before you go in. One point, though, I'd like to make clear from the beginning. Tommy, you're senior in rank to Ken but he's running this show. While it lasts you're under his command.'

Tomislav nodded his assent. It made sense to him. Kershaw was far better qualified to lead a reconnaissance patrol of his own troops through unpredictable country than Tomislav was.

'The target. I'm sure you've both examined it closely, but let's leave no room for misunderstanding. Look at the highest peak on the skyline straight ahead. Four o'clock from that at the water's edge is a red-roofed white house on a small island with a lot of shrubbery on it. There's a causeway joining it to the coast road and a high whitish cliff behind the road. The house is the Villa Ribar. How do you pronounce that, Tommy?'

'Ree-bar,' said Tomislav, who had simultaneously been amused at the care with which the location of his own childhood summer home had been pointed out to him and impressed by Madden's thoroughness in avoiding ambiguity. Milords Lucan and Cardigan at Bala-clava could have done with orders framed with similar attention to detail, he reflected.

'We'll run through the whole job backwards,' said Madden. 'Tommy, how long will it take you to open this, what did you call it . . . ?'

'Cache.'

'This cache and establish whether the stuff's still there or not?'

'Depends on how much muck's on top of it. Probably not much. It's only a couple of months since Henderson's party were there. Say one minute for scraping off soil, twenty seconds for opening up, half a minute for checking the contents, twenty seconds for closing down. Then, if we're going to be thorough, a good five minutes for muck-spreading and concealing the thing again.'

'Just over seven minutes at the cache?'

'Yes. Plus two minutes to reach it from the cliff-top and two minutes back.'

'Total time on the island eleven minutes and a bit. We'll add something for contingencies. Say a quarter of an hour.'

'That sounds about right.'

'Ken. How many people do you want on the island with Tommy?'

'Two,' said Kershaw promptly. 'Maxby and me.'

Madden grinned. He had been expecting this. In Kershaw's view the optimum force required for any form of patrol, fighting, reconnaissance or standing, was 'Maxby and me'. Kershaw looked upon the presence on these occasions of anybody else as an embarrassing nuisance, an incubus for which he was expected to take responsibility at the cost of diverting his attentions from getting on with the job. He and Maxby were an unusual pair.

'How many on the cliff-top?'

'I don't want anyone on the cliff-top. We can get by okay without 'em. And they'd be a bloody nuisance on the approach march. Three of us could slip through much more easily than a larger party.'

Madden considered the point. With almost anybody else he would have dismissed the argument without further thought and changed it to one about whether the total should be six or eight. Kershaw was special. Kershaw could get through with a party of three and look after himself into the bargain. But even a natural fighting machine like Kershaw would be asking for trouble if he weren't covered when he was bottled up on the island. The only way out was by the neck of the bottle, the causeway.

'No dice,' said Madden. 'You must have someone up there. Three will do. They can take a Bren each.'

130

Kershaw looked sullen, but took the matter no further. Madden often sought opinions. Once he had made decisions it was pointless to dispute them.

'What about the route?'

Kershaw brought his marked map over and squatted down next to Madden. The blue markings indicated a wriggling six miles of mountain track. Red circles showed known German positions, most of them reported by Partisans.

'I think I've got most of it,' said Kershaw. 'I'd like to take another look from the Gunner OP and from X Troop's position. There'll be a quarter moon which is about right. But there'll be a lot of mucking around taking compass bearings. That'll slow us up a bit unless the Partisans produce that guide.'

The guide had been a source of contention for the past three days. A British Mission officer named Dixon, who had been parachuted in a month previously to replace the wounded Henderson, had been working vainly on Henderson's old friends, the Brigade Commander and the Commissar with a view to getting one. They had replied with some acerbity and considerable justice that their soldiers were too busy fighting for even one man to be spared for a task that to them had neither military nor political significance.

'I'm seeing Dixon this afternoon,' said Tomislav. 'I'll see if he's any further forward.'

'Right. We'll leave that aside for a moment. What's your estimate of the timing, Ken?'

'It depends on two things. The availability of the guide and the number of Jerries about. Navigating myself, even with a clear run, I reckon it'll take nearly four hours there. Longer still if we have to start making detours. Coming back should be shorter unless we bump something. We'll know the ground.'

'You're thinking of taking the same route both ways?'

'Yes. With minor modifications. I know it's against all the lore in the text books, but in this case I think it's

131

justified. The Jerries won't want to leave their positions by night and get their throats cut and their balls sawn off by the Partisans. They'll sit tight where they are.'

Madden pondered. Kershaw was right.

'Okay. Tactical misdemeanour approved. On that timing, and allowing for hold-ups, you might be unable to do the whole job in one night. You might have to lie up for a day.'

'Yes,' said Kershaw expressionlessly. He'd done it before in the islands, on several occasions. Sometimes for several days.

'Timing with a guide?'

'If he knows his way around, not much more than two hours each way.'

'Have you thought of having any special diversions? Gunners and mortars shooting up this and that. Or navigational aids. Tracer or gunfire on to the villa?'

'I've thought about it. Forget it. I'll settle for general, usual noise.'

'Okay,' said Madden again, conscious that he'd been saying okay rather too often that morning. 'That's about as far as we can go. Any questions?'

There were no questions.

'Meet at Troop HQ at 1800 hours.'

They climbed over the crest of the ridge, picked up the subsection that had unobtrusively been covering them from positions among the rocks, and went their separate ways.

Dixon, Henderson's successor, had a noisily confidential manner, an ill-disciplined blond moustache and a voice like an upper-class corncrake. He had news of a sort when Tomislav went to see him in the afternoon. The previous day the Deputy Brigade Commander, a man named Juraj, newly recovered from wounds, had rejoined the Partisan brigade. Juraj was a forthcoming character, less laconic than the Brigade Commander, not offensive like the Commissar, and full of gratitude

132

for some past help that he'd been given by Henderson. Something to do with a duffy at some villa in which Juraj had been wounded and from which Henderson had helped to get him out on a mule. Dixon had been unable to follow the whole story. Anyway, Juraj had made it absolutely clear that he was in entire agreement with the stand taken by his superiors over the provision of a Partisan guide. The Partisans were fully occupied with attacks on the forts around Risan and on the sawmill in the town, and they were taking heavy casualties. Juraj could however lay his hands on a chap who not only knew his way backwards, blindfold, around every square inch of the area, he was the finest natural fieldcraft expert that Juraj had ever seen. He simply blended into the background like a wild animal. He was great. The main drawback was that he was ten years old.

Dixon, thought Tomislav, was an ass. A compulsive talker of an ass, from whom words surged like oil from a gusher. Still, Tomislav had said that he would do whatever he could about a guide and he supposed that he'd better do it. He could imagine the scornful incredulity on the faces of Madden and Kershaw when he turned up with some ragged-arsed snotty-nosed kid and introduced him as the boy wonder cross-country mover, the Kim of the Balkans. Resignedly Tomislav said that he'd like to see the boy. Two minutes later he shook hands with Bogdan Bojanic, a wary little lad, but strangely sure of himself.

When Dixon had completed a few unexacting formalities, the brevity of which would have appalled any conscientious social worker, Tomislav found himself the slightly uneasy custodian of a small boy for whom he had undertaken to provide food, shelter and as much protection from physical danger as could be considered reasonable in turbulent times. At the last moment, feeling completely foolish, Tomislav made an

133

abortive effort to back out of the transaction. It was then that Dixon, for all his volubility, showed himself to be not quite the ass he looked and sounded like. He suggested a field test of Bogdan's navigational abilities.

'I take it that you walked up here along the road?' he asked.

'Yes.'

'Well tell him that you want to go back to Crkvice across country. Then see what happens. If he loses you, forget him and send him back here. If he doesn't, keep him.'

Before this practical examination got under way, Dixon passed over a last piece of information. That doctor woman, he said, the one Henderson wanted to send his best wishes to. She'd apparently been pulled out from the Brigade some weeks previously and was working in a Partisan hospital in Trebinje helping to set up some sort of improvised mobile ambulance unit. Juraj had told him that. Juraj had also told him that she was agitating to get back to the Brigade.

Tomislav did not disclose the nature of his interest. Dixon was too damned garrulous.

'I tell you the kid's a genius,' said Tomislav defensively, some hours later to a sceptical Madden and Kershaw. 'He's like a homing pigeon.'

They were in a long, battered two-storeyed house at Crkvice, Madden's temporary headquarters, christened the Bronze Dog after some crumbling canine statuary at its gates. Old planks and bits of broken furniture nourished a fire that put out as much smoke as it generated heat. They were sipping tea from mess-tins. Through the shattered windows they could see the rain bucketing down and torrents of water rushing down eroded channels in the rock of the hillsides. From time to time the drumming of the rain on the roof was supplemented by the boom of the guns, firing yet again into Risan.

134

Madden chuckled. Kershaw scowled. First of all he'd been lumbered with three extra people he didn't want. Now he was faced with a half-witted suggestion that he should add to his responsibilities those of a roving baby-sitter.

'This,' he said in disgust 'is a load of bollocks.' Madden, who had no intention of subscribing to the exposure of a ten-year-old child to unnecessary danger, was not above taking a rise out of Kershaw whom, among other more flattering things, he regarded as a humourless, emotionless iceberg.

'I don't know, Ken,' Madden said provocatively. 'Why not give it a try like Tommy did? You're going down to Pod Han tonight. Tell the lad to lead you there over the hills. You never know your luck. If he's as good as Tommy says he is he'll get you there in half the time.'

It was a half-jocular suggestion and not an order. To Madden's surprise Kershaw took him up on it. Kershaw and his escort left after sunset, in the still persistent rain. Bogdan didn't get them there in half the time, but he did the next best thing. He got them there in about three quarters the time and thereby posed a new problem for Madden. Kershaw, who rightly prided himself on his skill in such matters, was impressed to the point of near awe. The kid, he said, was the guide for him. He'd make the patrol to the Villa Ribar a pushover.

Not for the first time in the past year Madden wondered about Kershaw. Life for Kershaw was a simple matter of black and white. The Germans were the enemy and therefore by definition bastards. Kershaw's job was to kill them, a skill in which, like the rest of the Commando, he had been trained with care. Unlike most of the rest of the Commando, who got on with the task efficiently and killed their foes without regrets but with no particular enjoyment, Kershaw loved it. In off-duty moments, when his fellows

135

thoughts were focused on home, or women, or sport, or past piss-ups, or present grievances or demobilization, Kershaw worked out better ways to kill Germans. He was very good at it. Madden willingly conceded that there had been times in Italy and on the islands when the knowledge that he had a supremely competent, fearless near psychopath at his disposal had been a great comfort. Kershaw had a tactical sense that enabled him to read a battle like a book. Kershaw could be trusted to carry out any task entrusted to him with complete effectiveness. When things went wrong Kershaw could be relied upon to help put them right with some unexpected initiative that was never less than useful and was frequently devastating. Kershaw in action was a credit to the community. Kershaw out of action was a mean-minded, taciturn, self-centred, insensitive oaf. Kershaw would not be permitted to put at risk the life of a child in order to further the chances of success of a recce patrol.

Kershaw accepted this decision with an angry resignation that fell, and was calculated carefully to fall, just short of the military offence of dumb insolence. This was the sort of thing that he had learned to expect from that sentimental sod Paddy Madden. Madden, in Kershaw's judgement, was a good Troop Commander who would have been twice as good if only he'd show more ruthlessness. Kershaw recalled occasions on the islands when he himself would have cut a few corners by shooting prisoners who were a nuisance, beating the shit out of others for information and calling down mortar stonks on villages in which civilians were intermingled with German soldiers. Madden had refused to do so and had stopped Kershaw from doing so. Now he was getting all steamed up about some bloody Jug kid. The bloody Jugs were slaughtering each other in droves and being slaughtered in further droves by the Jerries and fucking Madden was willing to prejudice the success of an operation for the sake . . .

Madden, surprisingly, after consulting his map again, suggested a compromise. The first two miles of Kershaw's route would be across rough country but barring the appearance of an unexpected patrol was almost certifiably German-free. Bogdan could guide Kershaw that far. After that Bogdan must fall out and come home, escorted.

The patrol left X Troop's position at Pod Han just before last light. Earlier in the afternoon Madden had given his detailed orders to Kershaw, with Tomislav in attendance. Later Madden had listened in silence as Kershaw briefed his followers. Kershaw, as was his custom and as Madden expected, did it exactly right. He left nobody in doubt about his own intentions and their individual responsibilities, omitted no precautions, and clouded no minds with verbiage. Twenty minutes before departure time Sergeant Grant, who was to command the cliff-top Bren-gun party, fell in the patrol. He inspected their weapons and ammunition for cleanliness. He checked that grenades were properly primed. He made them all jump up and down to see if they carried anything in their pouches or pockets that rattled or clinked. He made sure that there was nothing in their pockets, private letters or photographs for example, that could be of use to enemy Intelligence. He satisfied himself that all wore on cords round their necks the fire-proof identity discs that might be of use to the International Red Cross. He checked that all carried first field dressings. Then he reported to Kershaw that they were all present and correct.

The clouds had abated and it was a cool, starlit night. Madden watched them slip away in single file into the darkness. The boy led, with Kershaw hard on his heels. Next was the burly form of the redoubtable Maxby, Kershaw's MOA*, talented night mover, weapon

---

*MOA: Marine Officer's Attendant. The Royal Marine equivalent of an army batman.

handler, bar-room brawler, womanizer, in action a model of aggressive reliability, out of action the scourge of the Military Police.

Behind Maxby was Tomislav. Hurd and Spence followed, carrying their Brens balanced comfortably over their left shoulders. Sergeant Grant brought up the rear with Corporal Truscott and the two marines who were to bring back Bogdan from the point where he was to be dropped off. They were all closed up sufficiently to allow each man to just see whoever was in front of him. They were spread out enough to minimize the target they would present if they were bumped. Each man had been allotted an arc of observation so that at any given time pairs of eyes covered the whole 360°. Madden watched as the darkness absorbed the last man and returned for a chat with the Battery Commander.

First back, and much later than they should have been, were Corporal Truscott and the two marines of the Bogdan escort group. Bogdan was not with them. The little bastard, explained Truscott indignantly, had given them the slip in the darkness within two minutes of their turning for home. They had spent a futile half-hour hunting for him but since they couldn't call out without risking unfriendly attentions being drawn to Mr Kershaw's party, and since even without calling out they were making too much noise scrabbling about in the rocks, he had decided to call it a day. Or night.

Madden was angry. At himself, not at Corporal Truscott. Truscott was a steady, unimaginative countryman who always did his reasonably adequate best. In this case he had made the right decision and for the right reasons. Madden told him so and sent him and his companions away for the rum and cocoa awaiting them at X Troop's galley. Madden considered the possibility that Kershaw had somehow quietly arranged for the boy to make a token departure and then to rejoin him.

138

He rejected the thought. Ken often argued before a concept became an order and sometimes sulked after it had, but he was too good a soldier to disobey a direct order. Even if he had wanted to he lacked the means in this instance. His Serbo-Croat was about as good as that of everyone else in the unit. He could say good, not good, tea, vino and brandy. No, it was his, Madden's, fault. He should have realized that a wild young natural savage like Bogdan, who had doubtless suffered his share of the personal tragedies that dogged the lives of almost everyone in this luckless country, would be unlikely to respond to an instruction that did not tally with his personal inclinations. A realization that did nothing to ease Madden's conscience. The war was bloody enough without children taking a hand in it. Madden should never have taken the risk.

Madden, sleeping by invitation on the earth floor of a peasant's cottage that was currently being used as X Troop's headquarters, had arranged to be awakened at four o'clock in the morning. It was a superfluous piece of administration. Madden suffered from a disability shared by many junior and some senior commanders. Superficially imperturbable, he was always unhappy when he had committed troops to an operation for which he was responsible, but at which he was not present. Had he overlooked something in planning? Was he right in over-ruling Kershaw and insisting on the inclusion of Sergeant Grant and his Brens? Kershaw's skill was indisputable, but would his luck hold? If Kershaw became a casualty would the navigation of the others be good enough to get back by themselves? Tommy was good, but inexperienced at this kind of thing. Would he make some incautious mistake that would prejudice the safety of the others?

Madden, as ever, forced these disquieting scruples from his brain by presenting himself with the argument he always used in these private, worried self-examinations. He was committed. Whatever he'd done, he'd done it. He owed it to those whom he led to get some solid sleep so that he would be fit and fresh enough to make sound decisions if problems arose while Kershaw's patrol was returning.

He methodically relaxed himself, closed his eyes, and was two parts on the way to slumber when eight 25-pounder gun-howitzers of the Royal Artillery, from their positions two hundred yards behind X Troop's shack, each fired five rounds gunfire at the sawmill in Risan. Madden opened his eyes again and noted irritably that he seemed to be the only person present not to be discommoded by the deafening noise. The three X Troop officers, the aged peasant, the peasant's wife, daughter and two grandchildren who shared the floor had seemingly become immune to this type of disturbance, like city dwellers who lived near railway stations. They slept on, regardless.

The noise ceased, abruptly. Madden dozed for twenty minutes. He was awakened by a boot placed heel first on his chest, followed temporarily by the pressure of the weight of a well-nourished man moving towards the door, who had accidentally treated Madden as a raised part of the floor.

'Sorry,' whispered the voice of X Troop's duty officer, off to inspect his sentries. 'Forgot you were here.'

Madden tried to sleep again. He was successful for an hour or so, until gunfire broke out once more, now from one or two guns at a time, firing at irregular and unpredictable intervals. Madden thanked God that he was not in X Troop, pulled on his boots, the removal of which for sleep in this kind of warfare was the equivalent of donning pyjamas in more orthodox societies, and went for a walk.

The Battery Commander, up and busy, gave him a mug of cocoa. Madden asked him what he was shooting at.

140

'I've never known anything like it,' said the Battery Commander, with professional gratification. 'There's no limit on ammunition expenditure. As soon as we get it up from Dubrovnik we can bang it off at anything we like.'

'What's it you like tonight?'

The Battery Commander pointed to a set of China-graph pencil markings on his talc-covered map.

'Risan, of course. Ledenice. The forts. They're all regular customers. This random shoot we're doing now is aimed at odd targets here and there – road junctions, bridges and so on – chosen by me. My only specific orders are to drop up to half a dozen rounds a night around the Villa Ribar. Not tonight of course while your people are there. But if we have to shoot you in on a seaborne assault it won't look too unusual. Jerry'll be accustomed to gunfire by then.'

At half past four in the morning Madden sent out a reception party to welcome Kershaw. It was led by Peter Sims, Madden's other subaltern, and it went to the spot where young Bogdan had, or should have been, dropped off. It consisted of a subsection of three rifle groups and a Bren group and was accompanied by the two-inch mortar team, carrying plenty of smoke bombs, a medical orderly and a wireless operator. This last was netted into X Troop's set, beside which Madden sat with a gunner officer. If Sims reported trouble for himself or Kershaw the guns were ready to join in.

Sims came on the air on the 38 set at five fifteen to say that he was in position. No sign of Kershaw.

At five forty five, six fifteen and six forty five Sims sent identically terse bulletins. No Kershaw.

At four minutes past seven, as a diluted milky dawn light was slowly developing, Sims said that the boy, Bogdan, had joined him. The boy was trying to pass on news of some sort but nobody present could understand a word of what he was saying. Madden felt relief to hear that Bogdan was safe and some concern about the nature of the information he was trying to pass to Sims.

At eighteen minutes past seven, when the sun had risen but visibility was blurred by patches of mist, Sims reported the noise of a firefight. It was to the east of him and he could identify the sounds of Brens, spandaus and a grenade or two. He could see nothing. He was now closing down his set and heading for the noise. Madden felt a pang of worry and spared an appreciative thought for Sims. No hesitation there. Coming along well that lad. Sims had joined as a replacement on Vis and had been with Madden for only three months. He was still short of his twentieth birthday.

Madden, impatient, awaiting a further report from Sims and not getting it, told Troop Sergeant Major West to put another subsection, fully rigged, on immediate stand-by. Madden, more impatient still after a further quarter of an hour without information, told the X Troop signaller to try to raise Sims. The signaller, like all signallers using throat microphones, looked slightly insane as he chattered his repetitive jargon into space, seemingly a robot talking to himself. At the end of an apparently interminable chant imploring Yoke Sunray Minor to contact Yoke Sunray Major the signaller reported deferentially that he had been unable to make contact. He hadn't expected to and he doubted if Madden had expected him to either. He wondered whether Madden was going round the bend. Madden had a word with the Battery Commander who without demur conjured up a large-sized Forward Observation Officer with a proportionately-sized moustache and an under-sized signaller with an over-sized set. Madden walked back to the X Troop signaller and told him to have a last go at getting Sims. When, as expected, this was unsuccessful Madden, accompanied by the FOO and his bowed signaller, Troop Sergeant Major West and the stand-by subsection, and four spare parts

142

carrying stretchers, set off in search of one missing patrol, one missing subsection, two missing subalterns and one missing British Mission Officer. The expedition was guided by Corporal Truscott who knew the first leg of the route. Troop Sergeant Major West had included him, without orders from Madden and without fuss. West was a good TSM.

They marched fast, in single file, five paces between each man, along stony tracks, across small grassed patches of rock-surrounded grazing, through rocky valleys, over rocky hills. Truscott, the navigator, showed a sureness of touch that enhanced his promotion prospects. After twenty minutes they heard some desultory shooting. Occasional single shots. Short bursts, the ripping sound from spandaus, the more deliberate pop-pop-popping of Brens. They made towards the noise, on a zig-zag path that took them steeply upward on the southern side of a sharply sloping hill. Just below its crest Madden beckoned them to go to ground, and made come-with-me gestures to the Gunner officer and Truscott. The three of them advanced cautiously, now crouching, now crawling, now walking, careful not to show themselves on the skyline. From the cover of a scattering of boulders they looked out on to a curious panorama.

Immediately in front of their viewpoint the ground fell away in a scree, perhaps two hundred feet deep, to a narrow plain. This in turn dropped to a bowl-shaped valley, across which ran a thin lateral road. Beyond the road, about one hundred and fifty yards from it, there projected from the valley a small dome of a hill on which was a tiny red-roofed chapel. As a backdrop to the dome was the towering, contorted limestone of the mountains. Reading from furthest to nearest, shots were being fired from the area of the chapel, from the road and from the nearby plain. The ones from the plain and the chapel were directed at the road. The

143

ones from the road, which was littered with dead mules, burst panniers and some dead Germans, were aimed at the chapel and the plain.

It didn't take long for Madden to work out the details of this interesting deadlock. Kershaw was on the chapel hill and couldn't cross the road because of the Germans on it. The fact that he wasn't trying to double back on his tracks and come out by an alternative route suggested that he was probably burdened by casualties. The single shots and rare short bursts he was using indicated that he was low on ammunition.

The Germans firing from cover beside the road were presumably a replenishment party who, on their way back from taking supplies to one of the forts, had blundered into, or had been blundered into by, Kershaw on his way home. There seemed to be about two platoons of them. The people on the nearby plain were Sims and his subsection. They were strong enough to bother the Germans on the road, but not strong enough either to break through to Kershaw or to cover a breakthrough by Kershaw to them.

Madden made some brisk decisions. He told Troop Sergeant Major West to put the subsection with him in an all-round defensive position straddling the crest, nobody to be on the skyline. He told the Gunner officer to call up the Battery with a request for it to range on the road. And taking Truscott with him he set out to confer with Sims. As he left he ordered West's Bren gunner to fire a few bursts at the road. He could choose his own target, but if he hit it that would be an incidental bonus. The object was to make clear whose side the group at the crest was on. Sims and Kershaw would identify the distinctive sound of the Bren. Madden, to whom it had happened before, had no wish to be shot up by his own troops.

Madden and Truscott reached Sims without incident, aside from a badly aimed few bursts of spandau from the road. Sims, a tall elegant youth who believed in formality in action, saluted gracefully and said 'Good morning, Sir.' Madden, amused, returned the salute and said 'Good morning, Peter.' They got down to business.

Sims had three casualties, two from spandaus, one from a mortar which the Bren group had since neutralized. Corporal Warnock, hit in the stomach by a mortar bomb splinter, didn't look too good. Sykes, with bullet wounds in the muscle of his upper right arm, didn't look too bad. Richards, the wireless operator, was mourning at the same time the loss of half of his right ear and the whole of his 38 set, both victims of the same burst of spandau fire.

'You okay, Richards?' asked Madden.

'Fuck it, yes, Sir,' said Richards, who was holding a blood-stained dressing to his lug. 'I'm all right, Sir, fuck it.'

'Fucking good show,' said Madden genially. He had long since ceased to marvel at the conversational eccentricities of people wounded in action. Richards was a normally earnest and pious young man, ambitious to become a Methodist Minister in peace time.

'Now, Peter, what's the score?'

Sims told him. He had arrived when Kershaw's party was established around the chapel. He had assumed that they had had an unsuccessful go at crossing the road and had gone back to think again. They had been getting a bit of a pasting from the road when Sims had arrived. All from fire. The Jerries had made no attempt at an assault. In his view (with which Madden concurred) the Jerries had been shit-scared of becoming wounded and captured (and hence dead) by the Partisans they had doubtless assumed Kershaw's patrol to be. Sims had given them something to think about by shooting them up with his Bren and rifles and, when they had turned to take him on, Kershaw had livened things up with some carefully placed shots. But as matters stood there was a stalemate. Sorry he'd been

145

unable to report any of this. Set broken up. His next trick would be to put down smoke from his two-inch mortar around the Germans on the road and to see if Kershaw could break loose under cover of that. Sims would take out a party to meet him and cover him in.

Madden liked both the economy of words with which this account was delivered and the common sense of the next proposed move. He vetoed it.

'We'll let the Gunners do some work,' he said. And then a thought struck him. 'How's the boy guide?' he asked anxiously.

'Oh, him,' said Sims. 'He's buggered off again.'

When Madden reached the crest again, the distant guns, directed by the Forward Observation Officer, had been individually registered on their target, the road. One by one they had fired, their shells too far, too short, corrected, now accurate. As he climbed, Madden had heard their sibilant whispering and whistling, developing to a screech, before they crashed noisily into cloudy, flaming detonations about the road. The noise had ceased, preparation over. The guns were ready to do their job.

'Ever been to sheep-dog trials?' asked Madden.

'Yes,' said the Gunner. 'My father's a farmer.'

'Well, see if you can shepherd that lot off the road,' said Madden. 'Start at the right, well clear of 'em. Let them know what to expect. Then shift your fire by intervals towards them and then into them. I want them to break left.'

The Gunner had the whole Battery at his disposal. The impact of eight 25-pounder shells, precisely delivered at the same point, followed by a series of eight more moving along a defined track at exact intervals of twenty-five yards, is alarming. The Germans on the road broke and fled to the left. Sims, following Madden's order, did nothing to impede their withdrawal. Neither did Kershaw, who recognized a good thing when he saw it.

'Now smoke,' said Madden.

The guns switched from high explosive and the western side of the plain was obliterated by palls of thick white chemical cloud from smoke shells. Madden, watching the chapel through his binoculars, saw Kershaw's patrol rise to their feet and in diamond formation move slowly over the valley towards Sims' position. Their weapons were at the ready and they looked alert and efficient. They moved slowly to conform with the speed of their slowest components. Two men helping two others who limped. One man, carrying another.

Sims' Bren and the one with Sergeant Major West fired steady bursts into the smoke to cover Kershaw as he crossed the road. Sims went towards him with six men to take over the carrying of the wounded. Madden left the crest, accompanied by three stretcher parties, and went towards Sims' position. They all met up there, with the smoke cloud still drifting compactly about to the west and the two chattering Brens still shooting into it.

Kershaw looked tired and sweaty but as impassive as ever. The huge Maxby, behind him, looked more tired and sweatier. The front of his clothes was soaked in blood. In the background Lance Corporal Burge, the medical orderly, crouched down among the stretchers, bandaging, injecting, disinfecting. Madden, whose personal urge on occasions when speedy decisions were of no particular importance was to give first priority to seeing to his wounded, checked himself. He would only get in Burge's way. He turned to Kershaw.

'Short outline, Ken. Details later.'

'We got to the island okay and looked at the cache. The stuff's still there. Then we got bounced in a cluster of bushes by somebody. There was a lot of wild shooting in the dark and Tommy was hit. Sergeant Grant opened up from the cliff-top. He fired well clear of the row we were making and frightened the wits out of the opposition. They went to ground or buggered

147

off. I don't know which. Then we beat it back to the cliff.'

'Could Tommy walk?'

'No, Maxby carried him. That slowed us down. By the time we reached the road here it was first light but there was a thick mist. We were crossing the road under cover of it when a breeze suddenly came up and blew bits of it away. Including the bit we were in. That's when we found ourselves mixed up with all those bloody mules and Jerries.'

Kershaw paused and nodded towards the road below them.

'At first I hoped that we could simply shoot our way through but Sergeant Grant and Spence were both hit early on and bringing them in as well as Tommy ruled that out. You know the rest.'

'Thanks,' said Madden. He glanced at Burge whose ministrations seemed to be almost complete. 'Let's have a look at the wounded.' They walked over to the stretchers.

Burge had cut away most of Sergeant Grant's left trouser leg. A neat brown bandage had been tied round a shattered shin bone. Grant was clearly in pain but managed to accompany his Good morning, Sir with a smile. Spence, shot through the lung, was by now unconscious. Burge reported that he should be all right.

'This is the one I'm worried about, Sir,' said Burge as they approached the third stretcher. 'He got a close-range burst behind the right shoulder blade. The exit wound is massive. I've bandaged him up and heavily sedated him with morphine but if he gets through this lot he'll be a very lucky man.'

He wasn't lucky. Tomislav died in the Gunner's Regimental Aid Post that same night. At no time did he recover consciousness.

Back at their temporary headquarters in the Bronze

148

Dog, Y Troop found themselves in unexpected affluence. Their NAAFI ration had come up. The NAFFI – the Navy, Army and Air Force Institute – had been founded in the previous century by philanthropists who had been rightly distressed at the meagre standard of nourishment and recreation available to the off-duty sailors and soldiers of Queen Victoria. Later the airmen of her grandson became beneficiaries. At most major naval, military and air stations the NAAFI provided canteens at which were available such simple wholesome edibles as char and wads, trainsmash* and other delicacies named with similar exoticism by the customers. NAAFIs sold toothpaste, razor blades, chocolates, chewing gum, cigarettes and other useful odds and ends. By 1944 the system had been elaborated to the point that even obscurely sited side-shows like that run by Foxforce got a monthly delivery, randomly timed, of desirable groceries accessories, financed by troops who were actually saving their pay because where they were there was nothing they could spend it on. A residual caste-system, disputed by none, still prevailed. It was based on generations of Imperial experience and it was enshrined in the slightly shaky doctrine that while officers who drank spirits in excess could reasonably be expected to make fools of themselves in private, Other Ranks who did so were in danger of indulging in looting, rape, pillage and similarly embarrassing disciplinary offences that could land them in trouble. The consequence of this piece of paternalistic philosophizing was that the NAAFI monthly provided the troops with three bottles of beer and the officers with one bottle of Canadian Rye whisky. There was no such discrepancy in the cigarette ration, which was less likely to stimulate deplorable social by-products.

Madden, an unashamed paternalist who had many a time shared a tot or two of his whisky with Troop Sergeant

*Char and Wads: Tea and buns. Trainsmash: Two sausages with a smattering of tomato ketchup.

Major West, the Sergeants, the Corporals and on one occasion that had amused him, the reprobate Maxby, felt no pangs about not extending hospitality on this day. He detested Canadian Rye but it would serve his purpose. The business of the patrol had been tidied up. Y Troop, apart from looking after its own defences, had no role other than to prepare for Operation Croesus. The casualties had been despatched via Dubrovnik to Italy for treatment. Kershaw, with the aid of three stiff slugs from his own bottle of Rye, had been de-briefed with thoroughness and was now catching up on his sleep. Young Peter Sims was orderly officer and would look after controlling the protection of the Bronze Dog. The Troop Sergeant Major would be his usual vigilant self. Madden, in the manner of many of his fellow countrymen down the ages, decided to get reflectively plastered. In the manner of a Continuous Service Officer of the Royal Marines he decided to do it with a comprehensive discretion.

The starting point of Madden's musings was Kershaw's detailed report on his patrol. Who could it have been who'd jumped Kershaw's party on the island? Kershaw didn't know. He didn't much care either. Anyone who attacked him was an enemy and would get what he was asking for by having the temerity to be one. How many were there? Kershaw didn't know exactly. At least four. Not more than six. What there was of the moon and most of the stars were hidden by cloud at the time and they'd just been milling about in the dark. He and Tommy had dived right when the first shots had been fired and Maxby had broken left. After that it had been a matter of firing bursts at muzzle flashes and noises and getting out of the way before someone fired back at your own flashes. Maxby had thrown a couple of grenades. That quietened things down a bit and Grant's Brens had finally closed down the whole show. Tommy seemed to have had little experience of this sort of stuff and must have been hit fairly early.

No, Kershaw hadn't seen it happening. He'd hardly been able to see what he was doing himself. When the noise stopped he'd gone back to look for Tommy and had found him lying face down beside one of those bloody bushes whose name he didn't know, but which were all over the bloody place. Tommy was out cold and bleeding badly. Maxby had turned up about half a minute later. Between them they'd put a field dressing over Tommy's wound and then Maxby had lifted him up. Couldn't carry him over his shoulder in case Tommy lost too much blood so Maxby had carried him cradled in his arms. Yes, the whole way. Up the cliff and the four miles to the chapel. Strong as a horse, Maxby.

Kershaw himself had carried Maxby's Tommy-gun and Tommy's as well. How long had they been on the island before the excitement started? About twelve minutes. They'd opened the cache, had a quick look at the sacks of sovereigns, closed it again, re-spread the earth and were on their way out. No, he certainly had *not* taken Maxby to the cache. Maxby had been on watch, which was his job. When Kershaw and Tommy had rejoined him on the track through those bloody bushes, Maxby had reported that he'd seen and heard nothing. Christ knew where the bastards who later turned up had come from. They could have been asleep in that little cottage thing beside the villa. Probably deserters or stragglers or somesuch. Chetniks possibly. That was what Henderson had run into there some time back wasn't it? It made no difference to Kershaw. What was over was over and he'd been too busy getting Tommy out to be able to spare the time to look for enemy bodies. If there were any, a matter about which he was uncertain. And that was that.

But was it? thought Madden later, sipping at his Rye. War did strange things to people and this bloody war had gone on for far too long. Kershaw's account and his answers to questions had been given in his familiar blunt, unemotional, couldn't-care-less fashion. But there had been traces of a new element, a tenseness that Madden had never seen before. They were only faint traces but they were without doubt there. Could it be that Kershaw, he of the seemingly unbreakable nerve and physique, was beginning to crack? Madden had seen it happen to others. No man's courage was inexhaustible and every man's breaking point was different. The timing of the onset of the malaise was unpredictable. Madden remembered an unusually hardy corporal, a former Imperial Services middle-weight boxing champion, winner of the Military Medal for gallantry at Anzio, twice wounded on the islands, the sort of junior non-commissioned officer that any Troop Commander would prize. One day on Vis, just before embarkation for a job on Hvar, the corporal had begun suddenly to tremble and weep. He'd reached his limit. Madden had seen to it that he'd suffered no punishment nor disgrace for an unfortunate end to what had been a consistently honourable performance. Madden had shown a similarly understanding leniency over several cases of the breakdown of people who had done their best, and a corresponding ruthlessness with two or three who hadn't. It was part of his job to keep a close eye for the first signs of the symptoms. He had never thought that he'd detect even a hint of them in Kershaw because he'd never regarded Kershaw as courageous. Courage was what made people overcome fear. Kershaw, Madden had always thought, was fear-less; which was different.

Come to think of it Maxby, too, had been behaving slightly out of character throughout the day. Madden was inclined to put it down to simple exhaustion. Maxby's strength and endurance were legendary and were developed to a degree far beyond that of anyone else in Madden's experience. But as with courage so with strength. Every man had his limits. Even Maxby must have been pressed pretty close to his limits after carrying about twelve stone of inanimate Tommy along four miles of mountainous tracks. Whatever the cause, Maxby the extrovert skate, the irreverent humourist whose comments and demeanour had not infrequently enlivened disciplinary, formal and operational proceedings presided over by Madden, had today looked drawn, almost worried. Madden had never before known Maxby to worry about anything at all, even when faced with the prospect of some immense charge-sheet listing the extravagances of his last shore leave. That business in Naples after Anzio was vintage Maxby and it still caused Madden to chuckle to himself. Maxby, after vanishing for ten days, had reappeared in the custody of four bruised and embittered Military Policemen. When the case came up the charges, prefaced by the standard 'While on Active Service, Conduct prejudicial to Good Order and Naval Discipline', embraced a comprehensively gaudy range of events involving *inter alia* absence without leave, being drunk and disorderly, resisting arrest, assault, being improperly dressed, being in an out-of-bounds area, failure to shave and much more besides. A Sergeant of the Military Police was the first witness, red-capped, short-necked and smart as paint. He gave, in a formalized near shout, evidence of arrest, which had been effected in a brothel.

'Sir,' he bawled. 'On the twenty-first of the second, forty-four, acting on information received, I proceeded to number 48 Via Roma which is in the Out-of-Bounds Area, Sir! The lady in charge directed me to a room on the first floor. I hammered on the door and demanded that the accused open up. He declined.'

'In what terms?'

The Sergeant consulted a note book.

'He said, Sir, I quote "Fuck off!" unquote, Sir.'

Maxby's innocent eyes caught Madden's. Madden looked hastily at a point a foot over the Sergeant's head.

'I then broke the door down,' roared the Sergeant, 'and found the accused lying on a bed, naked. On his left was a lady, also naked. On his right was another lady. She was naked too.'

The Sergeant refreshed his memory from his note book again.

'I immediately said to him, I quote, "I suppose you realize you are violating the anti-malarial regulations . . ."'

Maxby guffawed, a great infectious belly laugh. Sergeant Major West, facial expression immobile, began to shake silently, like an African dancer in a tribal ritual. Madden produced his handkerchief and covered the lower part of his face in a feigned bout of sneezing. The Sergeant bellowed on relentlessly, through an account of a surrealistic fracas in which a nude Maxby, with some efficient supporting work from his equally bare fair companions, had taken on the Sergeant and three other Military Policemen. Two had been knocked out cold and the accused had only been secured when he had been temporarily unsighted by a cloud of feathers released from a bolster which burst when one of the ladies had hit the Sergeant over the head with it . . .

Throughout this narrative Maxby smiled appreciatively, a craftsman listening with modest satisfaction to a flattering account of his work. When the Sergeant had completed his evidence, had been given permission to fall out by a choke-voiced Madden, had saluted vibrantly and had stamped out, Madden broke down uncontrollably. So did TSM West. Maxby watched them benignly. At last Madden was able to speak, just.

'Maxby,' he said, 'you're a bloody fool.'

'Yessir,' said Maxby proudly.

'Remanded for CO's orders.'

For that little caper Maxby had certainly earned, and in other circumstances would have got, several weeks or months in the Glass House, the military prison. He had yet to be sentenced. The unit was off to Vis the following day and the Colonel, after consulting Madden, had deferred hearing the case. There were times and places in which someone of Maxby's calibre could put his talents to more constructive use than the resources of a military prison offered.

And on the islands Maxby had given extensive justification of the decision to keep him out of the Glass House. There was Maxby's strange devotion to Kershaw, so unlike him in character, that had led to an incomparable patrolling partnership. Maxby on Korcula, under heavy close-range fire, rescuing two badly wounded marines. Maxby on Brac exploding the Bangalore torpedoes under the German barbed wire in a brave but unsuccessful attempt on an impregnable position. Maxby on a boarding party, jumping on to a German lighter and knocking its steersman senseless with one solid punch. Maxby all over the bloody place, in short. Madden topped up his glass.

Madden wondered what would have happened to Maxby had there been no war. Almost certainly he would have been in gaol. The trouble with people like Maxby was that they had no concept of a society that extended beyond their immediate surroundings. Maxby's virtues were bravery, determination, hard work, willingness to sacrifice his life for his comrades, good humour and loyalty. But the loyalty was selective. Maxby would stand by his friends and by those companions of whatever rank whom the chance of war had brought him amongst. He was an outstanding performer at the job he was currently being paid to do. But turn him loose, with his trained skills, on a wider society to which he was at best indifferent, otherwise contemptuous, and on occasion hostile, and all hell was likely to break loose. Madden genuinely liked Maxby. He considered gloomily that if Maxby survived the war he was headed inexorably towards the gaol that the war had preserved him from. Which was a great pity. There were plenty of men in the Troop who came from backgrounds as deprived as Maxby's had been and had first been trained in and had then practised killing. Madden couldn't think of one who would be unable to readjust to the requirements of peace-time society. Some would doubtless take longer than others but he would bet on none going to gaol except through pure ill luck. He himself possibly.

It was interesting to speculate on where it would all end. This time next year where will we be? An unforeseeable number would be dead. A further number, on the rough and ready ratio of four wounded to one dead, would be wounded. Of these latter a few would have lost limbs, eyes, or suffered severe internal injuries. Others, the majority of those wounded, would have odd flesh wounds, bones broken. The highest proportion of both dead and wounded would be among the officers and the sergeants, followed by junior NCOs and with the real goers like Maxby the greatest risks of all. There would be some, perhaps many, psychological scars that would remain undiagnosed for years to come. Exact forecasting on the statistics of these matters was impossible but barring unusually good, or unusually bad, luck there was a thread of consistency in the trends.

Madden, the professional, the regular, had always accepted the chance of premature death as an integral part of the life he had chosen. He wouldn't have joined if he hadn't. But he never stopped marvelling at the equanimity with which the young men he commanded, in their early twenties and in their late teens, factory hands, farmers' boys, coalminers, bus conductors, clerks, shop-assistants, unemployed, nearly all of whom had left school at the age of fourteen, and none of whom had much cause to be grateful to the stratified society in which they and their families had been nurtured, faced the uncertain prospects of survival.

156

They lacked the dog-like trust and discipline of their
fathers' generation, when whole battalions had had
ninety-five per cent casualties in one morning on the
Somme, and in Madden's view it was a good thing that
they lacked it. His uncle, the member of the Irish
Republican Army whose existence so upset the Colonel, had, before he turned his warlike attentions upon
the British, commanded a company of the Munster
Fusiliers on the Somme. He had told the young Madden all about it. Madden wanted no repetition of that.
He wanted a discipline and trust tempered by self-
reliance, initiative and common sense, the whole
directed by a leadership at the top which understood
the requirements of modern war and was not obsessed
by how to get the cavalry through the barbed wire.

Something wrong there somewhere in that last
thought, reflected Madden. Too compressed. Essential
intervening stages omitted. The point really was that
there were plenty of idiotic Generals in this war but
most of the Generals had been junior officers in the last
war. However they buggered the troops about now
they didn't bugger them about in the way that they
themselves had once been buggered about. Casualties
had to be accepted but there was now more care and
preparation in planning, closer assessments of what
risks were justifiable, more economy over men's lives.
And a knowledge and understanding of that fact,
however imperfectly perceived, had percolated down
to the troops who did the work. That was why they
would follow Madden and Kershaw and young Peter
Sims and TSM West and the NCOs into action. They
were given all the information available, had plans
explained to them in detail, and were treated as intelligent participants, not mindless obeyers of orders.
Some of course were mindless obeyers of orders, but
most weren't. The second lot looked after the first.
Yes, this really was a bloody good Troop. One more
tot and then sleep. Good God. Three quarters of that

bottle of Rye gone. Why not, in the privacy of his own home? Discretion was the better part of Godliness, or something similar.

As he fell virtuously asleep in his little ruined room, Madden heard through the door a whispered admonition by TSM West to somebody who could only be Sims.

'I wouldn't go in there, Sir,' West was saying protectively. 'The Troop Commander's pissed.'

Operation Croesus was mounted forty-eight hours later. Its concept was simple, its support was elaborately efficient, its execution was perfect and it failed to achieve its object. Which last didn't matter very much.

The agent accidentally responsible for frustrating a carefully prepared little *coup* which had engaged the attentions of a Cabinet Minister, an Army Commander, the SOE top brass and a Force Commander, dignitaries who would not normally concern themselves with the details of a Troop attack, was a conscientious German transport sergeant named Becker. Becker was a thirty-year-old mechanical enthusiast who took a pride in his work. The standard of maintenance on vehicles for which Becker was responsible was famous. Becker never abandoned a truck nor squandered a spare part. If he set out to take a convoy of trucks from A to B, all the trucks reached B or if they didn't there was a very good reason for their non-appearance.

Shortly after midnight on the morning of Operation Croesus, Becker, in a scout-car, had been leading four German supply trucks along the narrow, winding coast road from Kotor to the beleaguered Risan. For safety's sake they drove without lights, a lesson drummed into them by recent attentions to incautious night convoys by the Tommi's guns. The sky was clear and starlit and the moon just past the quarter, an adequate light for a well-sighted man to drive by. The driver of the second truck was astigmatic and of a romantic disposition.

Charmed by the effect of the moonlight on the rippling waters of the Gulf he let his attention wander, hit a sharp-edged small rock that had tumbled down on to the road after a previous artillery shoot, and shredded the tyre of his offside front wheel.

Becker swore, stopped and inspected the damage. A lesser man, or a man less proud of his record, would have towed the truck into Risan on the rim of the wheel and written off the damage. Becker fastened a tow-rope all right, but he had no intention of arriving in Risan with a crippled vehicle. He led his little convoy to a place he'd marked down a few days before as a suitable site for emergency repairs. Becker, on the narrow Balkan roads, always marked down areas where he could pull off for emergency repairs. This was one of the better ones, a small island approached by a short causeway. There were too many oleanders on it for Becker's liking, but there was enough flat space to park all the trucks and change the damaged wheel. Ten minutes later Becker was dead. Corporal Truscott's Bren group killed him.

The Colonel came up from some rather boring operations at Niksic to watch the job. Madden felt no irritation at this. The Colonel would not interfere in the detailed arrangements made by a Troop Commander he trusted. What the Colonel would do was provide support and encouragement, make a suggestion or two and use his influence, which was more than Madden's, to help get what Madden wanted. The Colonel enjoyed his little jaunt. It was a happy respite from having to dream up a constant series of arguments, which had to be simultaneously convincing and courteously expressed, to counter the Foxforce Commander's more fanciful concepts. The last one had been something about creating artificial avalanches, triggered by parachuting a Troop on to a razor-edged mountain top and ordering them to roll snowballs over the side. This

159

Croesus affair was more to the Colonel's liking. There was a clear objective and means available to attain it. It was led by a man who knew what he was about. The Colonel, with sour recollections of the shambles of Dieppe, made only one suggestion. If the resources were available, over-insure. Use all eight 25-pounders instead of the planned two. The Battery Commander agreed with enthusiasm.

Thus it was that Sergeant Becker, calmly and methodically changing the wheel at the Villa Ribar, was distracted from his task. First there were two parallel streams of medium machine-gun tracer, spaced about one hundred metres apart, firing steadily at God knew what on either side of the island. Then there was the growing screech of a concentration of shells that crashed into the cliff-top beyond the road. Further concentrations, mostly directed at the two bends in the road below the cliff. Three salvoes on to the island itself, one of which wounded two of Becker's drivers and took most of the engine out of one of his trucks. The shells lifted to the road again to be replaced by a whining, thumping shower of three-inch mortar bombs. Becker, baffled and angry, lay flat on his stomach through the hideous crashes of the explosions, the zinging of mortar, shell and stone fragments flying about, the tangy smell of cordite and clouds of smoke and dust. What in God's name was happening? Surely no one had detected his arrival on the island? And even if they had, was this not an unnecessarily extravagant reaction to his presence? The mortaring stopped abruptly, but the noise of the shelling on to the cliff top and the road continued as deafeningly as ever. Becker and his transport team did not hear the sound of running feet coming towards them from the direction of the stone jetty.

Sims' Section was in the first flight of three collapsible assault boats. Madden, with Troop headquarters and

160

Kershaw's Section was in the second flight, a hundred yards astern. To the surprise of all, inured to that military gremlin the buggeration factor, everything went exactly right on the short crossing. The light from the quarter and a bit moon was ideal. The racket made by the guns and mortars covered the noise of the outboard engines. Not an engine failed, a rare bonus. Navigation between the lines of parallel machine-gun tracer was kids' stuff. The timing of the mortar stonk on the island was exact.

As the stonk lifted, Peter Sims, pistol in hand, jumped ashore and led his Section at a fast run straight towards the causeway. Looking after the causeway was his job. Kershaw's people would tidy up behind. Privately Sims had thought that far too much fuss was being made about landing on an unoccupied island, an opinion that he revised smartly when he noticed that the bloody place seemed to be swarming with trucks and that somebody was shooting at him with a Schmeisser. He ran on, cracking off two pistol shots as he went. Both missed. Never mind. Keep going. Somebody else could deal with that sod. Must get to the causeway. He heard a Bren firing behind him and the Schmeisser quietened at once. A minute later his Section was in position, the causeway was covered, and he was taking reports. No casualties in either subsection. One dead Jerry NCO. Four prisoners, two of whom were wounded. One intact scout car and one wrecked truck in the Section area.

He turned to try to identify the source of extensive bangings and crashings behind him. Kershaw cleaning up the rest of the island. Still some resistance apparently. He could hear at least two Schmeissers and some German grenades in among the short bursts from Kershaw's Brens and Tommy-guns, and the crack of rifles. He could see tracer from a Bren homing in accurately on to a truck stacked high with what in the dim light looked vaguely like cylindrical drums. The

161

accuracy of this piece of observation did credit to Sims' eyesight. They *were* cylindrical drums, filled with the petrol that was to fuel the evacuation of the German garrison of Risan. At the spot where the flashes of the tracer bullets were grouped, there was a sudden, brief, small, red glow. This was immediately followed by a massive, whoomphing explosion and a protracted and spectacular illumination of the night sky, modified erratically by palls of thick black smoke.

'Well fuck me,' said an amazed Marine MacIntosh, whose Bren had inaugurated all this unexpected havoc. 'What'll the buggers think of next?'

Chapter Nine

OH JESUS, THOUGHT the Colonel four hours later, after he had heard Madden's full report. He was thinking of how the Foxforce Commander would take the news that Y Troop with only two minor casualties and extensive singeings had secured the island, killed six Germans, captured nine and destroyed one scout car, four trucks and an unknown quantity of charred and unidentifiable equipment, but had returned without a single sovereign. The gold had been denied to them by the convoluted red hot ruins of three, by now fused together, trucks that had been parked over the top of the cache.

'Couldn't you have blown the bloody things away, Paddy?' asked the Colonel wistfully.

'We'd no explosive with us. Even if we had we couldn't have got near the mess. It was white hot to start with. Still red when we left.'

'You're sure they were parked over the cache.'

'So Ken said, Sir. He's the only one who knew the exact position. I've never known him wrong on a thing like this.'

'What do you think are the prospects of shifting them? Or it I suppose it is, now it's cooled off.'

'I think we'd need a recovery vehicle or a bulldozer. We could try explosives but I can't see how we could set off a charge without risking blowing in the top of the cache and causing fresh complications.'

Oh Jesus, thought the Colonel again. He could imagine the Force Commander getting his teeth into this one. A dockyard gantry flown in on barrage balloons, with fighter cover, support from the Mediterranean Fleet, a salvage team with oxy-acetylene blow lamps, an assayer from the Bank of England to confirm that the gold was still in mint condition . . .

Three days later Karla Bilic solved the problem for everyone.

The German troops at Risan belonged to 21 Mountain Corps. They were one of three advanced guards of the German forces in the Southern Balkans engaged in an attempt to break out before the advancing Russians, and possibly the British from Northern Italy, sealed the exits across the head of the peninsula. The German Command were military realists and they knew better than to reinforce a failure. British guns and Partisan courage had made the Risan route too expensive. Two nights after Operation Croesus the Germans withdrew quietly from Risan, headed south along the coast road through Kotor, and went inland to join their fellows in trying a more promising route further to the east. Because Marine MacIntosh's Bren had disposed of Sergeant Becker's collection of petrol the German disengagement did not go as smoothly as had been planned, but it was nonetheless effective and, but for one officer left behind, complete. Early in the morning Partisans, and some British, entered a deserted, wrecked Risan littered with rubble, abandoned damaged equipment, dead mules, a plenitude of graves.

The Partisans mounted a follow-up along the coast road. They were mostly on foot but they had a small motley collection of transport with them, battered old cannibalized civilian trucks and cars, equally battered captured German and Italian vehicles. Among these, grouped under a Red Cross flag, were a dilapidated charabanc, two Italian trucks and a barely mobile

164

Volkswagen. They trundled slowly southwards down the road, and turned right over the causeway on to the island of the Villa Ribar. There they halted, dispersed around the now-blackened house and the charred vegetation, and were unloaded. Tents were set up, two marquees and several bell tents, gifts of the American Red Cross. Stretchers and equipment were distributed. Within half an hour of crossing the causeway Doctor Olga's mobile field hospital was treating its first patients, wounded from the Risan fighting who had been ferried in on the shuttle service provided by the charabanc. It was a busy day and busy half night. The following morning the pressure of diagnosing, treating, bandaging, injecting and amputating had eased. Karla experienced her customary reactions of sorrow and pride. As much for a distraction as for any other reason she turned her attention to the cache.

Madden had spoken in terms of the need for a bulldozer or a recovery vehicle to clear the obstruction made by the welding together at a high temperature of the remains of three large German trucks. It was certainly not a job that could have been done by manpower alone. The problem had, however, been simplified partially by the fact that substantial bits of truck had been blown away in the initial explosion. Karla was no engineer. But she was a Yugoslav Partisan, a natural improviser indifferent to the conventional limitations put upon machines by their manufacturers.

The power of the charabanc driven in reverse gear and supported by a scrum of medical attendants, walking wounded and patients who should have stayed in their tents but who would not have missed the fun for anything, soon got the wreckage on the move. With crunches and squeaks and some temporary set-backs it was slowly pushed towards the jetty whence it eventually dropped into the Gulf with a spectacular splash and amidst a round of applause. The rest of the mess was tidied up by hand. After which Karla decided to re-site the bell tent that housed her meagre supply of surgical stores and in which she herself slept. She chose an oddly inconvenient part of the island. It was an order that was obeyed without question. Pretty Doctor Olga, sweet natured and tough as old boots, competent, kindly, tireless and caring, veteran of over three years of grim campaigning which included the Durmitor epic, was held in immense respect and admiration. Her wish was a command.

That night, with the help of one of the torches that had come in amongst the growing tide of supplies from the Western Allies, Karla re-arranged the stores inside her tent. Then she scraped away a layer of fire blackened earth. The steel pivot bar had warped slightly in the heat of the fire and the stone wedge had cracked, but with a bit of extra effort she was able to swing the top of the cache open. She lowered herself inside and shone the torch around her. The gold was intact. The two wash-leather bags of jewellery were gone. And in a corner, leaning against one of the sacks of sovereigns, was a bulging crocodile-skin briefcase, the flap of which was embossed with the initials V. B. Karla recognized it instantly. Her father had given it to her brother Vlado as a present when Vlado's thesis on Croatian History and Culture had been such a success.

Four days later, after some brisk signalling, a motor gun boat of the Royal Navy tied up alongside the jetty at the Villa Ribar. Henderson, his limp nearly gone, disembarked followed by a party of bemused Military Policemen, torn uncomprehendingly from their normal task of hounding deserters, drunks and lechers in Bari. Henderson saluted Karla with the casual courtliness that so enchants the female recipients of military salutes and she smiled her lovely smile. But it was, thought Henderson, a sad brave smile. Something was

166

bothering this poor girl again. She looked almost as wan and as tired as she had for days after his last visit in different circumstances to this island, when she had almost cracked up after the death of that gallant idiot Yeti Challoner. God knew what she had seen in Yeti and God presumably also knew why a girl with this one's looks, character and record . . . He forced his mind back to the business of the day. He was, he recognized, as besotted with Karla as Yeti had been. He was damned if he'd betray the symptoms.

That same evening, after an efficiently conducted day's work, Henderson, bearing gifts, was rowed ashore in a dinghy from the MGB, now at anchor some two hundred yards offshore. He reflected on the day's events. Karla had stimulated curiosity among the patients, but prevented its being satisfied, by placing a line of walking-wounded sentries across the corner of the island where her surgical stores tent stood. The sentries' orders were first not to look back towards the tent, an edict that irritated them, and second to permit no one else to come close enough to be able to see what was going on behind them, a popular injunction that they fulfilled enjoyably by throwing stones at all suspected transgressors, plus anyone else that they happened to dislike.

The Military Policemen had come woodenly ashore, marched to the tent and removed it and its contents to a point in front of the cache, where it provided further cover from view from the inquisitive. Henderson had, for the first time, briefed the MPs on the nature of their task, stressing the importance of absolute accuracy and honesty in delivering the sovereigns back to Bari. The Military Police Sergeant then roared out an unexpected intervention on the general theme of the appalling retribution that would fall upon his followers should one single sovereign be misappropriated. Maxby would have recognized an old adversary, the enthusiast for

167

antimalarial precautions, reducer of Madden's Troop Office to choking hilarity. The recipients of the Sergeant's message on this occasion had looked suitably terrified and Henderson didn't blame them. Counting began, followed by loading into the MGB, followed by a suggestion from the Sergeant. For the safeguarding of the gold on the MGB, he explained, he had devised a sentry rota system of such complicated ingenuity that only collusion by the Captain, the entire crew and Henderson himself could lead to the loss of even one sovereign. In the known light of human frailty, however, it would ease his mind if that boat could be stuck well out to sea to prevent some clever bugger seizing an armful of coin of the realm and disappearing with it into the interior of whatever this country was called, Sir. Henderson and the MGB Captain, who knew his crew, agreed.

Henderson's gifts, compliments of the MGB's wardroom, were a bottle of scotch, a bottle of gin, a small bottle of Angostura bitters, four tins of baked beans, two tins of spam and two hundred cigarettes. He took them, clanking in a webbing big pack, to Karla's surgical equipment tent, where they were received with warm gratitude. Juraj, passing through on his way to Lovcen mountain, had called in to visit some of his wounded and had stayed longer than he should when he heard from Doctor Olga that his Scotski friend Henderson was due to appear. Juraj greeted Henderson with uninhibited delight, a hug that nearly cracked his ribs, and a noisy kiss on each cheek that, to Karla's huge amusement, brought to Henderson's face a blush of residual Presbyterian prudishness. The three of them passed a happy, reminiscent half-hour. Juraj displayed to Henderson the intricate scars of his shoulder wound, 'healed by this pretty quack here.' Henderson initiated his hosts into the mysteries of how to prepare pink gin and competed with them in drinking the product. Karla

168

joined in the fun charmingly and amusingly and privately reached a positive conclusion to a tentative line of thought that had been running through her mind since Henderson had first stepped on to the jetty earlier that morning.

Karla was a complex girl with an active conscience and a logical turn of mind. Faced with a choice of apparently irreconcilable alternatives she would mentally muster the arguments for and against, consider them with ruthless honesty, discard dishonourable easy ways out, temper her conclusions with an element of feminine inconsistency and reach a decision. The decision made, she acted upon it, with neither second thoughts nor regrets. The irreconcilable alternatives that she had been wrestling mentally with since her discovery of Vlado's briefcase had concerned a conflict of two deeply-felt loyalties, one to the Party, one to her family. Karla had cut open the briefcase and had been appalled by its contents. There were bundles of photographs, each carefully annotated on the back, showing dead Serbs and Jews and gypsies hanged or shot or burned to death, the bodies often surrounded by laughing Ustasha. There was a precisely kept diary, evidently designed as notes for a future historical treatise to the glory of a triumphant Independent State of Croatia, which listed in sickening detail the punitive operations in which Vlado had been engaged over the past three and a half years. In separate folders were tidily filed draft press releases, draft speeches for the Poglavnik, and a series of scholarly analyses of the past role of Croatia in European history which led on to closely-argued recommendations about what Croatia's future role should be. The contents of the briefcase made up a brilliantly presented case for the furtherance of the interests of a talented and sturdy race that had been hamstrung by geographical and historical coincidence in its search for its just destiny and could only achieve it by a preliminary pitiless clearance of anyone who stood in its path. The only weakness in the presentation, thought Karla miserably as she read through the papers, was the basic one that insulated academic theoreticians from reality. The world was populated by people and most people were irrational, stubborn and uncomprehending. Vlado's tragedy – she still thought of him as gentle Vlado – was that by an accident of timing he had been given an opportunity to put his theories into practice and that a keenly developed sense of duty had led him to suppress his natural kindliness in the interests of the pursuit of what he conceived to be a sacred cause. Vlado was mentally unbalanced. Vlado was a war criminal. Vlado's papers named sufficient names, and linked them with supporting evidence to sufficient specific incidents, to keep the People's Courts busy for years after the war was over. It was Karla's clear Marxist duty to hand the briefcase and its contents over to the Commissar and to hell with the consequences.

Karla worked out the consequences. To her, if she chose to take a detached view, they would be only beneficent. Praise for a devotion to truth that had led her to put principle before sentimentality, party before family. Karla was unable to take a detached view. Memories of her happy childhood made up a central part of her life. She could not escape a debt of loyalty and gratitude for that. She had seen her brother Branko shot dead before her eyes and she had revealed his identity to nobody. She could do what she should do with Vlado's papers and bring him an immediate death sentence. As a Ustasha lieutenant-colonel he would get one anyway, assuming that he was caught. Since he had now equipped himself with the two wash-leather bags of jewellery it was reasonable to assume that he was taking active steps to ensure his own safety, and in the confusion of contemporary Yugoslavia he might well succeed in finding his way out. But the people about whom Karla were most concerned were her father and mother. It was nearly four years since she had heard of either of them but she had no reason to believe that they were not still alive. Karla recalled them fondly as honourable and tolerant. They would find hard to understand her own secession from Catholicism to Communism, but they would forgive her. They would find Branko's role as a Chetnik more credible, and would comfort her with a sympathetic love when they heard that she had been present at his death. But they would be destroyed utterly if they discovered that Vlado, kind, artistic and intellectual Vlado, had developed into a psychopathic butcher of his fellowmen.

Party or family? Family or party? Right or wrong? Karla had hardly slept since finding the briefcase. Looking at the cheerful, reliable, tough figure of Henderson, in his battle dress and black beret, expatiating on the merits of pink gin and laughing happily with the boisterous Juraj, Karla made up her mind. She would temporarily put the matter of Vlado's dossier into abeyance by removing it beyond the reach of both the Communist Party and the Bilic family. She would confide in Henderson in whom she had developed a complete trust. She would ask him to take the briefcase into his personal custody and not to disclose its contents to anyone else. She would tell him about Branko and Vlado. Much later, when the war was over, she would consider whether the interests of justice required disclosure to the People's Court of the detailed information which she alone among the Partisans possessed. If in her judgement it did, she would find a means to contact Henderson.

Karla also gave a less cold-blooded consideration to some other, womanly, thoughts she had had about Henderson. She decided that in certain circumstances she would. Four years was a long time for a healthy girl of twenty-four. If one breach of party discipline, why not two? Karla chuckled.

171

Later in the evening the one led naturally to the other. Karla took the coughing, decrepit Volkswagen into Kotor to deliver to the forward Brigade some of the growing volume of medical supplies that were coming in through Dubrovnik. Henderson, not due to sail until dawn, went with her. On the return journey Karla stopped the car at a ruined house not unlike the Villa Ribar. Together they admired the lovely silvered Gulf under the splendour of a full moon in a clear Mediterranean winter night sky. Karla said that there was something she must tell Henderson, but he must promise to treat it as a personal confidence. Henderson, fired by pink gin and the proximity of Karla, would have promised anything and did so. Karla, in a steady firm voice, told Henderson about the placing of Ivo's jewels in the cache three and a half long years ago. About the identity of the Chetnik officer shot by Yeti (her voice wavered here, but recovered). About the identity of her Ustasha brother Vlado. About the disappearance of Ivo's jewels. About the content of Vlado's archives.

Henderson, listening with a cumulative appalled sympathy, marvelled, not for the first time, about the practical stoicism with which the people of this country met personal and national calamities. Here was this delightful girl, still in her early twenties, who had come through nearly four years of hard, cruel, merciless fighting, her spirit undaunted. She must have marched thousands of punishing, mountainous miles. She had been bombed, shelled, mortared and machine-gunned repeatedly. With inadequate and sometimes nonexistent medical resources she had tended undernourished, lice-ridden wounded and sick who if abandoned would have been murdered. If captured, so would she, after torture and, since she was young and attractive, rape. For long periods she had been near to starvation, and in the winters near to frostbite. She would inevitably have known of, and on occasion would certainly have

172

witnessed – by God on one occasion at which he had been present *had* witnessed – the massacre of captured wounded, a deed repugnant to her nature. She was aware that her comrades tortured their captives for information or in retaliation. She had consciously adapted herself to all these horrors, secure in the firm faith that present sacrifice was necessary to secure a better future for generations to come.

Henderson had deep doubts about whether the faith was justified. But he envied it and felt humble when he compared the sacrifices these people were making compared with those of his own. His brother, in action for the fourth time, had lost a leg on a mine at Mareth. The whole Henderson family had been sunk in sympathetic gloom. How did that, distressing as it was, begin to compare with what these people were going through?

And on top of her own awful personal experiences Karla had had one brother, fighting as an enemy, killed in front of her. Had discovered that another brother, also an enemy, was a large-scale murdering maniac. And did not yet know, and Henderson had no intention of telling her, that a third brother, admittedly a half-brother, had recently died of wounds incurred at the same place where the first brother had been killed. Karla, thought Henderson with boundless admiration and love, was indomitable.

Karla ceased to be indomitable and reverted to being a woman at the end of her account. Since she had dried her eyes after saying goodbye to old Ivo in Zagreb she had cried twice. Once when little Bogdan had run to her and embraced her. Once when Branko was killed. Now, in the Volkswagen, in the bright moonlight, in the company of a sympathetic foreign man who had no obligations to Partisan discipline or party solidarity and for whom she had developed a cheerful affection, Karla caught up on her necessary feminine weeping. She sobbed with no attempt at restraint. A stream of tears

173

poured down her beautiful convex cheeks as she keened and wailed and purged herself of accumulated suppressed terrors and horrors and frustrations.

Henderson, moved as he had never been moved before, put a comforting arm around her shoulders and pulled her towards him. Karla sobbed on, her face to his chest. Henderson stroked her hair and gently kneaded the muscles in her neck. Henderson, through the serge of her battle dress jacket, massaged the muscular ridges on either side of her spine. He mopped her eyes with his handkerchief. He kissed her salt-tasting eyelids. Karla's heaving sobs, after a long, long time, diminished to sniffles, dealt with efficiently and kindly by Henderson's handkerchief. Henderson, in the manner of a father comforting a bereaved daughter, kissed Karla's forehead and cheeks. Karla, comforted, smiled tentatively and tearfully and said that she was sorry. Henderson said that she had nothing to apologize for and hugged her with sympathy. Karla shifted her weight, her breasts pressed against Henderson's chest and she hugged him back. Henderson . . . Karla . . . Karla . . . Henderson.

The second breach of party discipline proceeded on its way from a possibility to an inevitability.

In the small hours of the morning, on the jetty of the Villa Ribar, Karla and Henderson had their last sad frantic embrace. A disgruntled and blasphemous Ordinary Seaman, his sleep interrupted by a summons from the island, rowed Henderson, clutching a crocodile-skin briefcase, out to the MGB in a dinghy. The MGB started up her engines at dawn and set a course for Bari. At the same time, Doctor Olga, renewed spiritually and physically, began her rounds in the tents that served as wards.

In the middle of January, 49 Commando left Yugoslavia for the last time and returned to Italy. There Madden, promoted, left the Troop he had raised, cherished and led, and went to France to become the Brigade Major of No. 6 Commando Brigade, at that time preparing for the Rhine crossing.

In Italy 49 Commando rejoined the rest of No. 5 Commando Brigade just north of Ravenna at the extreme right of the 8th Army line, their right flank on the Adriatic Sea. And there in the line, in patrols in front of it, in major actions at Commaccio and Argenta, 49 Commando had fairly heavy casualties. Of Y Troop, Kershaw and Peter Sims were both wounded, the first at Commaccio, the second at Argenta. Sergeant Grant, he whose shin had been shattered on his way back from the recce patrol to the Villa Ribar, was killed while with Kershaw on another patrol along an Italian beach. Maxby was wounded in the thigh, also while on a patrol with Kershaw. Kershaw's luck held and his nerve remained intact throughout the closing stages of the war, although those who recalled his single-mindedness in the islands noticed a marked diminution of his zest. Troop Sergeant Major West continued to be a good Troop Sergeant Major.

Henderson, the sovereigns safely delivered to Bari, was dropped into Yugoslavia again, this time to Slovenia. A second, not too serious wound, brought him out in March 1945 and he was repatriated to Britain in time to play Rugby for the Army against the Royal Navy at Twickenham at the end of the year. In those days, when hookers were not noted for their speed, Henderson was exceptionally fast. He nearly scored two breakaway tries but was brought down flat on each occasion by inspired crash tackles by a familiar looking Navy wing forward, to whom he made jocular remonstrations in the bar after the match. Henderson and Madden became firm friends.

PART TWO

SO FAR AS ITS effects on several lives was concerned, the matters triggered by the abstraction and secreting of old Ivo Bilic's gems in 1941 stayed dormant for many years to come. They became cumulatively active again through the chance agency of a reunion package tour. There were in the interval some connected episodes, the relevance of which went unperceived at the time.

PART THREE

Chapter One

IN 1964 PROFESSOR Ian Kincaid Henderson, of the Department of Slavonic Studies at the University of Carleton, Ottawa, found himself engaged in an erudite correspondence with a man he'd never heard of. It had started with an unsought but fascinating commentary on a monograph published by Henderson in a learned journal. Somebody named Richard Atkins wrote from Toronto, giving a box number as an address. Richard Atkins commended the professor for an outstanding piece of scholarship, but begged leave to differ with him over some minor points concerned with the tombs of the Bogomils in Northern Montenegro and with an assortment of details about the sculptures of Mestrovic. Henderson in reply thanked Atkins for helpful criticisms which had brought a new light to bear on some matters that had hitherto puzzled him, said that he would make appropriate amendments in subsequent teaching and research, and acknowledged his gratitude to a man who was clearly a master of his, and Henderson's, subject. Could they perhaps meet?

Atkins' reply was courteous but evasive. He would enjoy few things more than a meeting with somebody who specialized in a subject that was his private obsession, he wrote, but he was a businessman who spent most of his time flying to one part of the world or another. Back in Toronto he consolidated and followed up the fruits of his journeyings and then, frankly, slept.

Would the professor accept his apologies, postpone a meeting and agree to an arrangement by which they would continue to correspond on matters of mutual interest? The professor did. And for many years made the most of an anonymous rich vein of knowledge and interpretation, freely and willingly given, that did much to boost the reputation of the Carleton School of Slavonic Studies.

It was fifteen years until Henderson met Atkins. The occasion followed an official visit to Canada of a Yugoslav Medical Delegation, charged with exchanging views about the proliferation of contagious diseases brought about by the increasing number of passengers travelling by air. One of the Yugoslav delegates was Karla Bilic.

The delegation visited most of the Provincial capitals – Vancouver, Edmonton, Winnipeg, Toronto, Quebec City – before its final discussions with Canadian officials in Ottawa. The Canadians, as was their wont, were brisk, friendly, efficient, thorough and hospitable. Part of their hospitality was a reception at the Château Laurier Hotel. Part of their thoroughness was to invite guests, non-official, with an interest in Yugoslavia. Henderson's name came naturally to the invitation list.

He did not know that Karla would be present and his encounter with her was thus surprising as well as delightful. It caused something of a stir among staid Canadian officials, unused to exuberance at Government Receptions. An academic, especially one with a Scottish name, was not expected to throw his drink, glass and all, into a potted plant, bawl out 'Karla!' at the top of his voice, charge roaring through scattering clusters of guests and embrace with fervour the only good-looking woman among the visitors. It was even more disconcerting when the lady concerned threw her filled glass over her shoulder without looking to see where it went (the Deputy Minister's shirt front), burst into laughing tears, hugged Henderson with all her strength and covered his face with kisses, the meanwhile shouting 'Henderson, oh Henderson.' The Yugoslav delegation, more used to this sort of thing than were the Canadians, watched the spectacle with sympathetic amusement. They gathered round the happy pair, saying bravo; and when Henderson had stopped saying Karla, and Karla had stopped saying Henderson and both had recovered sufficiently to offer brief explanations for their behaviour, the Yugoslavs burst into applause and the Canadians began to look less austere. A photographer bustled over, Henderson and Karla posed smilingly with their arms around one another's waists, and flashlights popped.

The following morning the picture was carried by the *Toronto Globe and Mail*. It was captioned 'War Heroes Surprise Reunion' and below it was printed a highly coloured version of the damage Henderson and Karla between them were supposed to have done to the Nazi hordes in wartime Yugoslavia.

That evening Richard Atkins telephoned Henderson. Could they at last meet, he suggested. He would be passing through Ottawa on the following Tuesday. Henderson invited him to lunch at the Cercle Universitaire.

Over the vichysoisse and rare steaks in a University Club whose members prized the best cook in Canada, Henderson sized up his guest. He was tall, lean, grey-haired and elegant. He had graceful manners and a comfortable line in amusing small-talk. His accent was unmistakably Canadian but carried mid-Atlantic traces that suggested a not wholly Canadian upbringing. His lined face hinted at a past confrontation with, and an overcoming of, much suffering, physical or mental. He looked to be in his late fifties or early sixties. He was reticent about his background and

Henderson considered that it would be discourteous to press him on the subject. In any case the talk soon turned to a paper Henderson was drafting on Croatian immigration to North America. Richard Atkins' oral comments were as helpful as his written ones had always been. Henderson found the conversation absorbing. It was not until the coffee and liqueurs that Atkins unloaded a surprise.

'Saw your picture in the *Globe and Mail* last week,' he said.

'Yes. Wish they hadn't written all that embarrassing rubbish under it.'

'Didn't know you'd been in Yugoslavia during the war.'

'Only for eighteen months or so.'

'Didn't know either that you knew Karla Bilic. I remember her as a kid. Used to visit London a lot. I knew her brothers better.'

Henderson combed his memory.

'Yes. There were three weren't there? All killed in the war.'

'Not all,' said Atkins, 'Vlado survived. As a matter of fact I met him in Valparaiso last week.'

Henderson stared.

'Karla thinks he's dead,' he said at last, 'she mentioned it only the other night.'

'Well,' said Atkins, smiling, 'if you'll let me have her address I'll write and tell her that he's not. It'll be a happy surprise.' Henderson took a small address book from his inside pocket and slowly read out an address in Split. He felt an unease as he did so and couldn't think why. Perhaps it was because mention of Vlado had reminded him of an obligation to Karla that he had not yet fulfilled. After the Minister's reception the previous week he had, while dining with Karla, remembered suddenly Vlado's monogrammed briefcase and its ageing contents, entrusted to him all those years ago on the jetty at the Villa Ribar. He had never heard from her about its disposal and for twenty years or more it had lain, forgotten, in a locked metal box in the vault of his bank. What, he had asked Karla, should he do with it?

'Please, please, please,' Karla had said, with tears in her eyes, 'destroy it without delay. All those horrible things happened a long time ago. I never want to see or hear of it again.'

On the day after his lunch with Atkins, which had ended with cordial farewells and an invitation from Atkins for a return match when Henderson was next in Toronto, Henderson went down with a troublesome bout of 'flu. Recovered from that he went to Simon Fraser University in British Columbia for a four-day seminar. Returned to Ottawa he made a note in his desk diary to retrieve the briefcase and destroy its contents. Before he could put the plan into effect a telegram arrived for him from Split.

'If not already disposed of,' it read, 'please retain, repeat, retain briefcase. Karla.'

Muttering to himself about inconsistent bloody women Henderson deleted the entry in his desk diary. What the hell was Karla up to now?

Chapter Two

OVER THIRTY YEARS after the end of the Second World War an ageing group of survivors of 49 Commando went on a sentimental pilgrimage to their old haunts in Dalmatia and Montenegro.

There were fourteen starters on the expedition. Eight brought their wives. One brought somebody else's wife. Of the other five one was a homosexual, two looked forward to a wine-sustained rest from matrimony, and two, over ambitious and disregardful of the precedents, put a misplaced confidence in their luck with the local ladies. The Yugoslav authorities, through the agency of the Partisan Old Comrades Associations, SUBNOR, were charmingly hospitable. There were battlefield tours by launch and coach. There were visits to industrial enterprises, war memorials, Venetian churches, mayors, chambers of commerce. Resigned and affectionate British wives watched husbands, customarily tentative about a second helping of cornflakes, eating five course breakfasts lubricated by *travarica* and red wine, followed by song. The tour was a huge success. Personally, because the people on it enjoyed it and admired the achievements of their hosts' country. Diplomatically, because the mutual expressions of good will were genuine and genuine expression of goodwill across national boundaries are beneficent. Medically it was probably less of a *tour de force*, as some disgruntled National Health

Service doctors made plain whilst attending subsequently to a variety of misshapen livers. There was also the matter of a curious statement made in Croatian by an otherwise silent Yugoslav who got drunk at a farewell dinner.

Of the former Commando visitors and their womenfolk, only one had a knowledge of the Croatian language, and that a smattering. He had once been an earnest signaller in Madden's Troop and one of his ears had been heavily modified by spandau fire. The upper half of it was missing. The lower half, which looked like the distorted remains of the sail of a windmill struck by lightning, was only partially capable of fulfilling its true function of channelling sound. Because of this artificial deformity Richards was never completely certain if his ear was receiving correctly messages transmitted to it. Two years after demobilization he had abandoned his theological studies for the Methodist ministry, dabbled for some months, because he couldn't think of anything better to do, at a Linguaphone course in Serbo-Croat, and had subsequently become a bank clerk. He was now a bank manager, trained and conditioned to precision. Making allowances for the inadequacies of his acoustic equipment and the rustiness of his linguistic training, he would have been prepared to have given a conditional affirmation about what the man sitting opposite him at the long table in the dining-room of the Jadran Hotel had said. The man, named Bogdan something, much younger than most of the others, earlier steeped in vignac-swilling reserve, had remarked on the strange habits of English soldiers. They at first seemed to be friendly to each other, he said. Then they killed their comrades. He'd seen it happen he said. Then he fell asleep, quietly. Richards gave the incident a little, a very little, thought and decided to dismiss it as an unpleasantly provocative piece of drunken maundering, out of keeping with the friendly spirit of a nostalgically happy evening. It would be wrong, thought Richards, still guided by Christian principles if no longer attracted to sectarian dogma, to mention the subject to his fellow guests.

Towards the close of the farewell dinner there were speeches and toasts. The most popular of these was a tribute to the volunteer interpreter, a handsome sturdy lady in her fifties who had clearly once been beautiful, whose English was colloquial and nearly faultless, and whose record as a Partisan doctor, so said the ex-Partisans privately, had been peerless. Karla Bilic-Markovic blushed, still prettily, as she listened to the praise being heaped upon her for her cheerfulness, energy, kindliness and expertise throughout the visit. She blushed further when fourteen ageing former commandos spontaneously abandoned their chairs, formed a jostling queue and kissed her energetically on both cheeks to the delighted applause of her compatriots and the more restrained approbation of the visitors' wives and one mistress. She accepted with a graceful little speech the commemorative present she was given, an enamelled Globe and Laurel set in semi-precious stones. She joined, tunefully and cheerfully, in the subsequent singing. She promised to be early at the hotel on the following morning so that she could shepherd the party through the relaxed formalities at the airport. She left for home after a further cluster of friendly embraces. And there she sat down and worried. She had overheard Bogdan Bojanic's remarks to Richards.

Chapter Three

WHEN HE WAS in his early fifties Peter Sims, a successful importer-exporter, subjected his life and his achievements to a thorough self-scrutiny. He concluded that he'd done well enough but that it was time for a radical change. As was his habit, foreshadowed by the manner in which he had won Madden's approval by marching to the sound of the guns when Kershaw's returning patrol from the Villa Ribar was in trouble, Sims' action was drastic, speedy and thorough. He sold his business and his house. He divorced his wife, settling upon her a handsome trust fund. He gave similar bounties to his only children, two married daughters. He searched for a small house in remote country by the sea where he could walk, swim, fish, garden, read, do *The Times* crossword puzzle and assuage a formidable thirst. He tried, unfruitfully, Argyllshire and Cornwall. A BBC Radio 4 programme on some of the more exploitable byways of the European Economic Community made up his mind for him. Instead of one small house he settled for two smaller ones, the first near Holyhead in the island of Anglesey and the second in Dunlaoghaire, County Dublin. To the puzzlement of his neighbours in either country he renamed the Welsh one Duty Cottage and the Irish one Free Cottage. Sims the liberated, who had long objected strenuously to excessive taxation, had discovered a new way of life. He was the first permanent Duty Free commuter. He divided his time between Ireland and Wales roughly in the ratio of three parts in the first to two in the second. At both termini he put in a satisfactory measure of walking, fishing, gardening and reading. He was equally happy in either. The determining factor in the relative lengths of his stays was that the Irish let in more duty-free stimulants than the British did. The Sims programme carried a pleasingly simple rhythm. When he'd finished off the booze he'd bought on the ferry from Holyhead to Dunlaoghaire he re-embarked and bought some more for consumption in Wales. That finished, back to Ireland. And so on. He was a generous host at both ends.

It was whilst he was sitting in the bar of the ferry during one of these replenishment pilgrimages that Sims was distracted from his crossword puzzle by the shadow of a man who paused in front of his table, cleared his throat and said,

'Excuse me. Mr Sims?'

'Yes, I'm Sims,' said Sims, mildly irritated, courteous.

'You won't remember me,' said the man, who had only half of one ear. 'Richards. Y Troop, 49 Commando. Jugland.'

Sims stared at him, grinned, stood up, shook him by the hand, said Christ Almighty and offered him a drink. Then he distantly remembered Richards former canonical aspirations and apologized for his blasphemy.

'Something soft, I mean,' he added stupidly.

'Large scotch and soda, please.'

They got on very well. They discussed old times. Sims, who had never in his life called Richards anything other than Richards, was soon calling him Dicky. Richards called Sims Peter.

'You weren't at the reunion, Peter.'

'What reunion?'

'Two really. One in London. One in Yugoslavia last year.'

'I'd have rather liked that. I've been right out of touch. I ran into Paddy Madden when he came back from Malaya in the early fifties, but I haven't seen him since. I heard somewhere that he'd been on that bloody awful Suez operation. Otherwise I've met no one.'

'I'm going over to see him now.'

'Who?'

'Paddy. He lives in County Wicklow.'

'Well, well. I own a house in Dunlaoghaire. Where in County Wicklow?'

'Kilmacanogue.'

'Just down the road. What are you doing tonight?'

'I'll put up in some hotel. I'm having lunch with Paddy tomorrow. I'm his sort of honorary banking adviser.'

'Look, Dicky, come and stay with me. You can pay the rent in duty free.'

'Thanks,' said Richards.

They were still talking at three o'clock in the morning, the comfortable, immemorial, partly fictional shared reminiscences of old soldiers. The islands (of which Sims had only partial experience). Montenegro. Italy. The Colonel, Madden, Kershaw, Maxby, Truscott. All that strange buggering about with that island villa place whose name neither could remember, for a purpose that neither had ever known. That luckless British Mission chap who'd been knocked off with Kershaw. That kid, the boy navigator, who kept popping in and out and who eventually disappeared without . . .

'That's him,' said Richards suddenly.

'Who's who?'

'The kid. Was his name Bogdan?'

'You've a bloody good memory. Yes. I think it probably was.'

187

'He turned up at one of the dinners last year when we visited Yugoslavia. He just got quietly pissed.'

'Occupational hazard of reunion dinners.'

'He only made one remark before he passed out cold. Look I've never told anyone else this. Didn't want to spoil the mood of the tour. At one time I did a course in Croatian. It's pretty rusty but I'm pretty sure that I got the gist of what Bogdan said. It was something about the odd ways of British troops. They all looked very pally but later they killed one another. He'd seen it happen.'

Sims laughed.

'Well he was talking balls wasn't he?' he said. 'Let's have the other half and go to bed.'

They did both. Sims' derision did not prevent his exceptionally retentive mental filing system from tucking away a small fact, or allegation, or suspicion, or fantasy, or whatever it was into a distant safe corner. There it would lie, to be obliterated or retrieved according to necessity.

'Hallo, Paddy.'

'Hallo, Peter. Good to see you.'

'Dicky said he was calling so I came for the ride.'

'Have a tot.'

'Gin and tonic thanks.'

'Dicky?'

'Horse's neck if you've got it. I seek revival. Peter's hospitality is lethal.'

Madden busied himself with bottles, ice, lemon, openers. Sims looked around the small serviceable cottage, with its shelves of books, a mixed fire of turf briquettes and logs, and its enchanting views. The tall rough cone of the Big Sugar Loaf behind the house, to the west, bracken and furze and rocky outcrops, the colours shifting under the constantly changing Irish sky. Sheep safely grazing. The occasional sound of traffic from the road in the valley to the east, winding gently southwards into Glen o' the Downs. Birdsong and church bells. The asymmetric bulk of the Little Sugar Loaf to the east beyond the valley, stone-walled green fields in a patchwork, more sheep, more rocks, some horses, a white-walled cottage, woods, a few houses, glimpses of the sea, a church tower in Bray.

'Good-looking spot this,' said Sims appreciately.

'I agree.'

'I thought Ireland was supposed to be green.'

'Popular illusion. The best-looking bits are varying shades of brown and mauve.'

They chatted easily and comfortably, like men who had lived next door to one another for years. They had last met twenty-five years previously. Must be something to do with companionship in battle reflected Sims. A friendship born of common liking, respect and experience that had survived exposure to stress, danger and the testing of the wisdom of decisions by counting the numbers who survived them. It wanted little nurturing. No need to bother with Christmas cards, letters, messages and assurances of goodwill. Just turn up. Carry on where you left off. No fuss.

Gaps to be filled of course. Madden: Hong Kong. Malta. Malaya. Malta again. Suez ('Shut up Peter'). Cyprus. Aden. Small Colonial wars which for some obscure bloody reason were inseparable from the biggest Colonial Empire the world had known divesting itself voluntarily of its colonies. Married. Widowed. Two children, the elder in his last year at Trinity; the younger in her first. Retired eight years ago. Brigadier's pension not all that much. That's why Dicky here was advising him on his investments, such as they were.

Dicky here, who had long since been through all this before with Madden and who was becoming reconciled with life after his second Horse's Neck, assumed the role of barman. He was efficient at it.

What about Peter? Nothing much really. Economics at Cambridge. Sold things for other people all over the

189

place. Stretches in India, Australia, Canada. Then set up on his own. Very profitable. Marriage broken up. Sold up business. Initiator of new concept of living: Duty Free Commuting.

'Duty what?'

Sims explained in detail. Madden, not for the first time since he had met young Mr Sims on Vis, was immeasurably amused.

'When will you be over again, Peter?' he asked later.

'Don't know. It's an eccentric schedule. Depends on when I've finished off the next lot in Wales.'

'Well, can you tidy it up a bit? Jock Henderson's coming to stay in early April. Why don't you come to dinner and see him again.'

'Love to. Only who's Jock Henderson?'

'Of course. I'd forgotten. You've never met. He was in the British Mission in Montenegro. He did two jobs at the Villa Ribar on either side of ours.'

Sims and Richards looked at each other.

'That's what it was called,' said Richards. 'The Villa Ribar.' Sims nodded.

'As a matter of interest, Paddy,' said Sims, 'what the hell were we supposed to be doing at the Villa Ribar? Dicky and I were talking about it last night. There seemed to be an amazing amount of excitement about bugger-all.'

Madden thought briefly and decided to break a trust that he no longer held to be valid.

'Picking up a lot of SOE gold,' he said. 'It was all very secret at the time. But it can't matter now. So far as I recall the secrecy was only to keep all you bloody thieves in Y Troop from pinching the stuff.'

Sims and Richards laughed.

'The orders came from way up in the sky,' went on Madden. 'Apart from me the only person in the Troop who knew what it was all about was Ken Kershaw. We had to tell him because the whole point of his recce was to find out if it was still there. And of course Tommy Daunt knew.'

Further conversation was prolonged and inconsequential. Sims' computer of a brain registered, without noticing it, another fact, not necessarily to be used.

During his Irish sojourns, Peter Sims became a frequent visitor to the cottage at Kilmacanogue. He loved the scenery. He enjoyed tramping about the Wicklow mountains. And his liking and respect for Madden had been undiminished by time and prolonged separation. They talked endlessly, inevitably in the main about old times. Sometimes they just sat in companionable silence.

On one of these calls, Sims found Madden looking troubled. 'Read that,' he said tersely, handing over an envelope, 'and let me know what you think.'

Madden went to get the drinks.

The envelope was addressed to Brigadier D. O'C. Madden, OBE, MC, RM (re'd), c/o the Royal Marine Barracks, Stonehouse, Plymouth. 'Please forward' was written at the top left-hand corner, a request that had been met so many times that there was no space left. The typing of the letter itself was adequate but clearly the work of an amateur two-finger practitioner. The sender's address was The Presbytery, St Brigid's Church, Liverpool 8, Merseyside and the signatory was F. X. Quinlan, PP. The contents were disquieting.

'Dear Brigadier,

Henry Maxby, one of my parishioners, died last week fortified by the rites of the Holy Church. He had for some time been suffering from cancer. A month before his death he made a strange request, not to be implemented until after he was gone. It was that I should then write to you, for whom he retained the highest affection and admiration from his time

191

with you during the war, and explain to you something that had long been on his conscience.

Frankly, I find myself in a difficulty over this. I feel a moral obligation to honour the wishes of a dying man. The dilemma is that if I do so I shall risk disclosing the identity of a man, who may still be living, who was Henry's accomplice in a very serious crime.

I have no doubts about Henry's truthfulness in this matter. He was in a State of Grace when he spoke of it and he did not retract his statement when I administered the Last Sacraments to him. But if I repeat his words to a third party I might cause grave hurt to someone who for all I know has, as Henry did, long since repented of his sin and has expiated it. If the man is dead I could cause sorrow to his family. And whether he is alive or dead, the transmission of an unsupported allegation made by a known criminal – Henry had served five terms in gaol, as you perhaps know – could have serious legal consequences.

After much heart-searching, I have therefore decided to take a middle course. I am telling you of Henry's request and of its nature. If you are prepared to leave it at that I will say no more. If, however, you request more details, and in fairness I must say that Henry was insistent on full disclosure, I will take spiritual and legal advice before deciding on how to proceed.

Yours in Christ,
Francis Quinlan.'

Sims put the letter on the table and sipped at his whiskey.

'So old Maxby's had it,' he said.

'Yes.'

'Henry. Christ. I'd forgotten he was called Henry.'

'I hadn't. I've not forgotten much about Maxby. He left indelible memories wherever he went. Ask the Military Police. I wonder what his serious crime was.'

'Probably picked the padre's pocket when he was in the nick. Parish priests and dying penitents get exaggerated ideas about what's serious.'

'But why was he so insistent that I should know about it?'

'Because you were the only real Daddy he ever had. He was inconsolable when you left us in Italy. I'd forgotten this. He came to my billet one night in Ravenna when he was pissed and spent about two hours telling me what a marvellous chap you were. I tell you he was swaying about with tears in his eyes, going on and on about you.'

Madden felt retrospectively glad and currently flattered. 'Well, I suppose that's one good reason for honouring his wishes to the letter.'

'Could be. But has it occurred to you that if this skypilot overcomes his scruples and comes clean, and then it turns out that Maxby wanted to tell you all about his and some other bugger's undisclosed part in the Great Train Robbery or some such, you'll be up the legal creek as well as the Rev. Quinlan, PP? It's called withholding material evidence.'

'Good point,' said Madden.

They kicked the problem about for half an hour. Madden hadn't changed in over thirty years, reflected Sims. This was like his wartime preoperational consideration of opinions and suggestions before deciding on a course of action and framing his orders. The pattern finally fell into place in Madden's mind.

'This is what I'll do,' he said. 'I'll say that I only want to know the details if whatever it was happened when Maxby was with us. And if the crime, and I'll want it specified, was sufficiently bad.'

'That should give the good Father a breath of comfort. I'll post the letter on my way home.'

Father Quinlan replied by return of post. The crime was murder of a comrade-in-arms. It had been committed when both its perpetrators were under Madden's command. Under the letterhead the priest had inked in his telephone number.

Madden's telephone call to Father Quinlan evoked one expected response and one minor bonus. He would certainly see the Brigadier but not yet. He was sorry to be repetitious but he badly needed spiritual and legal advice which he would now set about taking. But no real need for Madden to go to Liverpool unless he particularly wanted to. Father Quinlan would be having a short holiday in Limerick with his sister in three weeks' time. He would gladly meet Madden in Dublin if that would be more convenient. Madden invited him to lunch. He sounded a sensible and civilized man.

When Sims, after a briefer than usual stay in Wales, next saw Madden he thought to himself that Paddy looked bloody terrible. Sims could understand why. Madden customarily hid his views under a light-hearted surface. But those who knew him well soon discerned a fundamental outlook that in some respects was rigid, out of fashion and, in Sims' opinion, wholly admirable. Madden believed in, and practised, a code in which duty and honour were paramount. In the teeth of much contemporary evidence he was convinced that soldiering, properly conducted, was an honourable profession. He had soldiered in many parts of the world but to him the most satisfying, and the most memorable, experience of doing his job had been the wartime command of a Commando Troop. He had moulded it, controlled it, chided it, encouraged it and led it. He had brought it up to his own high standards. He had stamped down mercilessly on weaknesses that were capable of correction and had tolerated others with amused indifference. He had put his trust wholeheartedly in the men he led. To him it was inconceivable that that trust would not be reciprocated. To be told now, years later, when he was in retirement and living more and more on probably idealized memories, that two of the men he had cherished had murdered another of them was a savage affront and not only to his sense of honour. It was a reflection on his efficiency, which was a component of his sense of honour. Christ, thought Sims, poor betrayed Paddy.

'Paddy, you look bloody awful.'

'I feel bloody awful,' said Madden bitterly.

'Are you sure that this Father Quinlan knows what he's talking about?'

'Wish I wasn't. He sounded thoroughly balanced. What really convinced me was that he used to be a naval chaplain. He's used to troops.' Sims pondered and mentally eliminated one reservation that had been bothering him, the meticulous use by a Liverpool parish priest of the correct service forms of address; decorations and all.

'I've been thinking,' said Sims. 'I've reached some tentative conclusions. Well, tentative speculations,' he corrected.

'Oh yes?'

'I don't think Maxby and whoever it was knocked off one of our chaps at all. They knocked off somebody else.'

Madden gazed at him. He had a high regard for Sims' intelligence. Nothing had ever induced him to tell Sims so.

'Okay, Peter. Tell me more. Try to cheer me up. It'll be nice to know that the lads only murdered outsiders.'

Sims told him more. His hypothesis did little to cheer Madden.

Henderson was a very busy man. Research, lecturing, membership of two Royal Commissions, writing, seminars. He loved his work and detested distractions from it. One came from a telephone call.

'Professor Henderson?'

'Speaking.'

'My name's Peter Sims. We met at dinner at Paddy Madden's last year in Ireland.'

'*Hallo*. Where are you?'

'In Ottawa. Can you join me for a meal? Your choice of time. You're the worker.'

Henderson consulted his diary.

'Lunch on Thursday? Oh me. I'm on the home beat.'

Sims demurred but gave in gracefully. They ate at the table in the Cercle Universitaire at which Henderson had recently entertained Richard Atkins.

'Dear Paddy,

I'm off to Calgary to stay with a daughter for a couple of weeks so I'll send you an interim report. I was wrong. I apologize in his absence to Ken Kershaw. I'm now convinced that it wasn't him. The evidence pointing in his direction was of course circumstantial and I concede that I gave it too much weight. As I told you when we last met I disliked him. To my mind he was a callous, greedy, insensitive, selfish opportunist whose defects were not compensated for by his bravery. I now admit that my judgement was over-influenced by past prejudices.

Essentially there were two roots to my deductions. The first was Dicky Richards' account of the Boy Wonder Bogdan talking drunkenly of witnessing British soldiers first liking and then killing one another. As you know, Bogdan bolted from my patrol when I went out to pick up Ken and, given his fieldcraft expertise, it seemed reasonable to assume that he could have shadowed Ken to that island. The second was your recent revelation that the object of the job at the Villa Ribar was to recover SOE gold. From these factors I miscalculated the addition of

196

two and two. As I worked it out, Kershaw would have been totally unscrupulous about anything that would have got in the way of his stealing some gold. Maxby was devoted to Ken, looked upon loot as a normal by-product of War, and with his weird social values restricted his loyalties primarily to the Troop. Bumping off somebody outside it for a large profit wouldn't have troubled him much. Why not that British Mission chap, Tommy whatever it was?

This whole argument fell apart as a result of a lunch I had today with Jock Henderson. I posed my questions discreetly and got an answer that blew my assumptions to pieces. I hadn't realized that Henderson had been in at two crucial phases of the act. He helped plant the gold and he subsequently recovered it. It was counted carefully both before and after. After, none was missing. Hypothesis exploded. QED.

Let's start again when you've heard from the Rev. Quinlan, PP. I'll see you early next month.

Yours ever,
Peter.'

Chapter Four

FOR THE FIRST time in years Henderson found himself
with nothing to do. The university was on vacation.
The two Royal Commissions were in recess. He had
completed his paper on Croatian immigration to North
America and had not yet decided what to write next.
Fishing and walking in the Gatineau Forest Reserve,
relaxations that normally balanced his absorption in his
work, began to become tedious. Childless, and separated from his wife, he found no charm in domesticity.
His thoughts turned more and more to the past, when
life had been simpler and cleaner with clear objectives,
a satisfying job and little thought for tomorrow because
tomorrow was what occurred only if your luck held.
Careful. Don't over-romanticize. A lot of that stuff had
been messy, shapeless, cruel and unsavoury. Yes. But a
lot of it had been rewarding and interesting and ideal-
istic and companionable. Companionship of a quality
that was unmatched in the grubby, self-seeking, acqui-
sitive peace-time society of North America. That's
unfair. Lots of Canadians are kindly, selfless, responsible. True. But not to the extent that, say, Karla Bilic
had been. Karla . . .

Henderson leafed through the barren pages of his
desk diary, lifted the telephone and spoke to a Travel
Agent. Four days later he landed at Split Airport. He
wanted to see Karla simply because she was Karla. He
also wanted to satisfy his curiosity about why he had

been asked to hold on to that damned monogrammed crocodile-skin briefcase.

Henderson's previous twelve visits to post-war Yugoslavia had been shaped by current political exigencies and by a common-sense self-denying ordinance. Until Tito's break with Stalin in 1948 former British Mission officers were unwelcome and suspect. After the break they were more welcome, but because the security apparatus was in the paranoid hands of Alexander Rankovic they, like the entire indigenous population, were still suspect. Since Rankovic's secret police kept tabs on all visitors and most natives, it was necessary to act on the working assumption that Henderson's contacts would be monitored. It followed that if the innate volatility of Yugoslav politics shifted the country back into the Soviet orbit police files would be scrutinized to identify people who had been in touch with supposed Western Agents, of whom Henderson would be regarded as one. Henderson, remembering the way in which the Commissar in Montenegro had dealt with those he took to be ideologically suspect, was not prepared to put at risk old friends he had soldiered with. He would greatly have liked to see Karla and Juraj and the rest of them again. He eschewed the temptation. He moved exclusively and with circumspection in academic circles. By the time that Rankovic was disgraced and dismissed when it was discovered that his mania for snooping had led him ludicrously into the surveillance of President Tito himself as well as everybody else, the frequency of Henderson's visits had diminished. Once in Ljubljana and once in Zagreb, after Yugoslav life had become freer and more normal, he was told that Karla was somewhere in Dalmatia. But neither of his informants knew her address. The chance meeting in Ottawa had been his first sight of her since that jetty departure years before at the Villa Ribar. Henderson was in for a surprise or two.

They dined under the trees in the open air restaurant of the Hotel Park. Fairy lights were strung among the branches. A half moon and a multiplicity of stars shone in a velvet sky. An enthusiastic band belted out the rousing strains of *Slatka Mala Marijana*. The wine was good, strong, red and Dalmatian, black wine in the local argot. There were black olives and mussels and squid fried in batter. The place was thronged with healthy, well fed, well dressed men and women, most in their twenties and thirties, a new generation, too young for the war. Did they realize, wondered Henderson, what their starving, ragged, lice-ridden, maimed, bereaved, indomitable parents had been through? Probably not. They'd have heard about it of course, and read about it and seen it depicted endlessly at the cinema and on the television. But they'd never understand. Probably as well that they didn't. This new Yugoslavia was infinitely better than the old and good luck to the . . .

'Henderson. What are you brooding about?'

'Just thinking of the contrast between this lot and what it was like when you and I first met.'

'Yes. I used to do that once. Not so often now. I prefer to forget the war.'

'Strange. I forgot it for years. Now I'm here again memories come crowding back.'

'Happy ones, I hope. The mind is very selective in these matters. Only the best bits get retained.'

'It's probably tactless of me to ask, *Gospoda* Bilic-Markovic, but where is Mr Markovic?'

'He was killed in a car crash five years ago. We Yugoslavs are terrible drivers.'

'I'm sorry. I shouldn't have asked.'

'You'd have asked anyway. He was your old friend Juraj.'

'Oh Christ,' said Henderson.

Karla smiled gently and then began to giggle.

'Henderson,' she said. 'Your language hasn't improved in over thirty years. You probably didn't know it, but your nickname in Montenegro was O'Christ. That awful Commissar man kept hearing people talking about O'Christ and reached the conclusion that there was an Irish spy wandering around. It drove him frantic.'

'What happened to that ghastly bastard?'

'He was killed in a hunting accident near the Hungarian border in '48 just after our break with Russia.'

'Hunting what?'

'An official euphemism. Hunting accident comes in inverted commas. He was shot by the border police while trying to defect to the Russians.'

'Party discipline seems to be pretty lax these days. You'd never have spoken like this in the past.'

'It isn't lax, but it's pretty relaxed. And I only speak like this to people I trust. In any case I'm more or less immune. I'm a war heroine. A legend. I'm the girl medical student who was in it from the beginning, and treated all those poor sick and wounded with hardly any drugs and amputated limbs without anaesthetics and . . .'

Suddenly Karla began to cry.

'Damn you, Henderson,' she said vehemently. 'You and your memories.' Henderson appalled, embarrassed, contrite, silently handed over his handkerchief, furtively squeezed Karla's hand under the table cloth, waited. Karla dried her eyes, snuffled, managed a sad smile and apologized. Henderson told her that she had nothing to apologize for.

'You said that once before. We don't meet very often but I always seem to cry when I'm with you. You've probably forgotten the last time.'

'I remember it very well.'

'Oh Christ,' said Karla; and chuckled through renewed tears.

During the next few days Henderson met at Karla's flat one person he'd known before and one that he hadn't.

The second one appeared first. Karla answered the doorbell, showed signs of maternal contentment when she was comprehensively embraced by a large man in his middle thirties, and introduced him.

'My son Miro. Professor Henderson.'

Miro was on his way to play water polo and could only stay for a few minutes. He had only dropped in, he explained charmingly, to meet a man whom his mother had spoken of with affection and respect for as long as he could remember. Miro was deeply sunburnt, had short curly black hair, huge broad shoulders, extensive muscles and looked as strong as a horse. Henderson took an immediate liking to him. Nice guy. Intelligent. Amusing. Courteous. Considerate to his mother. Built like a Rugby hooker. They chatted about sport.

'Pity you don't play Rugby in Yugoslavia,' said Henderson, and regretted the statement. Entrenched enthusiasms were in danger of turning him into an ageing bore.

'But we do. I play for Split. I'm the hooker. Getting a bit past it though. Had the time of my life on a tour we did to Australia.' Henderson felt his age. He'd even lost touch with developments in a sport that to him had been the nearest thing to a religion since he drifted out of Presbyterianism.

'I used to hook,' he said nostalgically.

They talked about hooking. Then:

'Well, goodbye, Sir. I must go. I hope we meet again before you leave. I've asked Mamma to put the squeeze on you to come round for a meal with my wife and me if you can fit it in.'

Miro's colloquial English was serviceable.

When the door shut Henderson sat down again and addressed Karla.

'Didn't know you had a son.'

'It's not uncommon.'

'He's a good lad. Bit larger than you, but you can see who his mother is.'

202

'I think he looks more like his father.'

'No-oh, Juraj was fair and tall.'

'Henderson, you're a bloody fool. Hooking at Rugby seems to be hereditary.' Henderson gazed at her, baffled. Karla stood up, took him by the hand and pulled him to his feet. With her free hand she picked up a half-finished *rakija* bottle.

'My dear love.' she said, 'You and I are both getting old. But we're not past it, despite the suspicions of the younger generation. Come to bed, and I'll explain to you in words of one syllable the natural consequences arising from a physical union between a lonely British liaison officer and a terrified young female unqualified medical practitioner.'

Henderson continued to gape. Karla adjusted her grip on the bottle which she now held by the neck.

'And before you say anything,' said Karla, 'you should know this. There are two circumstances in which I will kill you. The first is if you should ever reveal to Miro who his father is. The second is if your next remark is "Oh Christ".'

'Oh Chr . . .', began Henderson, and restrained himself.

Karla tapped him lightly on the skull with the bottle.

'Bed,' she said firmly.

Henderson, put to work in the kitchen at slicing tomatoes for the salad, felt relaxed, delighted, bewildered, hurt, confused, enchanted and incoherent. All his thoughts ended in question marks. What did a man in his late fifties do when after a lifetime of imagining himself to be childless he discovered himself to be both a father and a grandfather? When he liked his son enormously but for reasons which he respected had to forbear from disclosing his genetic contribution? When a girl whom he'd briefly loved when both were young had re-entered his life after more than thirty years and had put the old spell on him again? Was it all a bloody awful mess? Or could it be a marvellous re-birth? Or again might . . .

'Henderson. You're no good at slicing tomatoes.'

Karla was busy at the stove. Very efficient she looked too.

'I wish you'd stop calling me Henderson. My first name's Ian.'

'I can never pronounce Ian properly. It comes out like Jan.'

'What's that got to do with it?'

'Lots of South Africans are called Jan.'

'So what?'

'We're a non-aligned country.'

Karla chuckled and restored her concentration to preparing her fish soup.

Henderson cut his thumb and bled into the tomatoes.

Before Bogdan Bojanic arrived for dinner, Karla briefed Henderson very thoroughly. She trusted Henderson to act instinctively with common sense and kindliness. But the chance of something going wrong would be lessened if Henderson were to be put in possession of all relevant information. To pass it on was painful, but necessary. The essence of the matter was that there were protracted but unpredictable periods during which Bogdan was close to insanity. Harmlessly so, but it could be disconcerting. If Karla, with the full backing and help of Juraj, had not first simply taken care of young Bogdan and then legally adopted him, the likelihood would have been that he would have been locked up in some asylum shortly after the war ended, with tragic results. Psychiatric resources, human or material, were minuscule at the time.

Henderson would remember little Bogdan's part in his first meeting with that sweet idiot Challoner? Henderson did. Well, the boy came and went after that. Karla had heard that for a brief time he had acted as a guide with British troops, but that was when she'd been away assembling her Field Ambulance at Trebinje. He had finally and permanently appeared in her life a few days after Henderson's departure from the Villa. This was the old, silent, withdrawn Bogdan. Not the bubbling little boy who'd run to hug her with the exciting news of beings dropping out of the sky. ('He made me cry before you did you know, Henderson.') If anything he'd been in a worse emotional state than when they'd first picked him up from that cave. He followed Karla around everywhere. He slept on the ground outside her tent. If she had to go away to a conference, or to collect supplies, or even on her ward rounds, Bogdan became nervously agitated. But he resolutely refused to say a word.

He became a sort of mascot to the Field Ambulance Team. He accompanied them as they trundled slowly north, in a progress much interrupted by mechanical breakdowns, in the wake of the Partisan armies pursuing the retreating Germans. In the early spring she finally confirmed that a personal physical irregularity that she had almost absentmindedly put down to cumulative strain and rough living was incipient motherhood. ('Why do you always do things at the most inconvenient times, Henderson?') She was a girl in trouble ('And that's not meant to be a joke.') For a *partisanka* to become pregnant was still technically a capital offence. She had no intention of aborting. She wanted Henderson's child, as an earnest of a moment of tenderness and sanity snatched from years of brutality and madness, a pledge for the future. But if she had the baby, and regardless of what happened to her, what would become of little Bogdan? She worried and worried. Not for the first time her problem was solved by Juraj, now a Brigade Commander, passing by with his Montenegrins heading north. Juraj simply married her, partly out of friendship, largely out of compassion, to some extent she suspected because of his infuriating male chauvinistic porcine sense of humour. ('He kept

205

saying, Henderson, that he'd always suspected that you were a Scotski stoat. Then he'd laugh which made me angry. Then I had to laugh which made me angrier still.')

The war was drawing to its close. The Germans were on their way out. The Ustasha, Chetniks, Domobrans and all were being slaughtered, hunted, imprisoned. The Communist hard core of the National Liberation Movement was proclaiming triumphantly its ascendancy, discarding its transient non-Communist domestic allies, and for a time looking as if it would embroil itself in another war over the question of whether Yugoslavia, Italy or an international compromise would control the destinies of the port of Trieste. Juraj was there, making provocative gestures at British and New Zealand troops and thinking, without letting the thought influence his commitment, of his friend Henderson. Karla was not at Trieste. She was in a shabby, threadbare, single-storied house in Soijek with Juraj's sister, looking after Bogdan, preparing for the birth of Miro. At Juraj's suggestion, Karla had given herself a medical certificate that described her as a victim of tuberculosis. Given Juraj's connivance and influence, and the chaotic conditions of the era, few questions, none of them troublesome, were asked.

Later they set up house in a flat in Zagreb. Juraj stayed on in the army, as ready to fight the Russians in 1948 as he had been to fight the British in 1945 and as he had actually fought the Germans for nearly four years after 1941. As often as not Juraj, ultimately a General, was away for long periods at his various commands. When the baby was weaned Karla returned to the Medical School at the University of Zagreb to learn how to become 'a proper doctor'. Juraj's sister looked after the baby; and, as well as she could, after Bogdan. ('I'm sorry, Henderson, I've been talking more about myself than about Bogdan.')

Surprisingly and gratifyingly Bogdan began to talk again, always about the present. He did well at school.

He was quick and intelligent. He adapted with ease to a city life that was in total contrast to his childhood in Montenegro. He was a natural athlete. He spent much of his spare time among the beechwoods on the slopes of Sljeme. But he often had devastating, screaming nightmares from which he would awake sweating and trembling. He never spoke about his past and Karla was scrupulous over not enquiring about it. He was a solitary boy with few friends. He was entirely at home with animals.

For some years after she qualified, Karla practised in various hospitals in Zagreb. Then she went to Split. Bogdan and Miro went with her. Bogdan, by then eighteen, was superficially a quiet, reserved lad with delightful manners. But the nightmares continued. Karla, hastening, when they came on, to Bogdan's room with sedatives, began to pick out a recurrent pattern in his ravings. The predominant themes seemed to concern his witnessing as a small child of the murder of his mother and of his sister. Of his finding his brother's beaten body. Of the disappearance of his father. And, most puzzling of all, of an incomprehensible incident that had brought about a shattering disillusionment. A foreign soldier, presumably British, a man Bogdan admired, had killed another British soldier, a man Bogdan liked. This occurrence had been at night, near the sea. Karla gave careful thought to this last element in Bogdan's fragmented babblings and reached the conclusion that the incident was imaginary, the product of a tortured brain pressed beyond what it could withstand. That was her view, until the party from 49 Commando had come out the previous year and she had overheard Bogdan's statement to that nice man with half an ear. Bogdan hadn't said much but he had said it with simple conviction. It was the first time that she had ever heard him talk consciously of that part of his early life that troubled him. She had since been pondering on ways to get him to unburden himself of more of it, to share his carefully damped down sorrows. She thought an encounter with Henderson, a relic from the past, might help to open the flood gates.

'So you see, Henderson,' she said at last, 'I'm behaving like a bad hostess. I've invited you to dinner, but I'm really using you as a therapeutic stalking horse.'

Henderson, looking thoughtful, said absently that he would gladly do what he could. Then he asked a question that bothered him badly. 'Nothing to do with Bogdan,' he said, 'but about Juraj. We were friends right enough. But it takes more than friendship for a man to marry a girl made pregnant by his friend, bring up his child and make *jokes* about it. That really is heroic tolerance.'

Karla looked at him and tried, without much success, to look dispassionate. 'The point was,' she said evenly, 'that in one sense Juraj was no longer a man at all. He was one of my early patients, long before he was wounded with us at the Villa. To put it in laymen's crude terms he was shot in the balls in Bosnia.'

The Bogdan dinner carried the makings of a social disaster. Bogdan was half drunk when he arrived. He was tall and lean with thick spiky black hair streaked with grey, a lined long face and sad persecuted eyes. He embraced Karla wordlessly, shook hands with Henderson and helped himself lavishly from the *slievovica* bottle. His conversational contribution to the first two hours of the proceedings was to say Yes four times, No three times and Thank you each time he was offered something to eat or drink. But for Karla's earlier account Henderson would have dismissed him resentfully as a boorish oaf. As it was Henderson, sympathetic, left the running to Karla who chatted easily and amusingly to Henderson while seeing to it that Bogdan's culinary and liquid needs were attended to. The latter requirement filled Henderson with awe. His life had been less than sheltered, but he had seldom seen anyone put away the stuff in similar quantities and with similar dedication. Karla, he decided, had resolved a doctor's dilemma. Drinking on this scale would do Bogdan no good. But Bogdan, tight, in the presence of former British soldiers, had for the only time in Karla's experience talked about his unbearable wartime boyhood. Karla considered that only talk would ease Bogdan's suffering. Therefore fill him up to maximum capacity, introduce Henderson as a former British soldier who had served in Montenegro, and hope for the best.

Karla's judgement of the timing was exactly right. Bogdan's inhibitions were fading fast but it seemed that he was still, amazingly, sound on coherence and clarity of thought.

'Bogdan,' said Karla, 'I didn't tell you before but Professor Henderson here is the same Captain Henderson you and I met near Bileca during the war. Remember? He came up to see those two British parachutists you found.'

Bogdan stared sightlessly. Then, as if repeating phrases he'd used to himself time and time again he said:

'British soldiers. I've been thinking about them for years. They let me down. They were kind to me. They fed me and gave me tea and chocolate. I led them through the mountains. Their captain was a very kind man. He didn't want me to go near where the fighting was. But I ran away and followed the others to the coast because I thought they might get lost and I'd be able to help them if they did. They didn't know I was following them of course. They weren't as good at moving in the countryside as I was.'

Bogdan paused and gave a humourless drunken snigger.

'Then when I got on to the island and was just going to talk to the Lieutenant he shot the Captain in the

209

back. Then he bandaged him up and the big man carried him back to the others where the kind Captain was. Then . . . I couldn't understand it. I still can't . . .'

Tears poured down Bogdan's cheeks. He broke into huge, breathless sobs. Karla sprang to her feet, put her arms around his shoulders and crooned to him like a mother with a deeply distressed child. Henderson, sensing that Bogdan would recover himself more quickly if talk were kept on normal lines, said conversationally, and with little initial interest in the response:

'Where did all this happen, Bogdan?'

'At the Villa Ribar,' sobbed Bogdan. 'The place where I joined Karla's ambulances.'

Two minutes later he recovered his composure, poured himself another tumbler of *slievovica* and began to talk quietly and earnestly to Karla. About his mother, his sister . . . Karla beckoned to Henderson to make himself scarce.

Henderson went for a long reflective walk and bought himself a Turkish coffee and a glass of mineral water at a small Kavana near Diocletian's Palace. If Bogdan's story about the British soldiers was true, there were some thoroughly unpleasant implications to be considered. There had been, he knew, only two British operations at the Villa Ribar. He himself had been in at the planning of the first one, the recce, with Paddy Madden and Tommy Daunt in Bari. He had heard all about the second one and had seen its effect on the villa and the island a week or so after it was over. Bogdan couldn't conceivably have trailed his way into that one. Anyway it went in by sea. So Bogdan must have been talking about the recce.

The kind Captain was clearly Madden. 'The Lieutenant shot the Captain in the back.' That Captain would be Tommy Daunt. The Lieutenant would be one of Madden's two subalterns. Either Peter Sims, whom Henderson had met recently and liked, or the other one whoever he was. But why? Personal grudge over a woman or something? Unlikely. They couldn't have known each other for more than a week. Speculation on that could wait. He'd have to discuss the matter with Madden, and Paddy would find it hurtful. Not as hurtful as Karla would find it if she made deductions of her own and worked out that her half-brother Tomislav, a British officer, had been murdered by a British officer at the same spot, her father's summer villa, as her full brother Branko, a Chetnik officer, had been shot in her presence by another British officer, Yeti Challoner. Oh Christ. Henderson walked miserably back to Karla's flat.

Karla looked exhausted. Bogdan, she explained, was out cold. She'd put him to bed in the spare room. He'd talked without stopping for nearly an hour. Oh, Henderson, the things that man had been through when he was a little boy. It was horrible. She'd always known it must have been something very bad but she'd never begun to imagine just how bad. But talking it out of his system had helped enormously. It was only a beginning but she'd arrange for a psychiatrist friend of hers to take over and see what could be done. Of course he'd never be entirely cured but . . .

Henderson listened and watched with pleasure, affection and admiration. It took him back a long time. He'd seen her like this before with her patients in her mobile hospital and of course with the young Bogdan on Yeti Challoner's plateau. Karla the compassionate. Poor bloody compassionate Karla.

'I'm sorry, Henderson. I'm rambling on and on. But this means a lot to me. Bogdan's like something between a son and a young brother.'

'I know. I'm very glad for you.'

'Well, don't look so glum.'

'Karla. It's unpleasant, but I think it best to get these things over with. It's about Bogdan's story about the British soldiers at the villa.'

211

'The Lieutenant who killed the Captain? I think I know what you're trying to say. It's about Tomislav, isn't it?'

Henderson nodded. Dumbly and sympathetically.

'I've known for years that Tomislav was killed at the villa,' said Karla levelly, 'through that talkative young man who took your place with Juraj's Brigade when you were wounded. He passed on a message of goodwill from somebody whose name he thought was Anderson, but who could only have been you. He said that a new British Mission man named Daunt, who spoke perfect Croatian, had delivered it. Daunt, who seemed to know his way around locally, had unfortunately been killed in a purely British action on the island. It was too much of a coincidence. It must have been Tomislav.'

'Poor Karla.'

'For a long time I thought that Vlado had taken those jewels when he left his briefcase. From Bogdan's story I suppose it's equally possible that whoever was with Tomislav took them and then killed him to keep him quiet.'

'Poor Karla,' said Henderson again.

'Yes. Poor Karla,' said poor Karla, losing her temper. 'What you're really distressed about, Henderson, is not so much that Tomislav was killed, although I think you're sympathetic about that; but you're desolated because it seems that the man who killed him was British. A commissioned British thief. One of yours. Somebody let the side down. Well, I don't give a damn about sides. I'm interested in consequences, not their cause. My father and two of my brothers were killed in the war, by people on different sides. The trouble with you bloody British is that for centuries you've been running around fighting wars and winning them, and thinking that it's all very romantic and getting sentimental about your dead. You're very good at all of it. The only thing you've forgotten is that you always fight in someone else's country. You got some bombing in

212

the last war but fundamentally your mourning is always for young men who died away from home. A silent tear on Armistice Day at the village war memorial when they play the Last Post and a few drinks in the pub afterwards while everyone explains that that's the way that old Charley or whoever it was would have wanted it. With us it's different. We get fought over, regularly. Our families, our homes, our crops, our livelihoods get destroyed and desecrated and dispersed. To you war's a dangerous game. To us it's a bitter, recurrent, devastating reality.'

Karla was sobbing again. Henderson tried to comfort her.

'Don't try to comfort me, Henderson. You've stirred up more than you know. To be fair to you, more than you meant. I've tried for years to put the war behind me, to expunge it from my mind. To me it was a savage waste. To you it's the good old days, your lost youth, when you were young and strong and brave and effective and uncluttered with routine and household bills and pension rights. You came back here intending to re-live a golden past. You . . .'

Karla stopped, chokingly, and continued to sob.

Henderson tried again to comfort her.

'Okay, Henderson,' said Karla through her tears. 'Comfort me.'

The following morning Henderson apologized.

'I'm sorry, Karla. You're right.'

'Yes. I'm right. And before you go I'll have to refer once more to that damned war. I hope I never have to think of it again. It's about Vlado's briefcase.'

Karla went to her desk, opened a drawer and produced a letter.

'Your chum Richard Atkins,' she said. 'The one who had lunch with you in Ottawa. He wrote to me.'

'He said he would.'

'It was an odd sort of letter. That's why I sent you a telegram. I wanted time to think.'

213

'What sort of odd?'

'Well, there were two letters, a coverer typed by Atkins and a manuscript letter from Vlado. They were worded very carefully. All allusive and elliptical and wouldn't mean a thing to any outsider who intercepted and read them. Atkins said that he'd flown down to somewhere in Latin America and met an old friend of mine. Letter enclosed. Vlado's handwriting hasn't changed much and he clinched the identification by references to childhood events that only he could have known about. You know the type of thing: "How is Beba?" That's what the boys called me when I was small. It all led up to a request. Obscurely phrased, but clear. He'd left some personal belongings in a cupboard to which I had the only other key and he couldn't spare the time to collect them himself. Would I look them out and send them to him, perhaps through Uncle Mladen?'

'Who's Uncle Mladen?'

'A brother of my mother's who once lived in Vienna. In translation, please get Vlado's briefcase out of the cache at the Villa Ribar. Contents too hot to send through the Yugoslav post. Smuggle it to Vienna and send from somewhere where random censorship is concerned with exchange control and not war crimes.'

'Oh, Karla,' said Henderson.

'You're right as usual, Henderson,' said Karla. 'Even if for a professor you're a bit less than articulate.'

'Don't be so aggressive, Karla. What did you do?'

'Nothing. I thought there might be some catch in it. I worried about possible threats, perhaps to Miro or my grandson. It seemed to me that while I had control of Vlado's papers I had the whip hand. That's why I sent you that telegram.'

'Quite right,' said Henderson sententiously.

'Christ, Henderson,' said Karla, 'I suppose it was. But you've bloody changed it. You've come here and resurrected the whole bloody war. The whole miser-

214

able bloody past. I want no more of it. When you get back to Canada will you please give that bloody brief-case to Atkins, tell him to give it to Vlado with my compliments, and say that I never want to hear of any of it again.'

Henderson knew what to do next. For the past few days he had made a point of carrying a spare clean handkerchief. Remarkable amount of weeping seemed to attend his activities in Split. He dried Karla's eyes and introduced a casual diversion into the discussion.

'Thing I've often meant to ask you, Karla,' he said, 'where did you learn your colloquial English?'

Karla sniffled.

'Christ, Henderson,' she said. 'You slay me. I spent three years being educated in England. By the fucking nuns.'

They both chuckled; and hugged companionably.

Three days later Henderson took the JAT flight from Split to Zagreb and there changed to the Air Canada flight to Toronto. In the course of the journey he read Karla's letter to him eleven times. She had thrust it into the breast-pocket of his suit as she kissed him goodbye and told him not to open it until he was airborne.

'Henderson My Love,

I've decided to write it down. Conversation with you always seems to find its way into strange, if amusing, byways.

Your idea was sweet. I was – still am – flattered and tempted. But it won't work. We may feel young at heart occasionally, but we're set in our ways. If I came to join you in Ottawa I would be happy for a time. But I'd soon start thinking of Miro and Zdenka and my grandson and my patients and my flat and my country that, for better or worse, has shaped my whole life. I'd get restless and resentful. And that would be unfair to you.

215

By the same token if you joined me in Split, you would have to abandon work you cherish and sever the links of a working life. And however you feel now, you too would resent that. And that also would be unfair to you.

Above all there would be the constant worry that by some hint or gesture or accident you might cause Miro to speculate about who his father was. That is a risk I'm unwilling to take.

So, dearest Henderson, let us do this. You come to me when you can. I'll go to you when I can. We'll . . .'

There followed a loving evaluation of the practicalities. Oh Christ, thought Henderson, she's right.

Chapter Five

PETER SIMS HAD news for Madden. Madden had news for Peter Sims. They both began together, stopped simultaneously and Madden brought the meeting to order.

'You first, Peter.'

'I'm in touch with Ken Kershaw.'

Madden raised his eyebrows and stared hard at Sims. 'How?'

Sims looked ill at ease. And *that* didn't happen very often, thought Madden. Sims, it seemed, had been overtaken by remorse. On the basis of patchy evidence, reinforced by prejudice and dislike, tempered by fantasy, clouded by increasingly dim memories, he had accused a man of murdering another in circumstances in which the victim had every right to assume a total trust in a colleague. Sims had been shown to be wrong by Henderson's assurance that the gold from the Villa Ribar had been recovered intact to the last sovereign. Sims' accusations had been delivered privately and to one man only, Madden, but Madden was a man to whom both Kershaw and Sims had once owed an absolute joint loyalty. Sims had concluded, admittedly with the help of an over-generous application of his Duty Free, that he owed Kershaw an apology. He had set about trying to trace Kershaw.

It had been much easier than he had thought it might be. There had inevitably been initial set-backs. He wrote to the Royal Marine Office and got a reply from its successor, an organism named grandly the Department of the Commandant General Royal Marines. They provided an address in Yorkshire, dating from Kershaw's service with the Royal Marine Forces Volunteer Reserve in 1950. Sims could find nothing in thetelephone directory and his letter was returned with an endorsement stating that the house had been demolished long ago to make way for a New Town. The ever helpful Henry Brown of the Commando Association offered an address, c/o a bank. The bank said that Mr Kershaw had closed his account with them over twenty years previously. Sims tried the Department of Health and Social Security. They replied primly that it was not their policy to disclose the addresses of their clients. Sims telephoned Dicky Richards. Richards said that he'd not seen Kershaw since the end of the war (and made it clear that he regarded this lacuna as no deprivation) but that at the last re-union somebody or other had said that Kershaw had emigrated to Rhodesia. Sims went to London to Rhodesia House in the Strand, seeking a Rhodesian telephone directory. Rhodesia House was closed and, said the caretaker irritably, had been since Mr Ian Smith's Unilateral Declaration of Independence in 1965. Sims telephoned Rhodesia Department of the Foreign and Commonwealth Office. They were courteous but cagey. They may or may not have had a Rhodesian telephone directory, but it was no part of their job to ease communications with people in a country that was in rebellion against the Crown. Unless of course it was a compassionate case. No, said Sims, it wasn't.

Sims returned to Holyhead, looked critically at the level of scotch in his last bottle, decided that a journey to Dunlaoghaire was imminent, poured himself a tot, and turned on his television set. A Rhodesian former member of the Long Range Desert Group was being interviewed. Terrorism in Rhodesia had reached a pitch that had convinced him that his growing family would have no satisfactory future in the country. He had immigrated to Britain. He had been helped enormously in settling down by a small organization sponsored by a retired General who had served with Rhodesians in the LRDG. Sims wrote down names and locations and the following morning with the help of Directory Enquiries did some telephoning. His second call hit the jackpot.

'I'm trying to trace the address in Rhodesia of someone called Kershaw.'

'Ken Kershaw?'

'Yes.'

'Well, don't bother with Rhodesia. He's here. Telephone for you, Ken.'

'How was he?' asked Madden.

'Sounded the same as ever. You remember that flat, emotionless voice he had? It's still there, but he's much more talkative than he was. Wouldn't stop. He's as bitter as hell about Rhodesia. I couldn't understand all of it, but so far as I can make out he's had to sell up and get out at a huge loss.'

'What was he doing there?'

'Farming. Did very well for himself for about twenty-five years. Then it all went wrong. There was a lot of stuff about the Terrs, and initials beginning with Z. And betrayal by British Communists like Harold Wilson and David Owen. He thinks Ian Smith's a left-wing softie. Then there's the munts and coons. I'm not sure if there's any difference, but whether there is or not, Ken doesn't think much of them. Also the Jaapies. Pretty poor crowd, the Jaapies, according to Ken.' Sims laughed.

'Did you get your apology in?'

'No. I thought I'd better do that in person. Not over the telephone. I've asked him to come and stay with me.'

'In Holyhead?'

'No. Dunlaoghaire. He's coming on Friday week.'

'What's your news, Paddy?'

'Two pieces. Jock Henderson will be in Ireland at the end of next week. Come to think of it, on Friday week. Same day as Ken. And I'm meeting Father Quinlan in Dublin on the Thursday. Why don't we all have supper here on the Saturday? Jock and Ken and you and me. Father Quinlan if he's still around.'

'Unfair to you. Who'll do the cooking?'

'No problem. My daughter in Trinity. Mary'll run us up a buffet. She's very good at it. Loves cooking. I pay her the going rate.'

'Well, thanks,' said Sims. 'I greatly look forward to it. Provided you let us all help with the washing up.'

'You're on.'

'I'll tell you a thing,' said Sims with a chuckle, 'I hope Father Quinlan can come to your supper. I'd love to see what he makes of Ken's analysis of the Rhodesian situation.'

Chapter Six

IN THE WINTER it was a ski lodge. Trail skiing along the tracks threading through the pines and birch, among the rocks, much of it easy going, unexpected steep curving drops to challenge the skilled, spill the unwary. The unambitious and energetic skied over the snow on the flat frozen surface of the lake. In the summer the lake accommodated power boats, water skiers, canoeists, swimmers, anglers of bass and pike and perch and assorted pan-fish. The design of the lodge was deceptively simple. Stone and huge baulks of timber. Steeply sloping shingle roof with an emphasized, Swiss chalet-looking, overhang. Stone dock. An enormous oil-burning boiler in the basement for central heating. Vast stone fireplaces in the spacious downstairs rooms, logs blazing. Kitchen like an operating theatre. Glass walled bathrooms with sunken baths and overhead heating. Thick carpets, deep armchairs, heavy dark old furniture and pictures of distinction. Lots of silver and brass. Persian rugs. Electricity by generator. It was all expensive, remote and isolated.

An excellent place for a clandestine meeting of seven very rich men from Canada, the United States, Australia and West Germany who were putting together the final details of a plan to demonstrate to the world that the cultural and historic role of the people of Croatia could not necessarily be subsumed indefinitely in that of a constituent entity of a bastard Federal Socialist

Republic of Yugoslavia. The plan was destructive, well-conceived, ruthless and unlikely to win the support of anyone not already emotionally committed. Its devisers were intelligent, successful, fanatical, sincere, and altogether alarming.

They sat at a long rectangular oak table, smoking, taking notes, commenting, offering suggestions, giving information. The sort of industrial boardroom meeting they were accustomed to, competent contributions, a strong chairman who kept everyone to the point.

Training? As good as it ever would be. Materials? Weapons and explosives delivered and held in secure hides. Manpower? Okay everywhere except Australia. Three of the boys in Canberra had become too exuberant and had been locked up after trying to blow up a Serbian-owned restaurant. Never mind, Munich would help. They'd send out three others, trained, eager and with bogus documents. Timing? Very important that everything should be simultaneous. Everyone to check scrupulously international time differences. Communications? Still the weakest link, but adequate. Simply-coded commercial telex messages. Trouble was that they were fine for reporting developments but less useful for transmitting instructions. Everything would depend on the training, initiative and common sense of the teams. Any other business? None. Contented silence all round.

'Well, I've just one item,' said the Chairman. 'Through a complicated chain of events I won't go into here, there's a man who just conceivably might compromise us. After the operation, not before. He knows who I am and what my background is.'

There was an immediately attentive silence.

'He's a man with whom I've been in touch for years on purely cultural matters. He recently returned to me an item of my property that had been missing since 1945. It contained papers and photographs. Nothing I'm ashamed of. Indeed everything I've every reason to

222

be proud of. A comprehensive summary of my past activities and present philosophy.'

The man from Los Angeles, irritated and uneasy, spoke.

'Look. If he gave this stuff back to you he presumably sympathizes with us.'

'Far from it. He was a British Liaison Officer with the Partisans. But he's devoted to our culture, our country and, I suspect, to a lady I used to know rather well. He's politically uninterested and in some respects remarkably naïve. He believes in letting by-gones be by-gones. He's typically British in an old-fashioned sort of way. For example he told me that he had not looked at my papers, which had been in his possession for years, because he regarded them as private although he had a pretty good idea from an outside source of what was in them. Oddly enough, I believe him. For another example, he's exactly the sort of civic-minded bleeding heart who after the big bangs will go straight to the RCMP in answer to the inevitable appeal for any relevant information, however seemingly trivial. His sense of duty will compel him to mention me, with reluctance. His sense of fair play will compel him to say that I'm a very long shot and all, but in view of the nature of . . .'

'How are you so sure he knows who you are?'

'Well,' said the Chairman, smiling sadly, 'when we met for lunch in Toronto last week he shook me by the hand and said "Good morning, Mr Atkins." When he left he grinned and said "Good luck, Vlado."''

'Where does this guy live?'

'Ottawa. He's a professor at Carleton. Slavonic Studies.'

'Waste him,' said the man from California, who had seen too many movies about the Mafia.

There were some objections, tactical not ethical. Murders in Ottawa were rare. The killing, or even disappearance, of a professor of Slavonic Studies shortly before the big bangs in Yugoslăv diplomatic and consular establishments could point to a possible connection between the two. All the professor's past contacts would be investigated, followed up. It could lead back to the Chairman. The Chairman smiled sadly again.

'I like that man very much,' he said. 'But I agree he must go. However, I told you he was naïve. He told me that he's going to Ireland in a week's time. I think we should eliminate him there. What resources have we available for activating a Special Operations Unit of, say, four men?'

They agreed on two from Munich, one from Milan and one from Minneapolis. The Chairman said that he would brief their leader personally. The meeting dispersed in some haste. It was Sunday and they all wanted to get to Mass.

On the same Sunday, more than three thousand miles away, a meeting with a not dissimilar purpose was held in a semi-detached modern house in Sanymount, an inner suburb of Dublin. This gathering was less elegant, less rich, less formal, more sparsely attended and of comparable potential deadliness. A burly, bald, red-faced man in his fifties in a roll-necked sweater and carpet slippers did most of the talking. He had a broken nose and sipped copiously from a succession of bottles of Guinness. He had two companions, one young and scholarly looking, one young and stupid looking.

'Well, human memory-bank, what's the state of the DHR?' The Designated Hostages Register was being compiled by a splinter group of the Irish Republican Army. The splintering had been forced upon them by the Provisional IRA who thought them too extreme. The register was of suitable targets for abduction in the lunatic hope that they could subsequently be traded for leading terrorist prisoners, international as well as Irish, held by the Irish or British authorities. It was not a written list. Names, addresses and habits were lodged in the retentive brain of the grandiosely entitled 'Intelligence Officer'. The scholarly-looking one. Those on the list were Irishmen with supposedly important English connections, or supposedly important Englishmen living in Ireland.

'We've checked out eleven out of eighteen so far. Five are too difficult. Too many kids, or neighbours or dogs or whatever. Three are possibles but could cause complications. Three are definite starters. Isolated houses, regular habits, few visitors, no resident children, wives dead, or deserted or bed-ridden.'

'Three's not enough. Who's the next check on?'

'Man named Madden. A lot of his mail's addressed to Mr Madden, or Madden Esquire, but some says Brigadier D. Something Madden, OBE, MC, RM (retired). Lives alone at Kilmacanogue.'

'Seems a sound choice. What's RM?'

'Buggered if I know.'

'Well the rest of it's good enough for me. When are you running the test?'

'Saturday night. The boys have had him under surveillance for six weeks. His movements don't follow much of a pattern but he's always in alone on Saturday evenings. Probably watches the telly or something.'

'I hope nobody's slacking off on these rehearsals. I want the whole works. Routes, timings, getaway cars, approaches, the lads armed. Everything short of being seen or doing the snatch. Who's on this one?' The Intelligence Officer nodded to his simian colleague.

'Mick's in charge. He'll take Liam with him.'

'Oh Jesus,' said the burly man. 'That's a real recipe for catastrophe. Let's have another jar.'

Vlado briefed the team leader in a motel room that he'd paid for in cash in advance in Kingston, Ontario. Experience and instinct had led Vlado to take no chances over being identified. After all there weren't many Ustasha Colonels who'd slipped by the 1945 carnage, evaded the mountain border guards near the Triglav and weaselled their way, through the Vatican, to Latin America and subsequent prosperity in Canada. Some though. Not all Colonels, but all with their hearts in the right place. Like his six co-evals at the planning meeting. Intelligent, hard-working, ambitious Croat exiles who had made a pile in their adopted countries and were prepared to put their money and their energies into the one Cause that counted . . . Vlado knew a thing or two about disguise. There had been times when he'd been unusually sophisticated about it. No need on this occasion. An auburn wig, false moustache, dark glasses, denim suit and gloves to conceal his hands were sufficient. Childish but effective. The motel manager clearly thought, as he was intended to think, that Vlado was some well-heeled businessman laying somebody else's wife. The team leader would never be able to identify him again. Until of course reason and justice triumphed and Vladimir Bilic, the national hero, returned to his rightful place in an independent . . . Stop daydreaming. Work to be done.

The team leader had flown in from Munich. He was in his middle thirties and looked strong and dependable. He was satisfyingly bitter. When he had been a small child his father had been shot by a Partisan firing squad, an outrage his mother had never allowed him to forget. Vlado gave him his instructions crisply, in an orderly fashion, and with an economy of words.

'A Professor I. K. Henderson, of Ottawa, is a threat to our movement. He is to be killed. It is undesirable that he should be killed in Canada. He is going to Ireland on Monday week. You will kill him there.'

The team leader nodded. He had done three of these jobs before. A Yugoslav consul, a police informer and a suspected paid traitor. 'You will have a team of four. For operational purposes you will be known as Matthew, Mark, Luke and John. You're Matthew.'

'Yes.'

'How you perform the execution is entirely a matter for you. But it's of the highest importance that it should be done by the end of the month and should not be traced back to the movement. If you have to dispose of Mark, Luke or John, you must do so. If you do, leave them unidentifiable, Matthew.'

'Yes,' said Matthew. He didn't like this bit much.

'Arrangements have been made for the team to assemble for briefing in London on Friday. Hotel Bristol, Bingham Square. Usual identification procedures. Work out your plan and tell them there. Then disperse. Then get on with it.'

Vlado smiled. Even through the false moustache Matthew thought that he looked unhappy.

'Any questions?'

'Yes. Do we know what flight Henderson's going to Ireland on?'

'We do,' said Vlado. 'He said that he's going from Montreal to Shannon. That's Aer Lingus E1 120 ETD 0850 hours. You can check the link flight to Dublin yourself.'

'Thanks. Money?'

'As much as you need for the task. Here's twenty thousand bucks for a start. If you want more draw on Munich.'

'Communications?'

'None from us. From you we want only confirmation of the result. Send a telegram, from England or France – not Ireland – to the Vienna group. Just say "Successful. Matthew".'

'Okay. *Do Vidjenya.*'

'*Do Vidjenya.* Good luck.'

Matthew shook hands cordially and left. Vlado heard his car start and drive away. Vlado felt a twinge of melancholy and pessimism. What a waste to kill some-

227

body like Henderson. And suppose that message read 'Unsuccessful. Matthew'. Vlado found himself almost hoping that it would. He left the motel unobtrusively and drove to Toronto.

He had never admitted it to anyone, but Henderson was a nervous air traveller. The cause of this malaise lay in earlier experience. All but two of his first twelve flights were preliminaries to parachute jumps, training or operational. A corollary of these journeys had been a largely subconscious feeling that if anything went wrong with the aircraft you could always jump out of the bloody thing. Passenger airliners offered no such comfort. Henderson customarily doused his forebodings by the pre-take-off ingestion of powerful quantities of anaesthetic pink gin. These medicaments usually made him sleepy, sometimes made him affable and occasionally made him irritable. On this flight, from Montreal to Shannon, he was affable. He welcomed the company of the tough-looking man who took the seat next to him and gave little thought to the man's curious procedure of scrutinizing the labels on the handbaggage in the rack before selecting a seat. They fell into conversation, eased by liberal recourse to the stewardess' drinks trolley.

They talked skiing, fishing and ice hockey. When the man, looking at a book written in Serbo-Croat that Henderson had put in the net magazine and sick bag holder in front of him, remarked that his mother had been Croatian, they talked Croatia. The man said expansively that he was going to Ireland on a golfing holiday. Did Henderson play? Indeed he did. Handicap of eight. So was the man's. Look, if Henderson had any spare time in Ireland why didn't they arrange a game? Excellent idea. They exchanged names and addresses. The man would be staying at the Royal Starlight Hotel in Bray. Henderson hadn't booked himself in anywhere yet. He'd fix a hotel on arrival.

But the man could always get a message to him through a friend of his. Henderson wrote down Madden's name, address and telephone number on a piece of paper and handed it over to his new chum. Luke tucked it carefully into his wallet.

On the Thursday morning, Father Quinlan telephoned Madden from Liverpool. Dublin Airport was blotted out by fog and according to the weather forecasters would stay so for the next twenty-four hours. He would cross on the night B and I ferry. He was sorry to cause inconvenience but he had rearranged his plans slightly so as to be able to meet Madden. He'd postponed his visit to Limerick by a couple of days and would first stay with another of his sisters in Killiney. No problem, said Madden, and invited Father Quinlan to supper on the Saturday. Father Quinlan accepted with great pleasure.

Matthew, looking comfortably out of the aircraft window at the night sky, made for the fourth time an assessment of the information passed to him by telephone, in carefully guarded phrases, by Luke. Luke had made contact with Henderson and could provide a positive identification to supplement the not very satisfactory photographs furnished by the organization. A plus. Luke had a covering address through which, without too much ingenuity, Henderson might be traced. A partial plus. Luke had inexcusably lost trace of Henderson at Dublin Airport. A minus. Luke had failed to discover where Henderson was staying. A minus. Luke had to some extent redeemed himself by telephoning Henderson's friend who had said that he too did not know where Henderson was; but if all else failed Luke could telephone him at the friend's house after 7.30 on Saturday. Henderson would be there for supper. Well that was something. Even if, in default of further information, it put uncomfortable constraints on timing and location. Luke's golf bag was safely through Customs. A plus. At least one gun was available. Luke was . . .

There was a rasping crackle on the public address system and a mushy voice announced that it was their Captain speaking. He apologized for being the bearer of disagreeable tidings, but Dublin Airport had just been closed because of fog. They were diverting to Belfast where alternative arrangements would . . .

Two hours later. Matthew was in a police cell being peered at balefully by three workmanlike members of the Royal Ulster Constabulary. Security at Aldergrove was much tighter than at Dublin Airport. A machine carbine broken down and hidden in a golf bag indeed! The man must be nuts. It was downright insulting.

Madden picked up the ringing telephone and said 'Madden'.

'Peter here, Paddy. In Christian mood. I've rented a car for the weekend to show Ken around a bit. If you'll tell me where Jock and the Reverend Father are staying. I'll collect your entire supper party for you tomorrow.'

'Thanks. Jock's at the Shelbourne. These filthy rich North Americans. He telephoned last night. He's been in the country. Father Quinlan – hang on a minute – here it is; 34A Thomastown Road, Dunlaoghaire. Dunlaoghaire's the postal address. It's behind Killiney Hill.'

'Okay. I'll pick it off the map. Better give me his telephone number and I'll warn him I'm coming.'

Madden did so and asked after Kershaw.

'Lost in the fog,' said Sims. 'His flight was cancelled. He's coming over on the day boat from Holyhead. He'll just have time for a quick wash and brush-up before we set out for you. I'll have to put off my little speech of apology until tomorrow.'

Mark had travelled, with golf bag and without interference, by the Fishguard-Rosslare Car Ferry. John had had a similarly uneventful journey from Cherbourg to Cork. Luke had joined them at the agreed rendezvous at Dublin Zoo. Matthew, sitting sorrowfully in his cell in Crumlin Road Gaol and pondering on what he regarded as disquieting character weaknesses in Mark's capabilities as a substitute murder gang leader, had not. It was standard practice that if anyone was more than six hours late for a rendezvous it was assumed that in one way or another he had been put out of the running. Whether through accident, betrayal, capture, incompetence did not matter. Mark took control. He listened to Luke's report, much as it had been delivered to Matthew, but amplified by the news that although Luke had spent the past two days tramping the streets of Dublin, looking into bars and restaurants, and telephoning every hotel listed in the Yellow Pages to ask for Mr I. K. Henderson, he had drawn blank. Mark, feeling the isolation of command responsibility, and apprehensive about the wrath that would confront him from on high if he made the wrong decision, hesitated as Matthew had feared he would. Then he made his mind up and gave his instructions.

They would give themselves the chance of two bites at the cherry. The first would be at Madden's cottage and would be subject to two considerations. Satisfactory approach and escape routes, to be determined by reconnaissance. And a reasonable certainty that Henderson would be eating alone with Madden. 'Supper', he had called it. That sounded private and informal. Madden would have to be killed too of course. But if there were more than two cars parked at the cottage they would switch to plan two. Wait until Henderson left, trail him, and dispose of him either at a convenient moment en route or at his destination. This made sense to Luke who, in any case, for reasons of discipline, would not have questioned it if it hadn't. John never questioned anything. He was an expert with guns, knives and explosives, but like that long-gone warrior Yeti Challoner needed somone to point him at the right place at the right time.

They took both Mark's and John's hired cars on the reconnaissance. Mark went by the Stillorgan Road, through Foxrock and Shankill and Old Connaught. John took the upper route through Stepaside, the Scalp and Enniskerry. By the early afternoon they met casually at the foot of the Sugar Loaf Mountain and climbed it together, bird-watching picnickers with binoculars.

'That's it,' said Luke, pointing to a compact white-walled cottage with a slate roof and a rocky furze-filled garden scattered with wind-bent conifers. It was one of the several things he'd got right. An enquiry at the Bord Failte Office, some map reading, the hire of a car and a word at a pub in Kilmacanogue had been followed by a discreet look around. It had been sketchy, but enough.

Later Mark and John walked leisurely down past the cottage, pausing at intervals to look at birds through their binoculars. They left Luke to make his own way back to his hotel. Henderson might already be at the cottage and that could lead to embarrassing questions. Mark paused at Madden's gate, raised his glasses and studied a pied wagtail that was pottering about in the garden. It was a satisfying piece of ornithology. He could see a small porch from which the inner front door opened directly on to a sitting-room. There was no Yale lock. A keyhole beside a brass doorknob proclaimed what Mark wanted. One good kick should fix that. It was all falling neatly into place. The obvious approach was down the mountain. Now to look for a place to park the getaway car in the valley.

Madden was a considerate and amusing host. All four of his guests had demonstrated that they too were considerate by contributing a bottle of something. Sims and Kershaw had simply plonked theirs on the sideboard without comment. Henderson, looking unexpectedly pre-occupied, had remarked that he liked to round off his evening meal with a shot of brandy. He couldn't expect an ignorant Irish peasant to have any. Hence his offering. Father Quinlan had shyly produced a bottle of Jamieson which he hoped the Brigadier would accept in recognition of the fact that the duty free was a splendid institution.

Madden, refilling glasses, gazed at his guests with affection. Kershaw, Sims and Henderson, thinning, greying hair, thickening waists, signs of age and all, took him straight back to days he looked upon with a wistful nostalgia. Father Quinlan had turned out to be a robust, entertaining character who had struck up an unlikely rapport with Peter Sims, with whom he was exchanging outrageous witticisms about religion and the lack of it. Kershaw, burlier and grey-haired, but still looking strong and light on his feet, was booming on and on about Rhodesia. Henderson was listening with impatience. Before their arrival, Madden had reached one firm decision. Hospitality first, bad news later. Father Quinlan's bulletin could wait until after supper. Jock Henderson, who seemed keen to impart some sort of urgent information, could wait too.

They moved to the buffet laid out stylishly on the breakfast-room table. Mary Madden, delivered three hours previously to the bus stop outside the Glencormac Inn by a loving and grateful father, had done them well. There was smoked salmon and vol au vents and tongue. Cold turkey. Spiced ham. Potato salad. Mixed salad. Crisp rolls. Butter. Trifle. Brie, Camembert and Stilton. Washed down by Beaujolais, supplemented by the offerings of Sims and Kershaw. They ate and chatted and reminisced contentedly. Over the coffee, and Henderson's brandy, Sims said:

233

'Do congratulate your daughter, Paddy. Bit better than the grub at the Bronze Dog.'

'What's the Bronze Dog?' asked Father Quinlan.

'Place we were in Yugoslavia. We used to live on Compo tea and corned beef fritters. I've been off corned beef ever since.'

'I don't know,' said Kershaw. 'Maxby used to make damned good corned beef fritters.'

There was a short silence, broken by Madden.

'Well that,' he said, 'brings us conveniently to what might be called the business side of a social evening. I'd hoped to do it separately but the fog ruined that. Peter and Father Quinlan know what it's about. Father, you can speak freely in front of everybody. Three of us were in the same Troop with Maxby and you can rely totally on Jock's discretion.'

Kershaw looked puzzled. So did Henderson.

'Ken,' said Madden, 'Maxby died recently. He was a parishioner of Father Quinlan's. Before he died he asked for a message to be passed to me. Touch of conscience. It seems that he and somebody else in the Troop committed a murder. Somebody on our side.'

'Oh, that,' said Kershaw off-handedly. He looked almost bored. The others stared at him. Henderson, scowling dangerously, jerked his chair backwards. To a position, it seemed to Madden, from which he could if necessary throttle Kershaw from behind. Kershaw, impassive, seemed not to notice. Father Quinlan reached into his inside coat pocket and produced a piece of paper.

'I'm sorry,' he said apologetically, 'but I think I'd better speak from notes. I want to be one hundred percent accurate.'

They were going over the route in reverse in the dark. Start at the farmhouse outside Blessington where a sound-proof cellar could hold a captive. Time and measure the journey to the Sally Gap where the cars would be changed. Time and measure the journey through Newtownmountkennedy and up to Kilmacanogue, to the place on the lane where the car would be parked on the night of the snatch. The last leg would be on foot to the cottage.

'Count every pace, Liam. There and back. I'll time you from here. We'll add three minutes for the actual pick-up.'

'How far d'you want me to go. The gate?'

'Every pace, I said. Into the garden and touch the house wall. Good practice for you. No harm in it. The old fella'll be watching television.'

Liam set out, an aspirant abductor who was developing doubts about the wisdom of his choice of calling.

It looked to Mark as if the prospects were good. They had left their car in an old quarry beside the road in the Rocky Valley. They had climbed steeply to the south, up the track that they had previously examined carefully. In a patch of rocks they unzipped their hold-alls and put on stocking masks, black nylon overalls and black silk gloves. They made sure that their machine carbines were ready for action. Mark's with the silencer, the other two without. Luke and John would only have to use theirs in an emergency and if there was an emergency a gun without a silencer would be more effective. There was an almost full moon, masked erratically by scudding clouds, driven by a near gale. Good. Reasonable visibility and the wind would help to drown any noise. Not that there should be any.

They slipped quietly down the hillside, scattering a few sheep as they went. Just short of the cottage wall Mark gestured to them to get down. He moved cautiously to the gate and peered in. Two cars only. Curtains of the cottage tightly drawn. Back to Luke and John. Plan one. They nodded and rose to their feet. They knew what to do. One to each side of the house. When they were in position Mark would walk to the front door, kick it in and shoot Henderson and Madden. Then shut the door, back to their car and away. All the best plans were models of simplicity.

'Where or what is Solta?' asked Father Quinlan. 'This business happened *on* Solta. Not in it or at it. That puzzled me.'

'It's an island off the Dalmatian Coast. Pronounced Sholta.'

'Ah. That explains it. Well on Solta Henry Maxby and somebody called Billy Truscott shot dead a marine named Rowlands. It was a deliberate act. Henry didn't go into details. He just said that I was to tell Captain Madden and say that he was sorry. Then he said some very kind things about you, Brigadier. I assumed that it was some drunken brawl while the three of them were on shore leave.'

'No,' said Madden, 'we did a four-day operation on Solta. I was told that Rowlands was killed by a mortar bomb. He was a big strong fellow.'

'He was also a yellow bastard,' said Kershaw unexpectedly. 'That's why Truscott and Maxby knocked him off.'

They all stared at Kershaw for the second time in a minute.

'I don't know how good your memory is, Paddy, but I remember that day very well. We'd been sitting on that damned flat hill for three days waiting for the guns to be landed. They were held up by a storm. There was a lot of mortaring and shelling and then that bloody great Coast Defence gun from Split kept landing twelve-inch bricks among us. Very trying it was.'

'It was indeed,' said Sims. It had been his first time under fire. As such it was graven deep in his mind.

'You told me to send a small party back to the beach to collect ammunition and rations. I told Corporal Truscott to take Maxby and Rowlands because they were the strongest. When they got to the beach Rowlands said he'd had enough. He was damned if he was going back to be shot up on that bloody hill again.'

'Go on, Ken,' said Madden quietly. Sims, looking at him, saw that he was controlling anger.

'Truscott and Maxby told Rowlands that if he didn't get off his backside and do his share of the work they'd knock the hell out of him. They also appealed to his better nature. You know the sort of stuff. "Unless you get stuck in the lads on the hill will be short of grub and ammunition." Rowlands still refused so they thumped him. Rowlands then picked up his load and they headed back. Half-way up they ran into a mild mortar stonk. Rowlands dropped his load and bolted back towards the beach. So they shot him,' concluded Kershaw with satisfaction.

'How do you know all this?' snapped Madden.

'Maxby told me.'

'Then why the hell didn't you tell me?' The anger was less controlled now.

'I did consider it,' said Kershaw complacently, 'but I decided against it. In the first place I reckoned that Rowlands deserved everything he got. I doubted if you'd share my view. If you didn't and fell back on the Rights of Man or the Holy Ghost or King's Regulations, there'd have been a court martial. Even if they were acquitted on some technicality two good men, particularly Maxby, would be out of play at a time when they could have been more usefully employed with us. And remember Maxby still had a bloody great charge-sheet hanging over him from his last excursion in Naples. At best we might not have seen him again for months. Lastly, I knew that you'd worry yourself silly about the whole thing. So I kept it to myself.'

'You knew damned well you should have told me.' The temper was rising fast.

'Look, Paddy, be reasonable. There were all sorts of things I didn't tell you. Same applied to Peter. There were all sorts of things the sergeants didn't tell Peter

237

and me. There were quite a few things you didn't tell the Colonel. All best kept in the family unless they got out of control. In this particular case, no one could have brought Rowlands back. He was no loss anyway. We kept Truscott and Maxby. And they both subsequently did a bloody good job of work.'

Father Quinlan looked as if he were making an unsuccessful attempt to reconcile expediency with morality and at the same time regretting irrelevant references to the Holy Ghost. Henderson had the air of a man who was on the verge of committing an inexcusable social gaffe, like hitting a fellow guest. Madden looked plain hopping mad. Sims, the coolest of them all, decided upon an emollient move that would simultaneously shift the emphasis of the conversation and let him get something off his chest.

'Ken,' he said, 'I owe you an apology.'

'What for?'

'I thought that you and Maxby killed somebody. I told Paddy so. Then I got some evidence from Jock that convinced me that I was wrong. That's why I wanted to get in touch with you. To tell you I was wrong. And to apologize.'

It was Kershaw's turn to stare. It was Henderson who broke the silence.

'Evidence from me? What evidence?' He was puzzled and aggressive.

'Well, when we got Maxby's deathbed confession, Father Quinlan was reluctant to tell Paddy who Maxby's accomplice was. Then I worked it out that Ken and Maxby had pinched some gold from the Villa Ribar and killed that British Mission chap to keep him quiet. You told me in Ottawa that there was no gold missing. So I knew I had it wrong.'

'There was no gold missing,' said Henderson grimly. 'What was missing was about half a million bucks worth of diamonds. Valued at 1941 prices.'

Kershaw's expression became more immobile than ever. His voice flatter and even more emotionless.

'I know damn all about any diamonds,' he said, 'but I did kill Tommy Daunt.'

It was Madden who prevented the rapid development of a ridiculous degrading punch-up among the middle aged. He was the host, the oldest man present and had held the senior rank. None of these attributes would necessarily have stopped a murderously inclined Henderson from throwing himself wildly at the man who had just owned to killing Karla's brother. Henderson had liked Tomislav well. Nor would they have stopped Kershaw from defending himself in the only way he knew. Dirty. By God, thought Sims admiringly, Paddy doesn't need to use it much, but he still has what he always had had, a natural, irresistible authority.

'Jock, sit down and shut up. Ken put that ashtray down. Peter, pour everyone a drink. Father, I'm sorry.'

Henderson sat down and shut up, sullenly. Kershaw put down the heavy crystal ashtray but kept it warily within reach. Sims, subdued, courteously asked everyone what they'd have and gave it to them. What the hell, he wondered, was Father Quinlan making of all this?

'Now, Ken,' said Madden briskly, 'you've made an admission in front of four witnesses which could land you in serious trouble. You can do one of three things. You can say no more in your own interests. If you do so, I must warn you that I'll send a statement to the Judge Advocate General's Department. There may be all sorts of legal complexities about the Statute of Limitations and so on. But there may not.'

Kershaw nodded. How does the bastard always manage to look so impassive thought Sims.

'Second, you can tell me about it privately. Third, you can tell me about it with Jock present. He's an interested party.'

'I'll take a fourth option,' said Kershaw promptly, 'I'll tell the whole lot of you about it. It was an accident. I've been ashamed of it for years. Not ashamed of killing Tommy Daunt. Ashamed of having an accident with firearms,' he added, as if determined to dissipate any hint of sympathy that a confession of shame might engender. In this he was successful. He paused, mustering his recollections in the right order. It had, after all, been a long time ago.

'To cut it as short as possible,' went on Kershaw, 'when we were jumped in the dark in the bushes on that island, Maxby, Daunt and I got separated at first. Then I could tell roughly where they were by the sound of their Tommy guns. I knew old Maxby would be okay, but I wasn't sure about Daunt. So I went over to give him a hand.'

Kershaw here gave a further demonstration of how to dissipate sympathy.

'In case he cocked it all up,' he said bleakly.

'And just when I was about five yards behind him, I tripped over a stone. My finger was on the trigger and not along the trigger guard where it should have been. When I fell the gun went off and put a burst into Tommy's back. And that was that.'

Kershaw sipped at his drink.

'Why did you keep quiet about it, Ken?' asked Madden gently. Sims thought he knew the reason. He thought that Madden knew it too. Henderson wouldn't. Father Quinlan couldn't have begun to guess. Kershaw thought for a moment.

'Call it injured pride if you like,' he said, without affectation. 'You see, I knew I was good. Better than you in my opinion, Paddy. I was good partly through natural aptitude; partly from having the right attitude to war, which you never had; and mostly through hard slogging application at getting the details right. I used to come down like a ton of bricks on the troops if there was any slackness in weapon training. I thought carelessness with arms was inexcusable. And then through a stupid bloody oversight, I shot Tommy Daunt. I'd have been a laughing stock if it came out.'

Madden's tone was still gentle.

'He was still alive when you brought him back. What would you have done if he'd recovered?'

Kershaw pondered again.

'I've often thought of that. I think I'd have taken a chance on his not knowing what hit him and then brazened it out. But I'll tell you one thing though. It shook my self-confidence badly. I think Peter'll confirm that after that I was never again the man I had been. Particularly in Italy after you left. Still good, mind you.'

'Yes,' said Sims. He remembered; and used to wonder.

'Can I ask a question, Paddy?' asked Henderson harshly.

'If he's prepared to answer it.'

'Certainly,' said Kershaw, 'anything you like.'

'In listening to all this,' rasped Henderson, 'I've formed the impression that you're a callous, self-important creep.'

'That's not a question,' said Madden reasonably.

'It's setting the atmosphere for a question. You've admitted to lying twice. Once over this fellow Rowlands. Once over Tommy Daunt. How do we know that you're not lying about stealing those diamonds?'

'I didn't lie about Rowlands and I didn't lie about Tommy Daunt,' said Kershaw levelly, 'I just didn't tell the whole truth. Which is different as Father Quinlan here will doubtless confirm. As for the diamonds, I'd never heard of them until you mentioned them just now.'

'Are you trying to tell us that when you looked in the cache you didn't even see 'em?'

'If I did I didn't recognize them. Look, this was all a long time ago. I can't remember all the details. My job – Tommy's job and mine – was to check that the sovereigns were still there. We didn't count the bloody things. We just poked about with torches for about a

241

minute, saw a lot of sacks, lifted some to test weight and kicked a few for hardness and jingles. What were these diamonds in? A box, a sack or what?'

'I don't know.'

'Well, nor do I. I don't mind telling you that if I'd seen some I'd have pinched them like a shot.'

'It may be incapable of proof, but it seems to me that the balance of probability is that you stole the diamonds and killed Tommy Daunt when he objected.'

'Jock,' said Madden, still gently, 'there's something you don't know. After Tommy was wounded Ken bandaged him up and brought him out. With this fellow Maxby we were talking about earlier. Ken went to a lot of trouble over it. Risked his own life if you like. When he reached me with Tommy, Tommy was still alive. Ken would hardly have done all that if he'd decided to kill Tommy.'

Henderson slowly absorbed the logic of this. Kershaw gave it reinforcement.

'I'll tell you another thing you don't know,' he said. 'After I was demobbed I spent two years as a draper's assistant in Huddersfield. I'd hardly have done that if I'd had half a million dollars' worth of . . .'

At this point there was one main, and one supplementary, distraction. The front door burst open with a rending crash and a figure dressed in black, wearing a stocking mask, and holding a machine carbine in a competent manner, sprang into the room. And hesitated. Simultaneously there was a loud bang outside the kitchen window followed instantly by the sound of a complaint being lodged.

'Jaysus, Mick,' roared an affronted voice, 'I been fuckin' shot.'

If it had been Matthew and not Mark there would have been instant massacre and damn the consequences. Mark was less adaptable and slower of thought. The sight of five men instead of the expected two put him off his stride. The shot and the shouting from the garden added to his unease. Four of the five men in front of him now took immediate action to unsettle him further. Sims rose to his feet in a quick fluid movement, raising his hands in the universally accepted gesture of surrender. When he was at his full height his right hand was inside the lamp shade. He squeezed the bulb which exploded with a pop and reduced the amount of light available by half. The only diversion that Madden could think of was to tip over a table on which was a large china bowl of flowers arranged by his daughter, four tumblers and a big lamp with a glass base. The noise was satisfactory. Kershaw's contribution was the most practical. His hand swooped down on the crystal ashtray that he had earlier earmarked for his anti-Henderson defences. In one motion, with a slip fielder's flick of the wrist, he had it flying through the air at the centre of the stocking-masked face. It hit with a crunching noise at where the nose must be. Mark stumbled back a pace, partially blinded by tears. He saw, with distorted vision, Henderson plunging to-wards him. The force of Henderson's tackle was a pallid shadow of those of the bygone days when he had laid waste many an opposing pack of forwards. But Henderson was weighty and his system was suffused with a surfeit of adrenalin, inspired moments before by fury with Kershaw. Henderson crashed destructively into Mark, carried him through the doorway to the floor of the porch and fell heavily, winded, on top of him. The impact forced Mark's hands above his head. He fired an involuntary, forlorn burst through the porch roof and stopped when Kershaw, following up fast, thumped his shoe down on Mark's wrist. The gun fell out of Mark's hand.

Sims, because he was too busy at the time, was never able to reconstruct the chronology of events with complete accuracy. Later he thought that it was at this moment that his attention was temporarily distracted

243

by obtrusive noises from outside the kitchen window again. In sequence these were an explanatory footnote, roared in injured tones: 'In the arse, Mick'; a grunting thud which Sims diagnosed as someone kicking someone else in the groin; a piglet-like screech, which Sims decided came from someone being kicked in the groin; and a second shot which could be assumed to be a miss because the bellowed outraged bulletins continued unabated.

'The bastards have sentries out, Mick. I just kicked one in the knackers.'

Sims, springing beside Madden to the window at the far end of the house, thought that Madden too must have picked up and registered the details of the kitchen window commentary. Madden, looking grim, had suddenly unleashed an unstoppable, schoolboy chuckle. Then Sims and Madden were at work together, dealing with a new threat, posed by the crash and tinkle of broken glass, a gloved hand tearing down curtains and the muzzle of a carbine poking into the room from where the window had been.

Madden was the first there, and just in time. He ducked below the window sill, thrust upwards with his right hand and grabbed the barrel of the carbine as Luke was loosing off his first burst. Madden continued to push upwards. The shots brought down a shower of plaster from the ceiling, most of which settled on and around a bemused Father Quinlan, still seated in his armchair. Sims, a second behind Madden and the taller of the two, reached further out and began to try to wrestle the gun out of Luke's hands. Luke had possession, was young, strong, afraid and angry and would probably have won the contest if in the middle of it he hadn't been shot in the back.

Mick did this. He too was young, strong and afraid, but he was angrier than anybody else present. He didn't know what had gone wrong or why it had gone wrong, but wrong was what it had bloody gone. The only thing to do was to retrieve that stupid clown Liam from the shambles he seemed to have created. It was time to get away the hell out before the complete strength of the Gardai Siochanna, reinforced by the Irish Army in its entirety, descended upon what was beginning to sound like a Hollywood movie about the United States Marines capturing a Pacific Island from the Japanese. Mick's car was parked a hundred yards down the lane. He raced towards the cottage, drew his pistol as he ran, and joined in the nearest part of the affray, helped by a bright patch of moonlight emerging from the wind-driven clouds. He wasn't much bothered by the puzzling details of what he saw. If Madden and his sentry or whatever he was wanted to fight each other through a broken window that was their affair. Mick shot the nearest one because he was in the way, noted that Liam was elsewhere, and moved round to the back of the house in search of him.

Sims, as puzzled as Mick and equally unbothered by puzzlement, decided instantly to exploit his luck. Luke had crumpled under the window, his carbine beside him. Dive out of the window for the gun or take the longer route through the front door? Front door for Sims. Too arthritic and brittle at his time of life to risk an eight-feet drop head first. Sims headed for the door at a middle-aged lope, noting as he did so that Madden was crossing the room fast towards the kitchen window. Sims heard Madden shout 'Get *down*, Father,' and the sound of a cleric being thrown forcibly out of a chair. A second later the last of the lights in the cottage went out. Madden had reached the mains switches.

In the moonlit porch Sims saw fleetingly a prostrate body in black with a curiously misshapen smear where its head should have been; and a groggy-looking Henderson with blood streaming from his nose, crouched on his hands and knees like a boxer trying to get up to beat the count. Henderson was muttering something about his intention of killing that bastard

Kershaw. Full marks for fixity of purpose, thought Sims, but let's get one war over at a time. He took the steps in three jumps, ran round to the right, turned the corner and picked up Luke's carbine. It was an unfamiliar model either jammed or with its safety catch applied, freakishly, by its dying owner. By keeping a continuous pressure on the trigger, pointing the muzzle at the ground, and shifting every knob he could feel, Sims found the safety catch. This discovery was signalled by a short, noisy burst that drew further unfavourable comment from the far side of the house where more complex events seemed to be in progress.

'The fuckers are at it again, Mick,' bawled a by now familiar voice. As a navigational aid the voice had its defects, but it was the best available. Sims stepped quickly towards the corner of the back of the cottage and moved uphill at a tangent to a point in some rocks and furze from which he hoped to see clearly what was going on at the kitchen window ten yards below him. He set himself up in a position to join in in any way that might be of use.

Madden, once he had doused the lights, followed Sims towards the porch at a jog trot slightly more hampered by sciatica than was Sims'. Madden took in at a glance the contorted body of Mark and the bloodied face of Henderson, who by now was stiffly pulling himself to his feet. Madden quickly abandoned a short, unsatisfactory conversation with him.

'Where's Ken?'

'I'll kill that murdering bastard,' said Henderson thickly. Madden sprang down the steps but unlike Sims turned left. This brought him to the side of the house where the kitchen window was, the epicentre of the major hullaballoo of the evening. Madden went as fast as he could to the shelter of a stunted oak some fifteen yards away. He was unarmed, a deficiency he put right by picking up two small rocks. He would intervene if necessary with the aid of the rocks, and possibly his feet, but he first needed to establish some facts. Who the hell were these people fighting in his garden? The fact that they were fighting each other suggested that one side might be friendly. But which? And why? And where was Kershaw? And Sims?

The moon was lost temporarily behind a cloud and it became harder than ever for Madden and Sims, thirty yards apart, unaware of each other's whereabouts, and on either side of the last remaining disturbance, to make sense of what was happening. There was a continuous muted sound of grunts, curses, bodies thrashing about, twigs snapping and stones rattling away in displacement. Then the moon relit the scene and the physical evidence became available. The reason behind it stayed obscure. To one side lay the splayed-out figure of Kershaw, unconscious or dead, a machine carbine beside his outstretched right hand. Between Kershaw and the kitchen window two intertwined figures were rolling on the ground in a deadly, no-holds-barred fight, gouging, biting, kneeing and elbowing. They seemed evenly matched, one in a ripped stocking mask and torn black overalls, the other bareheaded in a sweater and jeans. Jumping about beside them like a referee in an all-in wrestling match was another man in sweater and jeans, brandishing a pistol. His intention was clearly to try to shoot one of the wrestlers and he was showing signs of frustration. The combatants were rolling and jerking around at such a rate that he was having difficulty in picking one off without doing harm to the other. Finally he did it. Liam had an armlock on John and John's head protruded fractionally from the melee. Mick put the pistol to John's ear and fired. Liam rose awkwardly to his feet and opened his mouth preparatory to issuing another statement on how he viewed developments. Mick stopped him with a savage back-hander across the mouth and said 'Out. Quick'.

Sims saw and heard all this very clearly. He made a lightning assessment from the facts as he knew them and decided that since his known enemies had worn stocking masks and boiler suits, the sweater and jeans team must be friends. He lowered his carbine just before Mick raised his pistol and emptied his magazine into the kitchen window. Christ, thought Sims, Father Quinlan's still in there. Sims took as quick and as careful an aim as he could in the moonlight and squeezed the trigger as Mick and Liam began to hurry away, Liam limping badly, hand pressed to his rump. There was a click. All rounds gone in that trial burst the other side of the house. Bugger. Getting old and out of touch. Sims stood up, took a step in pursuit of Mick and Liam, and was halted in his tracks by an order from a voice he had been trained to obey instinctively over thirty years before.

'Stay where you are, Peter,' snapped Madden.

Madden waited until he was confident that the diminishing sound of receding footsteps and murmured talk meant what it seemed. As he stood up he heard a car starting up down the lane and driving off fast.

'Look to Ken, Peter,' he called, 'I'll just see if there are any more of these bastards about.'

Sims went to Kershaw and knelt beside him. Madden, making a careful inspection of the outside of the cottage, passed them without looking down. Nobody at the back of the house. A black overalled body outside the sitting-room window. Another on the porch. And Henderson, recovered, wiping blood from his upper lip and in a mood of seething belligerence.

'Where's that thieving, murdering sod Kershaw?'

Madden lost his temper.

'Now look, Jock,' he said dangerously. 'I'm getting fed to the teeth with you and your obsession with Ken. Those bloody people have shot my house to pieces. There are three bodies in the garden. I haven't the

248

faintest idea of what's going on or why. And all you can do is go moaning on and on about something that might or might not have happened over thirty years ago. I . . .'

'I'm talking about tonight dammit. Kershaw clobbered that sod in the doorway with that ashtray. Fine. Then I tackled the bugger. Kershaw stamped on his wrist and made him drop his gun. So far so good. Then bloody Kershaw picked up the gun, held it to the man's face and blew the top of his head off. *While I was still holding him.* It was sheer criminal butchery. I caught Kershaw's ankle but he banged me over the nose with the butt and disappeared into the . . .'

'Oh Christ,' said Madden. What was this, he thought. Shock? Scruples? Jock had scruples and they did him credit. Sensible scruples? How many scruples were sensible? And if an attempted murderer who didn't obey the rules, had a Henderson who stuck to the rules any right to criticize an action that . . . Anyway were there any longer any rules? Had there ever been any rules for that matter? It was all too bloody complicated at this time of night. Father Quinlan, powdered by plaster flakes from the ceiling, came out to the moonlit porch from the sitting-room. He was dabbing with his handkerchief at a steadily bleeding gash on the side of his head.

'You okay, Father?' asked Madden, with concern.

'Yes thanks. Just a surface cut.'

'What did it? That last fellow firing his pistol in the window?'

'No,' said Father Quinlan benignly. 'It was you actually. I cracked my head on the corner of the bookcase when you threw me out of that chair.'

'Oh,' said Madden, contrite. 'Sorry. Let's go and see how Ken is.' The three of them walked together to outside the kitchen window. Sims was rising to his feet. Kershaw stayed down.

'Ken's dead,' said Sims wearily. 'Must have been that stray shot when that Match of the Day character was announcing that he'd kicked somebody in the goolies.'

Father Quinlan, quietly and impartially, went to each body in turn. Madden, Henderson and Sims walked silently and slowly back into the wrecked house to the distant sound of police sirens, drawing rapidly closer.

Epilogue

KARLA FIRST HEARD of the events on the Big Sugar Loaf on the early morning news broadcast of the BBC Overseas Service. She gave the matter little heed. Another senseless piece of savagery in a crazy world. In the same genre as the topic currently exercising the Yugoslav press, television and radio to the exclusion of almost everything else – a series of co-ordinated attacks on Yugoslav diplomats, embassies and consulates throughout the United States, Canada, West Germany and Australia. An Ambassador, a Consul General, two First Secretaries and a Consul killed. Several others wounded. Others attacked, but safe. Car bomb explosions outside three embassies. One consulate burnt to the ground.

Ambassadors of delinquent countries were summoned to the Ministry of Foreign Affairs in Belgrade to be handed blistering protest notes about the criminally inadequate security measures of host governments with a legal and moral obligation to safeguard foreign diplomats accredited to them. Why couldn't they all rise to the excellent standard set by the Government of the United Kingdom of Great Britain and Northern Ireland who, with commendable efficiency, had promptly locked up a terrorist caught at Belfast Airport on his way to attack the Yugoslav commercial consul. It hadn't taken *them* long to check with Interpol and identify the man as a member of a Croatian extremist

251

exile organization. The text of the protest notes were published in full in the Yugoslav press, accompanied by a scathing official commentary.

Aside from her revulsion at these events, Karla had another, pressing, pre-occupation, Bogdan. The psychiatric treatment that had followed Karla's medically unorthodox methods of persuading the patient to unburden himself of his sorrows had so far been enormously encouraging. This week the status of the cure was being put to a crucial test. For the first time since the end of the war, Bogdan had returned to Montenegro, alone, to visit his boyhood haunts. It would doubtless be distressing, the psychiatrist had explained, but it was necessary if Bogdan were to finally exorcise his devils. Bogdan was due back on the Friday. It was now Tuesday. Karla worried. Was the psychiatrist moving too fast? Was there not a danger of regression? Was there . . . ? No point in going on like this. Nothing could be done about it now. *Stop* worrying. Karla worried.

On the Thursday came a letter from Henderson. She may or may not have seen or heard reports that he had been involved in an inexplicable fracas in Ireland in which four people had been killed, he wrote, but she was not to worry. He was a bit bruised and battered, but safe. There was one thing she should know. The man they had both suspected of killing Tomislav had admitted it. He had denied stealing her father's diamonds, but it was suspect testimony. He had shown himself to be a liar on other matters and Henderson was convinced that he was lying over this one. By a bizarre coincidence, which Henderson could only put down to the operation of some mysterious force dispensing natural justice, the man had been killed in the same fight in Ireland in which Henderson had been slightly hurt. Henderson knew Karla's views about resuscitating the past and he had hesitated about men-

tioning the matter to her, but after anxious consideration he had concluded that . . .

Oh Henderson, thought Karla. You and your
damned sense of duty and tidiness. You knew that your
news would upset me and you knew that I had to know
it for my ultimate peace of mind. Damn your eyes and
thank you. Knowledge, even disagreeable knowledge,
was a great layer of ghosts. Hers were nearly all laid
now, mostly sadly, but laid. Get Bogdan back to full
sanity and that would be the last of them. At five
o'clock in the afternoon of the Saturday, Bogdan,
carrying a small suitcase, presented himself to Karla.
He was smiling.

'It was horrible at first,' he said, 'but it worked.'

'Oh, Bogdan.'

She hugged him as hard as she had on that day many
years before, when a small boy had run to her laughing.
She cried as hard too. Later he opened his suitcase and
brought out a small shapeless bundle wrapped in oilskin. There were some earth stains on it.

'I'll tell you something I've never told anyone before,' said Bogdan. 'I couldn't. Because it happened at
the place where the Lieutenant killed the Captain. I
was never able to talk about that.'

Karla looked at him fondly. The cure had worked all
right.

'Well, I'd been watching them for some time. They
couldn't see me of course. At one stage they scraped
away some earth and opened up a sort of hole in the
ground. Then they closed it with earth again. They
went away and the shooting started. And one killed the
other. Then everyone went away.'

'What did you do?' asked Karla curiously.

'I hid on the island. When it was dawn I saw that
there was nobody in sight, so I opened up the hole the
way I'd seen them do it. There was a lot of stuff in
sacks. And two little leather bags. There were some
pretty shining stones in the leather bags. I took them

253

away to give to you as a present. I ran all the way back to the other Lieutenant, the young one, and tried to tell him. But he couldn't understand me. Then suddenly I changed my mind.'

'Bogdan . . .'

'Karla, I'm sorry, but I couldn't do it. It seemed to me that every time I saw you with them they'd remind me of the Lieutenant killing the Captain. So I ran away and buried them up at that grazing my father had. You know, where the two parachutists landed.'

'Bogdan . . .'

'I dug them out on Thursday. And here they are,' said Bogdan expansively, opening the oilskin package, exposing two decaying wash-leather bags and tipping a fortune in gems onto the tablecloth. He was pleased to see that she was sobbing again. In his experience she always had when she was unusually happy.